THE LAW OF
Attraction

by

N.M. SILBER

THE LAW OF ATTRACTION, COPYRIGHT © 2013 BY N.M. SILBER

ALL RIGHTS RESERVED. This book contains material protected under International and Federal Copyright Laws and Treaties. Any unauthorized reprint or use of this material is prohibited. No part of this book may be reproduced or transmitted in any form or by any means, electronic or mechanical, including photocopying, recording, or by any information storage and retrieval system without express written permission from the author / publisher.

Mendelssohn Levy Publishing

Philadelphia

http://mendlevypub.com/

First Mendelssohn Levy eBook Edition August 2013

First Mendelssohn Levy trade paperback edition, August 2013

Edited by:

Julie Roberts

isillote1@gmail.com

NOTICE: This is an adult contemporary romance novel and contains explicit love scenes and mature language. It is intended for readers over the age of eighteen.

This is a work of fiction. Names, characters, places and incidents either are products of the author's imagination or are used fictitiously. Any resemblance to actual events or locales or persons, living or dead, is entirely coincidental.

Library of Congress Control Number: 2013911094

Silber, N.M.

The Law of Attraction / N.M. Silber – 1st edition

ISBN 978-0-9895984-1-5 eBook edition

ISBN 978-0-9895984-0-8 Print edition

1. Romance - Fiction

Cover Design by Carrie Spencer

Formatting by Donnie Light

This book is dedicated to my family.
I know that it's your job to love me,
but you do it especially well.
(Don't read the dirty parts.)

⮎ CHAPTER ONE ⮌

IN THE COURT OF COMMON PLEAS OF PHILADELPHIA COUNTY, PENNSYLVANIA

Commonwealth v. Harris

I stood in front of the jury delivering my closing argument in a shoplifting case that my client had insisted on taking to trial against my advice and despite my begging.

"Ladies and gentlemen, we live in a country where every citizen has a right to trial by his peers. The prosecution must carry its burden of proof beyond a reasonable doubt, the *highest* legal standard of proof possible in this great country of ours. We are here today because my client is a citizen, and he has a right to a trial if he wants one."

We lawyers often couldn't let people know what we were really thinking. I often pictured the things that I would *like* to say and do, though, and I called those thoughts "inner-Gabrielle," for lack of a better term. Right now inner-Gabrielle was sighing and rolling her eyes because I was breaking out the old "right to a trial defense" again. It's what we public defenders did when we found ourselves addressing a jury without the one thing that would come in most handy under the circumstances – an actual defense. After all, you had to say *something*. Technically, my client did have a defense in this case. It was just *so* stupid that nobody in their right mind would believe it, so I figured what the hell, it never hurt to bring up the Constitution.

"You heard Mr. Harris tell you that he simply made a mistake," I went on, "one that perhaps you yourself have made. You go into a store, expecting to pick up only one item, and so you don't bother with a shopping basket. Then you see another item that you need. And then another."

I paused and gave the jurors a friendly smile to show them how very reasonable all of this was. I hoped that it said: "See, citizens of Philadelphia, who have put off your obligations, hired babysitters, and missed work; I'm a nice person, so you shouldn't hate me or my jackass client for wasting your valuable time." After all, this was all a big misunderstanding, right?

"Mr. Harris claims that's what happened to him on that day in May. He went to the store for one item and then saw another that he needed and then another. Rather than go all the way back to the front of the store for a basket, he simply stored some items in his clothing, fully intending to pay for them."

I looked into each juror's eyes as I slowly paced in front of the jury box. I could see that some of them actually wanted to believe me. That was nice of them. Obviously, not being clinically brain-dead, they didn't believe me, but they *wanted* to, and it was the thought that counted.

"That's his story ladies and gentlemen, and he has a constitutional right to tell it. If you feel the prosecution has not proven their case beyond a reasonable doubt you must acquit. Thank you."

I sat down with as much dignity as I could muster, as a tired-looking, fifty-something, assistant district attorney rose to his feet and addressed the jury. He cleared his throat and I could see that he held a list in his hands. Inner-Gabrielle cringed. *Oh shit.*

"Mr. Harris had three boxes of Melba toast, a can of smoked oysters, a wheel of Gouda cheese, two bunches of grapes, a package of smoked salmon, a can of sardines, a bottle of sparkling grape juice and a can of cocktail weenies in his pants. I simply ask you to please use common sense. Thank you."

He sat down again as I just continued to stare straight ahead doing my best, "Did someone say something?" look. (They teach you that one in law school.) The judge charged the jury and they left to deliberate as Mr. Harris went out for a smoke. I stood and gathered my things as the public defenders and the assistant district attorneys working on the next cases set up. I had seen two familiar faces among those waiting, so I was already prepared for the humiliation that I knew would be forthcoming. Adam Roth and Braden Pierce were good-looking young prosecutors – very good-looking. We usually worked the same courtroom these days and both of them liked to tease me. It fact, it seemed to be their favorite pastime. I didn't mind terribly, though, as I was deeply in lust with Mr. Pierce.

"A can of cocktail weenies." Mr. Roth fired the first shot.

"It would be a shame to have to hurt someone as pretty as you, Mr. Roth." I straightened my papers and tried to look busy. (They teach you that one in law school too.)

"Sounds like it was going to be quite a party," Mr. Pierce said.

"Feeling lucky, Mr. Pierce? I'm not afraid to take you down too, you know. I work with two hundred criminal defense lawyers." I saw him try to contain his laughter as I heard my friend, Jessica's, voice behind me. I turned around, eager to see a sympathetic face.

"I just tried one where my client claimed he was urinating in a back alley. Turns out he was jerking off on a street corner. The prosecution had twenty-one witnesses. They were nuns." She looked pained.

"I understand," I said gently, patting her on the back.

"Did you put on the 'my client has a right to a trial defense' too?" Mr. Roth asked.

"I loved it when she said 'that's his story and he has a constitutional right to tell it.' That was a classic moment in American jurisprudence," Mr. Pierce added, coming over to the defense table and leaning against it immediately next to where I was standing. I noticed that he had a very nice scent — spicy, with a trace of mint. Mr. Pierce even smelled attractive.

"I'm glad that we amuse you guys. You have no idea what it's like to have to stand there and say that with a straight face." I turned quickly to face him and my mouth almost popped open. *Christ on a cracker!* I had been looking at this man across a courtroom for months, and I had even sat across a table from him when negotiating a deal, but I had never been *this* close to him before. Wow. I realized that I was just staring at him stupidly and I managed to pull myself together. I really had to get laid soon.

"Poor Ms. Ginsberg," he said and smiled, looking at me curiously.

That smile made my girl parts warm. Mr. Pierce was too attractive for my own good. With him standing right here next to me, I could see that his eyes were a gorgeous sky blue ringed in indigo and his hair wasn't really blonde, but actually a shade of light brown with golden highlights. I couldn't help it, I started imagining how he could make me feel better with a nice massage and a warm bath together, maybe a glass of wine and some sexy music... "Yeah well, maybe you should comfort me..." I mumbled distractedly. My eyes widened. Jesus, Gabrielle! "Confront! Maybe you should not... confront me because I can be"... I searched for something... "dangerous." *Huh?* I rolled my eyes and felt my face get hot.

"I don't doubt it," he said with a cocky grin. "I think that *confronting* you could be very dangerous."

"I just hope they threw the grapes away," Mr. Roth said, completely snapping me out of my lust-fueled reverie. I had finished straightening up my own papers, so I started straightening up everyone else's papers too. I was tidying up the whole damned courtroom and Mr. Pierce was watching me do it with an extremely amused look on his face. I wondered what *he* was thinking — probably, "I wonder if she's off her meds."

The jury was back in ten minutes. Shockingly, they didn't believe Mr. Harris. I went back to my office in defeat. Inner-Gabrielle went out for a drink.

∽ CHAPTER TWO ∽

I sat there preparing my cases for the next day. I had to figure out a way to convince a six foot five, three hundred pound biker named "Tiny" that nobody was going to believe that he had just "found" 27 thirty-inch HD flat screen televisions in an alley behind his apartment. One had to tread lightly when telling someone like Tiny that even his lawyer thought he was full of shit. I wasn't really looking forward to it, or any of the sixteen other cases I had scheduled. Luckily, that was a light work day.

Jessica finally got back an hour later, looking like she had gone a few rounds with Mike Tyson. It had probably just been Mr. Roth being a dick, though. He did that from time to time. (Daily.) Jess and I had both begun working for the Defender Association at the same time almost a year ago and we had been office-mates from day one. As of a few months ago, we also shared an apartment in a building a few blocks from our office in the upscale Rittenhouse Square District.

To be perfectly honest, I didn't really need to have a roommate. My parents were very successful business people, so I guess you could say that I came from a wealthy family. I liked knowing that I could support myself, though, so I mostly tried to live on my own salary. Unfortunately, that worried my parents, but then everything worried my parents. They worried about me working with criminals. They worried about me living in a different city. They worried because I wasn't good at financial stuff. Most of all, though, they worried that I would eventually end up living alone with a bunch of cats and a couple of million dollars in a shoebox under my bed.

My social life wasn't exactly thriving at the moment. I did go out, but only if I were surrounded by friends because, frankly, I had spent enough nights fending off drunken players at bars and clubs. I didn't want to date anyone from my office, and I wasn't really meeting anyone new, so I hadn't been out with a guy in a few months. That was going to have to change, though, because I couldn't live like this anymore. My job created a lot of tension and I needed an outlet. I had to find a sex partner that didn't require batteries.

The problem was that the only guy who I was interested in was Mr. Pierce. We'd been working that courtroom together for months now, and while Mr. Roth could be a pain in the ass, Mr. Pierce just did his job. He always offered me fair plea bargains, although sometimes he made me work hard for them, and with him it was always a good clean fight, even if it made me want to be a dirty girl. Battling in court could be pretty stimulating to tell you the truth. Sometimes there's a fine line between pissed off and turned on.

I thought about him way too much though. I was becoming like a crazy fan girl. I might as well have hung a poster of him over my bed. Unfortunately, I was hardly his only fan. Everybody knew that he was a big time player. I didn't want a one night stand and I didn't want to share, so it seemed like Mr. Pierce was off-limits. Now, if someone could just explain that to inner-Gabrielle. And my vagina.

And then, of course, if that wasn't bad enough, there was also another issue; he reminded me of someone from my past who I didn't exactly associate with happy memories. That one wasn't a deal breaker, but it certainly didn't boost my self-confidence with him. It was a long story, but back in college I managed to lose my virginity in a one-night-stand with another player. I know – brilliant Gabrielle. Right? Wait, it gets even better, I decided to tell him the next day that I wanted to be his girlfriend. Let's just say he wasn't really on board with that plan. Can you say humiliation? Anyway, I'm not sure why, but something about Mr. Pierce reminded me of the player who deflowered me.

"Shake it off, Gab, tomorrow's another day," Jess said, breezing in and dropping a pile of case files that looked like it weighed more than she did.

"Is that supposed to cheer me up?" I asked, clearing a path on the floor so she could get to her desk. I tended to spread out when I worked.

"I would think you would be pretty cheerful already with all the attention a certain prosecutor has been paying you lately." She threw herself down in her chair, opened her bottom desk drawer and put her feet up. Okay, that got my attention. I hadn't told anyone about my little infatuation, not even her, but I guess that ogling him and then asking him to comfort me hadn't exactly been subtle.

"And what prosecutor would that be?" I asked lightly, sitting back on my heels.

"The beautiful blonde Braden Pierce," she said, smirking.

"Why would Mr. Heavy-hitter be paying attention to me?" I went back to sorting piles on the floor and tried to act nonchalant.

"Oh, I don't know. Maybe because you're good-looking and smart and funny?"

"Well, then he's just looking for a good time. I hear he doesn't date; he just hooks-up. Anyway, you're probably wrong. The women he likes look like Playboy bunnies."

"How do you know?" *Oh damn!* Caught by my own big mouth.

"He's a senator's son. I Googled him once."

"Hey wait…"

"Wait what? I know what you're thinking but I'm not a crazy stalker chick! I was just curious."

"Not that! The other thing. Screw the Playboy bunnies!"

"I'm sure he did."

"Like you're not attractive? Look at you with the golden brown hair and the big hazel eyes. You also have big boobs and a nice ass which tend to be popular features with the male sex. The drunken business boys are on you like a bad rash every time we go out."

"Thanks, but I'm just saying that he seems to have a type and I'm not a spray tan blonde with a two inch waist like the ones I've seen him with in pictures. Some of them were so Barbie-like I'm not even sure they had bendable legs."

"Type or no type, I still say that he wants you." She put her feet back on the floor and started clearing a space in front of her and stacking files.

"Yeah maybe for an extremely short-term relationship, like however long it would take to screw me. I don't want to have a one night stand with a guy I face in court every day. To tell you the truth, I don't really want to have a one night stand with anybody, no matter how hot they are."

"So maybe he'd be willing to invest more than one night for you. We should ask Mark." Mark Patterson was a fellow public defender who had been friends with Mr. Pierce and Mr. Roth in law school. They had managed to remain close even though they worked on opposite sides of the courtroom now. Together they were probably the three sexiest guys and the three biggest womanizers in the Philadelphia criminal court system, but Mark was still pretty cool just to hang out with, and he and Jess were really good friends.

"No! He would say something to him and then if you *were* wrong I would feel so embarrassed that I wouldn't be able to do my job. Besides, he would see me as just another one of his groupies and I want him to respect me." I was already having flashbacks to college. One adventure in complete humiliation was more than enough, thanks.

"And what if I were right?"

"Then he could always ask me out, couldn't he? It's not like it would be hard to track me down. I see him practically every day. I wouldn't hold my breath though. I think he's pretty content randomly screwing Barbie dolls that he meets in bars and clubs."

"Well, I definitely don't think he would ask you out unless you let him know that you were interested too. Sometimes you act so stand-offish around him."

"I do?"

"I know you well enough to realize that you're just attracted to him, but he probably wouldn't know that. Well, he might figure it out after today. You seemed pretty flustered when he came over to talk to you and you did ask him to comfort you." She laughed to herself as she started taking notes on a file.

"Oh God," I moaned. "I'm such an asshole."

"Don't be embarrassed. He always looks at you like he wants to toss you in the jury box and have his wicked way with you. He also keeps moving closer to talk to you. I thought he was going to sit on your lap today and you obviously liked it."

"Yeah, well, he smells good," I said and paused to think about that for a second. "I need to get out more. I'm sniffing the prosecutors."

Commonwealth v. O'Neal

The next day arrived, just as Jess had threatened, and once again I found myself up against Mr. Pierce in court, wishing that he had me up against the courtroom wall. He was becoming increasingly distracting, especially now that she had filled my head with all of her theories that he wanted me too. She was such an enabler sometimes.

"Okay Ms. Ginsberg," Judge Channing said at the conclusion of the preliminary hearing. "Time for argument. Will we be attempting to amend the Constitution today?"

"No, Your Honor. I wouldn't want to become predictable," I replied with a smile. Judge Channing wasn't exactly a fan of mine, by the way. "It's the defense position that the Commonwealth has not made out the charge of attempted homicide. Mr. O'Neal allegedly shot Mr. Anthony in the leg at close range. Clearly if he had intended to kill him he would have aimed higher."

"He would have aimed higher. I see. Mr. Pierce, your response?"

"Your Honor, Mr. O'Neal shot Mr. Anthony using a nine millimeter handgun on a crowded street in front of at least thirty witnesses. The Commonwealth has presented sufficient evidence to bind all charges, including attempted homicide, over for trial."

"I'm sorry, Ms. Ginsberg, I'm going to have to go with Mr. Pierce on this one. The fact that your client is a lousy shot doesn't provide a defense. All charges are held. Schedule it for trial." They led my client away and I headed back to the defense table to gather my things. Mr. Pierce came over to hand me the copy of the order. That was different. Prosecutors weren't usually that polite. Instead of walking away he stayed there – so close I had to look up to talk to him. Wow, he was tall.

"He would have aimed higher?" he asked with amusement.

"Look, when you represent a guy who shoots somebody in front of sixty witnesses let's hear what you have to say, okay?" I turned around and leaned over to put the order in the file and when I turned back I caught him totally checking out my ass.

"Thirty witnesses," he said, and quickly looked up at a group of cops coming in the door. I couldn't help myself, I totally checked out *his* beautiful body and when he looked back, of course he caught me doing it. I yanked my eyes away from him and cleared my throat.

"Thirty, sixty. What difference does it make? Were they nuns too, by the way?" When I glanced back I saw him trying to stifle a laugh.

"I must admit that I admire your creativity." I wondered if he meant it or if he was just teasing me as usual. I looked at him directly again and I saw his eyes drop to the bottom lip I was gnawing on nervously. I couldn't handle the way he was looking at my mouth like that so I turned to gather the papers on the defense table. I was always freaking gathering something when he was around! I really needed to have sex again soon, and God, I hoped that I wasn't thinking out loud again.

"Thank you, Mr. Pierce. I try. I'll be doing a second show later this afternoon. Just wait until you meet Tiny," I said, starting to pack up my files. He couldn't hold back anymore. The laughter escaped but he politely covered it with a cough. I glanced up and caught sight of his beautiful mouth and my eyes lingered there. I wanted that mouth on so many parts of my body.

"Did you say something?" My gaze flew back up to his eyes. *Shit!*

"Month. It's been a busy month," I mumbled and bit down on my bottom lip to prevent myself from saying anything else out loud. His eyes dropped to my mouth again and they actually seemed to get a little darker. I was starting to sweat and feel a great deal of tension in the room that had nothing to do with Mr. O'Neal's poor aim. I had to get the hell out of there. I went to grab lunch before I grabbed Mr. Pierce and found out if he tasted as good as he smelled. *Jesus!* I felt like I needed a cold shower.

Commonwealth v. Kaminsky

At one o'clock we were back in front of the judge. "Okay, Ms. Ginsberg. Can't wait to hear what you're going to come up with this time," Judge Channing said. Nothing like a vote of confidence from the judiciary.

"Your Honor, we all know that retail establishments sometimes discard unwanted or defective merchandise. It was perfectly reasonable for Mr. Kaminsky to have mistakenly believed that the merchandise in question here had been abandoned."

"Uh huh. Mr. Pierce, what do you have to say?" the judge asked.

"Your Honor, nobody discards twenty-seven HD flat screen TVs."

"You know, Mr. Pierce, I'm inclined to agree. All charges held for trial." Judge Channing banged his gavel and Tiny was escorted away by two rather wary-looking deputies. I was fairly sure Tiny wasn't anybody's bitch in the jail. I headed back to the defense table again.

"You were right. That was pretty good," Mr. Pierce said, handing me the order again. His hand brushed against mine this time and I jumped like I had just stuck my finger in a socket. He looked at me like I might be really be dangerous after all. Nice, Gabrielle – very subtle.

"I predict that I'll be breaking out the 'right to a trial defense' again," I said, trying to not act any weirder than I already was.

"You don't think he'll be willing to plead guilty?"

"Probably not. He firmly believes that claiming to be a complete idiot will get him off."

"You're very funny," he said, leaning against the defense table right next to me again.

"Mr. Pierce, in my line of work, one either laughs or cries and I would rather laugh." Oh Jesus H. Christ! I sounded like a country western song.

"You can call me Braden." He was looking at me kind of intently like he was curious to see how I would react. I felt my cheeks getting warmer and my heart started pounding like a drummer on speed. I was starting to wonder if I had high blood pressure or something. This couldn't be normal.

"You can call me Gabrielle then," I said, staring directly into those incredible blue eyes and hoping that my face didn't look as pink as it felt. We were only inches away from each other and I could feel the heat from his body. I was looking up at him and he was looking down at me and I felt that tension there again, but just then the judge called out.

"Mr. Pierce, I hate to break up your conversation with Ms. Ginsberg but we need a prosecutor to be involved in this prosecution." I looked over at the bench and saw that there was already another case waiting.

"Goodbye, Gabrielle," he said with a smile. Why did my name sound so damned sexy when he said it? I placed my wheeling briefcase full of files on the floor. My toned muscles didn't just come from walking everywhere. I could probably bench-press a Buick.

"Goodbye, Braden," I muttered and made my escape.

* * *

It was Friday and I wouldn't get to see him again for at least two days. I headed back to my office, probably the only one of the two hundred plus attorneys who worked there who wasn't thrilled that the weekend had finally arrived. I contemplated my plans for the next day. I could rearrange the kitchen cupboards, maybe catch a matinee, slit my wrists. The possibilities were endless. Jess was already at her desk when I got back and I unpacked my files as I thought more about my little exchange with Mr. Pierce — Braden.

"Mr. Pierce told me to call him by his first name and he also told me that I was funny."

"Oh really?" she asked, spinning around in her chair and sounding diabolically intrigued like some evil genius in a James Bond movie. "So admit it, maybe I was right." She had the "I told you so" look written all over her face.

"I don't want to hear it until I have some proof. Thanks to you planting your dubious theories in my head, I've gone from just lusting for him to pining for him too. I'm like Pepe Le Pew on Acid every time he gets near me now," I said, rolling my eyes.

"We could go out to O'Malley's with the other public defenders later," she suggested. "A lot of prosecutors go too on Fridays. Maybe he'll be there."

"And what then? I can gaze at him from afar over a pitcher of beer?"

"You can flirt with him. Maybe you could get something going that way."

"Because you know that picking up a guy in a bar is the best way to start a healthy romantic relationship. I'm not looking for a one-nighter Jess."

"You don't have to go home with him. Just flirt with him and see what happens."

"Just flirt with him and see what happens – those are famous last words if I ever heard them."

⤳ CHAPTER THREE ⤳

O'Malley's managed to seem upscale and still feel like the fun dive bar that every lawyer everywhere had hung out in when they were in law school. There was a large old-fashioned, central bar area, surrounded by tables lining the walls. When the place started filling up and the jukebox was playing, people tended to crowd into the open space between the bar and the tables to socialize and dance.

We had just walked in, and were navigating through the crowd, when we passed near a table surrounded by prosecutors laughing and drinking. We were en route to a table surrounded by public defenders laughing and drinking. After a week in the criminal justice system, laughing and drinking were necessary components for maintaining one's sanity. We had almost passed the prosecutors' table when I heard Mr. Roth call out.

"Well if it isn't Ms. Albright and Ms. Ginsberg!" We paused and moved in closer to them. My stomach started contortions that would have made the U.S. Diving Team proud when I saw Braden sitting there, leaning back in his chair with his jacket off, his sleeves rolled up, and his tie and collar loose. You could sell postcards of that sight, baby.

"Hello, Mr. Roth," Jess called out above the noise. "Drowning your sorrows?"

"Celebrating my victories, Ms. Albright. Perhaps you don't recall my impressive courtroom performance earlier?" Mr. Roth was also a very handsome guy but in a different way than Mr. Pierce. Braden was a golden boy but Adam had dark good looks – dark hair, brown eyes, and always just a touch of five o'clock shadow. He was one of those guys who always looked like he may have come directly to work from some woman's bed. And in Adam's case that was a definite possibility.

"Someone catch me. I'm going to swoon," I shouted dryly. And one can actually shout dryly – trust me. Mr. Roth needed to occasionally have a woman fail to worship him and I was happy to oblige.

"Such a saucy mouth on this girl," he said with a laugh, looking over at Braden. Their colleagues paused in their revelries to pay attention to this little exchange. Two attractive public defender women had ventured close to a table full of semi-drunk male prosecutors. That didn't happen every day. It was like one of those scenes from a wildlife documentary. You know, the ones where the baby gazelle decides to drink from the nice cool stream right next to the pride of hungry lions.

"You think I have a saucy mouth huh?" I decided that now was as good a time as any if I wanted to try my hand at some flirting. "What do you think of my mouth, Braden?" I asked, turning to him. By some small miracle I actually managed to sound calm and even a bit playful. The guardian angel of the socially awkward was obviously smiling down on me.

"I rather like it," he answered with a flirtatious smile, as his eyes very obviously dropped to my lips, this time in a practiced way that probably had women dropping their panties for him left and right under other circumstances. I heard some suggestive laughter and there were a few comments from his friends that I didn't quite catch – probably for the best. Dusty Springfield was singing *Son of a Preacher Man* in the background and it helped to set the saucy mood.

"There you go, Mr. Roth," I said, as I walked over to stand right in front of him, leaned down, and looked him directly in the eye, our faces inches apart. "Some men can obviously handle my mouth." Jess let out a startled laugh behind me. I stood up, smiled and started to walk away. After a second of stunned silence, their table erupted into laughter. *Wow, I really was kind of saucy wasn't I?* I was several feet away when I heard Braden call out and my heart slammed into my chest wall.

"Hey Gabrielle!" I turned around and quirked an eyebrow inquisitively. He gave a devastatingly sexy smile and then said loudly enough to be heard over the crowd, "I can handle your sharp tongue too!" More raucous laughter echoed around him and I dug down deep and found courage that could only be developed after three years of exposure to sadists who enjoyed destroying self-confidence (law professors.)

"Behave or I'll make you prove it!" I called back loudly, smiling as if I had issued a challenge, and then I turned back around and kept walking. Mercifully, I didn't trip over anything. That one went over very well at the prosecutors' table, incidentally. I thought for a minute that they were going to either give me a standing ovation or start shoving dollar bills in my stylish but sensible suit skirt. Jess looked over at me with an expression of stunned delight.

"Who are you and what have you done with Gabrielle Ginsberg?"

"So, that was kind of flirty, wasn't it?"

"Kind of? That gets at least an R rating," she giggled. I looked up and saw Mark waving at us.

"Hey Jessica, Gabrielle!" He had obviously heard that little exchange because he was looking over at their table and laughing with obvious surprise. But then most of the crowd had probably heard it. Jess and I changed course and headed over to join Mark at his end of the table.

"Having fun?" he asked.

"It's certainly been interesting so far," Jess answered, giving me a slightly bewildered look.

"Have some beer. I'm driving," Mark said. We filled up two plastic cups from a pile sitting next to a pitcher. "So, what's this about Braden and your tongue, Gabrielle?"

"They were teasing me and I just teased back a little," I said dismissively, taking a sip of beer.

Jess told him about our little back and forth exchange and he laughed again and looked at me, like he didn't recognize me and he was trying to figure out who I was.

"So, flirting with Braden, huh?" he asked, sounding both amused and surprised.

"Just being saucy." I smiled.

"Oh she was totally flirting with him," Jess corrected, giving me a conspiratorial look. She was so proud of me – I could just tell.

Mark looked back over at the other table. They were off to my side, and I didn't want to turn and look directly at them, but he seemed to be sharing some kind of unspoken communication with someone over there. I thought I saw him nod subtly and shrug. I wished that I knew what they were saying to each other. I took a deep breath and sat there for a second to let what I had just done sink in.

I couldn't believe that I had actually pulled it off! I had flirted with Braden Pierce. Geek girl had flirted with gorgeous guy, senator's son, the man who had his own fan club among the members of the Women's Bar Association. I felt mad, bad and dangerous to know! I had a feeling that it would be one of those moments I would relive mentally for years. Like the time that I had refused to pay the ten cent fine because the library had closed early the day before and the drop box was locked. In the world of a ten-year-old that was Civil Disobedience at its finest. (I was such a rebel.) I might never actually get to go out with this incredibly hot man, but for one brief moment in time, I was the sexy confident woman in the room. Inner-Gabrielle pumped her fist in victory. It was Miller Time.

Now that the adrenaline was hitting me full force, I was feeling a lot of nervous tension and without really thinking about it I downed a couple of cups of beer in rapid succession. That's a nice way of saying that I probably could have won a chugging contest at a frat house. Not long after I finished the second one, a waitress stopped over and handed me a piece of paper. It was a note. She told me that if I wanted to reply she would deliver it for me. By the look she was giving me I had a feeling that a monetary donation to her effort would be involved. I looked down and read while she waited, shifting her weight back and forth impatiently.

> **Dear Gabrielle,**
>
> ***I've never seen you this saucy before. You're not under the influence are you?***
>
> **Sincerely,**
>
> **Braden T. Pierce, Esq.**
>
> **Assistant District Attorney**

Oh great! He thought that I was drunk! So much for confident and sexy. I showed the note to Jess and Mark who found it highly entertaining. In fact, Mark almost did a spit take. That doesn't just happen in movies. Trust me. I thought he was *done* drinking by the way. He looked up at their table and laughed openly. Oh, he thought that was funny did he? I responded directly below and gave it to the waitress to deliver, along with a generous tip.

> **Dear Braden,**
>
> ***You've never seen me outside of court before. Are you implying that I am behaving in a drunk and disorderly manner?***
>
> **Regards,**
>
> **Gabrielle S. Ginsberg, Esq.**
>
> **Public Defender**

Just then another group of public defenders from our office came pouring through the door. Someone called out to inform us one of our colleagues had won a trial and it was time to drink and bond. I sighed and prepared. Here came the shots. I heard laughter coming from Braden's table when my reply arrived. About five minutes later, the waitress, who was probably making some good money with this, had returned with another note written below the other two.

Dear Gabrielle,

I assure you that I am making no such implication. In fact, I like the way you're behaving very much. I'm, frankly, intrigued by your threat to make me prove that I can handle your tongue. I must confess it makes me want to misbehave.

Best,

Braden T. Pierce, Esq.

Assistant District Attorney.

Oh shit! He was flirting back – big time! Now what? I hadn't planned this far ahead. Actually, I hadn't planned at all. I was winging it and flying blind here. While I desperately tried to think of how to answer that, a round of tequila shots arrived at our table along with salt and lime.

"Salud," Jess said and downed her tequila. I remembered again why I didn't usually go out with my colleagues on Friday nights. When there were more than two hundred lawyers in your office someone was always winning a trial.

"Viva Mexico," I said and drank mine distractedly in one swallow.

"Take mine, Gab."

"I can't, Mark. I hardly ever drink anymore and I just had two cups of beer and downed a shot of tequila within less than half an hour."

"You're not driving. Don't waste it. There are people going to bed sober tonight all over the world."

"Fine. Speedy Gonzales," I said making the only other Mexican-themed toast that popped into my head, and drank his shot too. I vowed that it would be the last one and I didn't care if someone came in who had just won the trial of the century.

"Are you trying to get her drunk?" Jess asked.

"Maybe." He laughed.

Finally I came up with something to write. I was going to have to sell some real estate to raise enough money to tip the impatient waitress who had been standing there the whole time.

> *Dear Braden,*
>
> *I wouldn't want to be responsible for encouraging an officer of the court to misbehave in public. That might actually be disorderly conduct – among other things.*
>
> *Yours Truly,*
>
> *Gabrielle S. Ginsberg, Esq.*
>
> *Public Defender*

My response was another big hit. I heard more laughter and comments that I couldn't make out. Actually, I could make out less and less of what was going on around me. My head was starting to feel a little fuzzy. Jess and Mark had been checking out this ongoing correspondence with great amusement. A few minutes later we received a reply from the other table.

> *Dear Gabrielle,*
>
> *Would you like to encourage me to misbehave more privately?*
>
> *Warmly,*
>
> *Braden T. Pierce, Esq.*
>
> *Assistant District Attorney*

My mouth went dry and I almost fell out of my chair but I had a feeling that people were watching my reaction closely, so I was careful not to get all flustered. Yep – you guessed it – law school. Really, the only thing they don't teach you there is law. Jess glanced over and quickly did a double take when she read that.

"What?!" she exclaimed. "Is that a question or an offer?" she asked Mark.

"Uh," Mark began with a laugh. "I think he might be asking her if she wants to hook up."

Oh fuck! The flirtation thing had worked a little bit *too* well. Although my position on the one night stand thing was wavering a little at the moment, the tiny little piece of my brain that wasn't yet swimming in beer and tequila was warning me that having a one night stand with the prosecutor who I faced regularly in court, and was insanely infatuated with to boot, was maybe not a good idea. Jess helped me to get a grip on reality.

"Mark, she was just flirting with him, not trying to pick him up. If he's interested in her let him ask her out on a date. You know — a date? Where you leave with the same person you arrived with?" I wanted to be just like Jess when I grew up. Then she turned to me. "Honey, you tell him that he doesn't get to misbehave with you unless he at least takes you out to dinner first." That sounded like a good response. It even sounded saucy. What the hell — I was feeling courageous. Alcohol will do that.

> *Dear Braden,*
>
> *If you want to misbehave with me, at the very least, you'll have to take me out to dinner first.*
>
> *Respectfully,*
>
> *Gabrielle S. Ginsberg, Esq.*
>
> *Public Defender*

"I suspect I'll be getting a summons soon," Mark said as we watched my response make its way

toward the other table. "So, you're saying that you're not interested in just hooking up with Braden but you would be interested in dating him?"

"I was under the impression that he didn't really do that – dating, I mean," I answered.

"He doesn't," Mark replied. "You never know though. I kind of get the feeling he may be a little more interested in you, but I can't make many promises, even if he is."

"See!" Jess smirked in triumph. "I told you so!" Mark glanced at her with amusement.

"Well, I might possibly be interested, but only if it was like a real dating thing and not just a one nighter with a meal plan," I said. Mark found that rather amusing.

"So, you would want there to be a *series* of dates?" he asked, sounding like he was negotiating a plea bargain.

"I'm not saying he's got to commit to a certain amount. I'm just saying that it would have to be more than "one and done" even if I got fed." I paused for a few seconds and then went for it. "And if he really wanted to date me then it would need to be exclusive."

"That's a pretty big demand." Mark looked like he didn't think I had a snowball's chance in hell of nailing that one down.

"I'm not making demands, Mark," I explained. "I just prefer that people who date me focus on getting to know me, which is easier if they aren't busy screwing a bunch of other women. Besides, I'm sorry, but I just don't want to stand in line at anybody's bedroom door. I was an only child. I never learned to share nicely." I didn't hold out much hope either, but I wasn't going to compromise on this and wind up miserable. I'd rather be frustrated than heartbroken.

"I think what she's saying, Mark, is that she would be more than happy to tire him out on a regular basis herself but she expects to be treated with respect." Jess summed things up well.

"Mark, I believe that Mr. Roth is trying to get your attention," I said. I had glanced over quickly and seen that Adam was grinning at us and gesturing for Mark to join them. Braden looked deep in thought but he was also looking at *me*. My tummy fluttered.

"I'll relay your position, Gab," he said with a smile. "We public defenders have to stick together." Mark was a champion negotiator. I didn't exactly anticipate success but at least I was in the best hands possible. If I ever committed a felony, (and mind you, the night was still young), I wanted Mark in my corner. When he left I decided to take advantage of Jess and I being left alone to hold a conference and I leaned across the table, speaking in a conspiratorial tone while breathing tequila fumes into her face.

"So, you really think that Mr. Player over there might agree to date me?"

"Anything's possible. Take off your jacket, by the way."

"Why? The air conditioning is set to subarctic."

"Just do it. All the booze you've been drinking should keep you warm." I slid my suit jacket off, hanging it on the back of my chair. I was a little self-conscious because the white sleeveless shell I had on underneath was snug, and it made me look like a waitress at Hooters, but the beer and tequila were really kicking in and so my self-consciousness was diminishing rapidly. Alcohol will do that too.

"What if he still isn't interested in anything but a one night stand though?" I asked. I had a quick flashback to my humiliating college experience. "I sense much awkwardness on the horizon."

"Then he isn't interested. You didn't ask him out. He asked you to hook up and you turned him down but said you *might* consider dating him. Big deal. Now let your hair down."

"What, am I going to bed?"

"Maybe – depends on what they come back with. Don't question it, just trust me." I sighed and reached up to do it. It felt good to take my hair down out of its elastic band and I shook it out and let it fall freely down my back and over my shoulders. Then I ran my hands through it to straighten it out a little.

"Anything else while I'm undressing?"

"Nope. That will do," she said with a smirk. "I think he's adjusting himself under the table." I noticed that at the angle she was sitting she could see the other table out of the corner of her eye.

"Braden? He was watching me do this?"

"Yep. Now that you've announced that he's man enough to handle your mouth he's barely looked anywhere else. He probably wants to throw you down on that table and make you see God."

"Well, at least we have that in common. He's not talking to Mark?"

"He's listening to Mark while watching you. It looks like they're engaged in some pretty intense discussion. It should be interesting to see if he's going to go for it."

Before I could ask her what she meant we were descended upon by herds of semi-drunken guys in business suits who had caught sight of us sitting alone. (Sometimes the hungry lions came to the baby gazelle.) One by one, and sometimes two by two, a steady stream of males smelling of beer, scotch, rum and various other potent potables, were stopping by to say hi and introduce themselves. They attempted to chat us up, buy us drinks, and stare at our boobs. I needed a whip and a chair. I was afraid that the whip might attract more of them, though, or at least the kinky ones. In between fending them off, we continued to talk.

"The problem is that I don't know what to say to him beyond making snarky comments." I was starting to sound panicky.

"What are you so nervous about? It's not like you've never attracted a guy before, Gabrielle. At least ten have tried to pick you up since Mark left the table"

"He's so sexy, Jess. He probably dated entire sororities in college."

"More likely they just blew him in the bathroom. If he asks you out on a date, Gab, then he seriously likes you. He doesn't date. He fucks."

"So, why are you encouraging me here?" Get it On by the Power Station was playing and I was tempted to start drunk dancing but nobody needed to see that.

"Because I think that he *does* seriously like you."

"Do you know more about this than you've shared?"

"Look, I don't know anything for sure, but I have a gut feeling and my gut's usually right. I'm also not sure that he'll do anything about it, even if he does like you, but he might now he knows that you're interested too."

"He doesn't even really know me, though. This is the first time he's seen me outside of court."

"Do you feel like you've gotten to know him by being in court with him practically every day for the past six months?" She had a point there. It was something I had thought about myself.

"I guess that I have gotten to know a lot about his personality."

"Well, he's gotten to know a lot about yours too. You guys *do* know each other well. You just don't know all the details." She looked up. "Uh oh. I think we're being summoned now."

That feeling I had before? That wasn't panic. *This* was panic. Even a bit boozed up I was nowhere near ready for a face to face flirt. Flight seemed out of the question, though, as Jess was already up on her feet and I didn't want to be left alone to face the horny drunken businessman brigade. I took a deep breath, grabbed my jacket and followed along. Several prosecutors had moved on and there were plenty of empty seats. Thanks to Jessica's decision to throw her body across three of them, though, I found myself seated directly across from Braden. This wasn't getting any easier.

"Was there something that you wanted?" I asked Adam, hoping that I just sounded saucy and not like my clients who worked the corner outside the Triple X Theater.

"Why don't you tell her what you want, Braden?" Adam laughed. I had a feeling that I could guess. Braden was giving me a really heated look. I had never seen him look at me like that, but then I had only ever been with him in court. It would be kind of odd to glance over in the middle of a carjacking case and see opposing counsel looking at you like he was picturing you naked. And I was pretty sure that's what he was doing. Although he wasn't being openly rude, he seemed to really like how I looked in a tight shirt in a cold room, if you know what I mean.

"We figured we would save you from having to turn down any more guys trying to buy you drinks," Mark said, tossing a peanut into his mouth.

"It's the least you could do, since thanks to you I actually *am* under the influence *now,* Mr. there are people going to bed sober tonight all over the world."

"Hey, it's not my problem you're a lightweight," he teased. "I didn't force you to chug those two cups of beer, Animal."

"I can't *wait* to hear what she has to say when she's been drinking," Adam joked.

"Perhaps I'll just sit here quietly and be entertained by your sparkling wit," I said and started torturing a napkin in a way that it had done nothing to deserve. Suddenly Braden, who had been quiet up until this point, reached down and picked up my hand. He held it up to examine it more closely and my pulse shot into the stratosphere. At this rate I was going to need a cardiologist soon.

"Yale?" he asked, looking at my class ring with amusement and then laying my hand back on the table. So, I picked up his hand and held it up for my own examination. It had seemed casually sexy when he had done it. I, on the other hand, was squinting, which made it look like I was giving him an appraisal. After two beers and two shots of tequila, I was lucky I could still see straight.

"You went to Harvard?"

"Go Crimson," he said, giving me a cocky grin. I put his hand down, afraid that if I didn't, I would yank him across the table and kiss him stupid for daring to be that sexy.

"The Bulldogs are ahead by ten games now you know." Way to be charming, Gabrielle. Maybe you should arm wrestle him too.

"That's just because Harvard's busy attracting world class scholars."

"You mean the ones who couldn't get into Yale?"

"I've heard that anyone could get into Yale."

"What?" I smacked him on the arm. *Oh shit*! I had just drunkenly hit a freaking prosecutor. I slouched down in my seat a little hoping to look less drunk and disorderly… and violent. He seemed to be highly amused though.

"Did everyone see that? She just assaulted an assistant district attorney," he said with a grin.

"She's a naughty girl. I think she needs to be punished," Mark said.

"Make sure you cuff her first," Adam said with a smirk. "I hear she's dangerous."

"I'm not afraid of a little danger and I like naughty girls," Braden said with a suggestive smile. He was openly flirting with me at close range. My heart felt like it was trying to escape my body through my throat and it occurred to me that it might be too late for a cardiologist. I forced myself to act cool and calm though. I held his eye contact and gave him a saucy smile. To that extent the tequila was actually quite helpful.

"You want to cuff me, you'll have to catch me first." I was getting pretty cocky over there myself, which was pretty impressive considering I was on the verge of having a nervous breakdown.

"Uh oh. I think we just hit foreplay," Adam said and I wondered what exactly would happen if I actually lost consciousness. Would someone try to revive me or would people just step over me on the way to the bar?

"We seem to have a rivalry, folks. I think we should see how Harvard matches up with Yale in beer trivia," Mark said, pulling out his phone.

"What is this, a frat party?" Jess asked.

"If it were a frat party we would play strip beer trivia," Adam explained. I could tell that Adam missed his fraternity days.

"Here you go, plenty of trivia online," Mark said. "And hey, there's sex trivia too. Hmm. The Harvard-Yale Beer Sex Trivia Challenge. I like the sound of that."

"How about a little wager that Harvard can take Yale?" Braden smiled. The look he was giving me was getting hotter by the minute.

You know how flames have that blue part? Well, that's what his eyes looked like. I felt like I was about to spontaneously combust.

"You want me to wager Yale's honor on Beer Trivia?"

"Beer *Sex* Trivia," Adam corrected.

"I'll respect Yale's honor," Braden replied, taking a swig of his beer. "Loser takes the winner out to dinner. That's what you wanted, right?" Out of the corner of my eye I saw Adam and Mark exchange knowing looks. *Jesus in a sidecar!* He was going for it!

"Maybe," I said hesitantly. This was only his opening offer — he was agreeing to one date.

"Oh yeah, Harvard's definitely going to take Yale." Adam smirked, watching us like he was watching two samurais circling each other. Or possibly like he was watching porn.

"Harvard's going down," Jess shot back, and I could hear barely suppressed excitement in her voice. She just couldn't wait to see what was going to happen next.

"Sounds like Yale will too, judging by our opening conversation," Adam retorted suggestively.

"Okay, forget the games," Braden said, sitting back and looking at me like he was ready to rumble. "You and I have been facing each other in court for six months and we've negotiated plenty of agreements. So, let's negotiate." The gloves were coming off. Bring it baby.

"Why don't you make me an offer, counselor?" I was hoping it would be an offer that involved getting naked at some point. I wanted to take off more than gloves. My chances of that were probably pretty good with Mr. Private Misbehavior over there.

I sat up straight with my shoulders back and my chin up. I may have had one fuckinormous crush on this guy, but I could be one tough broad when I needed to be. Hothouse flowers didn't allow themselves to be locked into ten by ten concrete rooms with guys who had "Blood Killa" tattooed on their knuckles.

"If I understand your position correctly you want more than a one nighter with a meal plan."

I shot Mark a deadly look. *Big mouth.*

"It was funny!" he said defensively.

"I'm stealing that line, by the way," Adam informed me.

"That's correct."

"I'll take you out to dinner tomorrow and you can choose where we go and what we do. Everything we do. I won't even try to touch you unless you ask me to. Nicely."

"Keep talking."

"We could also go out next Friday and you could choose again then if you wanted, although, there should be an implicit understanding that if we were hitting it off there might be some private misbehavior on the agenda. I'm not saying that I expect to hook up with you. I'm just saying that you should expect me to try. "

"Is that it?" I was playing hardball. I probably would have accepted it but I had a feeling he would offer more.

"You could also come over and join us for game night on Sunday at my place." I raised an eyebrow. Game night? "And I have a fundraiser for my family's charitable foundation that I have to attend next Saturday night. There would be dinner and dancing involved if you would want to come with me to that. So, that's four dates in two weekends and I'm not even anticipating any really good misbehavior until the third one. I think that's more than fair."

"Hold on," Jess broke in. "Game night counts as a date? As in she can come over and watch the Phillies, eat pizza and drink beer with you *and* your buddies here?"

"What, that's not romantic enough for you?" Braden joked. "I'm sorry, but that's what I had scheduled already and I don't plan to blow off my friends or my obligations. I also don't plan to drag this out for a month. If we want to keep doing this, we should figure it out quickly. Besides, she gets to choose what we do on two nights."

I could feel the expectant looks of everyone else at the table focused on me as they waited for me to answer. As usual, Mr. Pierce had made me a fair offer. I didn't really care what we did, to be honest. Frankly, I would have been willing to watch ping pong with the entire DA's office to spend time with him. Hell, I would probably have *played* ping pong with the entire DA's office to spend time with him. I took my time and held his gaze. Neither one of us was going to look away first. In the background *April Skies* by the Jesus and Mary Chain played. This had to be the coolest jukebox ever.

"It's a deal," I said finally. I had gotten what I had asked for. I was jumping on this opportunity before I lost my chance. I reached into my purse, grabbed my cell and handed it to him. He called his phone with it and we both typed in the contact info.

"The only thing is that I have to pick up my brother at Georgetown Sunday morning and move him back home, so I can't stay out too late tomorrow."

"Oh, perfect!" Jess muttered.

"I wasn't prepared for this!" Braden said defensively. "If I were, don't you think I might have picked something other than game night and a fundraiser?"

"What about the other condition?" Jess asked.

"When would I have the *time* to screw around during this little introductory dating period?" he asked her.

"Or the energy," Adam smirked. "She's going to tire him out eventually, right?" It was only the fact that my blood alcohol level was rising by the second that prevented me from dying of embarrassment.

"Seriously, Gab. Fridays and Saturdays are usually his only nights to pick up women," Mark assured me. "It sounds like by virtue of time constraints alone, you wouldn't have to stand in line at his bedroom door." Remind me never to tell Mark anything that I don't want repeated out loud to his two besties over there.

"I'm stealing that one too," Adam added.

"And if we get along and hit it off?"

"Then I guess we'll keep doing it," he answered. I waited. "Exclusively." I realized that I had been holding my breath and I released it.

"Fine. I accept."

"It's time to go home. You're agreeing to everything so easily that if we stay any longer you may wind up not going to bed sober *or* alone tonight." Jess started gathering her things.

"So easily?" Adam demanded. "He gave her everything she asked for!"

"And I'm sure she'll give him *plenty* of what he wants too. I have a newsflash for you, Mr. Roth. They wouldn't have agreed if they didn't *want* to. Come on honey. Time to go." She grabbed her purse and started for the door. "Enjoy your last night as a player," she called back over her shoulder.

"Make sure she gets plenty of rest," Adam called back.

"I'll call you tomorrow," Braden said.

"Bye," was all I replied. I wasn't sure I trusted myself to say anything else. I stood up, (steadily, I think), threw my jacket back on and followed Jess out the door. Well okay, technically, I walked face first into the door, but right after that I went through it. It was probably a good thing that I was leaving.

* * *

I knew what was coming as soon as we got outside. Jess did at least wait until we were about half a block away before launching into her "I told you so" speech. It was the start of a weekend in a major city so as we walked and talked, we navigated around many interesting sights and sounds.

"So, why would he be paying attention to you, huh?" She smirked.

"Okay, maybe he's a little interested," I admitted, stepping over a puddle of something I didn't want to contemplate too deeply.

"A little? If we had stayed any longer you would have had to break out a calendar."

"I said that I wanted more than 'one and done.' Besides, I amuse him. He's looking for some diversion," I replied, circling around a group of people who were either doing Thai Chi or line dancing – on a public sidewalk.

"Honey, Braden Pierce could easily find all the diversion he wanted. There were probably twenty women in that place who would have been happy to divert him on their knees in the men's room and at least a dozen who already had."

"Thanks, Jess! That image really puts me in the mood for romance," I said, passing by a six foot tall guy with five o'clock shadow dressed in a purple polka-dotted miniskirt and sensible pumps.

"Hey, I'm just stating the obvious. I told you that it would be significant if he asked you out."

"Tomorrow. He asked me out for tomorrow. Oh God," I muttered, avoiding two pretzel vendors who seemed to be purposely ramming their carts into each other.

"Yeah, and you should remember, this is one sexually experienced guy. God only knows what he's into. Maybe we should stop by that little shop. You know which one I mean."

"Look, Dr. Drew, he himself said that he would be playing by the third date rule unless I said differently, so I don't know about breaking out the sex toys yet."

"You haven't gotten laid in months. You might be the one to suggest it."

"I'm pretty sure that I should wait until at least the second date before buying a remote control vibrator," I noted, dropping a buck in the hat of a guy who was playing Feelings on the tuba.

"What, game night?" She rolled her eyes. "You should have held out for something better than that. I hope that this teaches you to listen to me from now on."

"Here it comes, three, two…"

"I told you!"

"You already said that."

"Okay. I told you asshat!"

∽ CHAPTER FOUR ∽

I had a hard time falling asleep that night and it wasn't just because of the tequila and beer induced bed spins. My brain felt like it might self-destruct every time I thought about the fact that my first attempt at flirting with Braden had been so wildly successful that I was now actually dating him. I was afraid that if I fell asleep I would wake up the next day and find out that it had all been a hallucination caused by some bad bean dip. So I laid there staring at my ceiling and not sleeping until about 3a.m. when my body finally told my brain to shut the fuck up if it didn't want me to look like an extra in Zombie Apocalypse tomorrow. Today. Whenever.

I crawled out of bed again at ten o'clock and staggered toward the smell of coffee in the kitchen.

"You look like hell," Jess said, glancing up from the paper.

"Thanks," I croaked. "You have no idea how much that doesn't help."

"Do us both a favor and have some coffee," she said taking a sip of her own. "So, where do you plan to go to dinner?"

"That little Middle Eastern place on Sansom." The coffee maker looked like an oasis sitting there on the counter as I staggered toward it.

"That little hole-in-the wall place? He would take you anywhere you wanted. Why not someplace fancy?"

"That place is really good and the people who own it are sweet. Besides, it's close by. Maybe afterward we can go down to Suburban Station and see if Stan's playing." I filled my mug and just as I was about to reach for the creamer I stopped myself. This was a black coffee kind of morning.

"Stan? You want your first date with a senator's son to include a trip to a railway station to listen to a street musician?"

"Stan's really talented. He's credited on albums put out by some real blues giants." I collapsed ungracefully into a seat across from her. Amazingly, I wasn't hung-over, but it felt like I had been hit by a Mack truck and dragged for a couple of miles.

"Yeah Gab, thirty years ago, but he's a street musician now."

"I think that if Braden doesn't like Stan and the Middle Eastern place, he's not going to like me much. Besides, I'm going to game night with him!" She smiled and shook her head like she thought that I was crazy but she loved me anyway. Then she got up and went over to the sink to rinse out her mug and put away the dishes in the drying rack.

I quickly finished my coffee and had just started to feel semi-human again when I heard my cell phone start ringing. I froze. Jess swung around and gave me an expectant look.

"Gabrielle! Answer your phone!" she ordered, diving at my purse. She grabbed it and threw a Hail Mary pass across our kitchen that would have had NFL scouts interested. I caught it… and fumbled… but Jess was on it. She threw her body on the bag and thrust her hand in just in time to click answer and pant into the phone like an obscene caller.

"Give me that!" I grabbed it away from her. "Hello?"

"Gabrielle? Are you okay? Was that a dog?"

"Braden? No, that was Jessica. She exerted herself a bit on the way to the phone." I gave her a "what the hell is wrong with you?" look.

"I see. I think. Uh, anyway, I hope it's not too early…"

"No. I've had my coffee and I'm not even hung-over this morning." I started straightening my pajamas like he could see me. And like it would matter that Betty Boop's ass looked crooked on my nightshirt.

"Are you usually hung-over on Saturday mornings?"

"No! I just meant that I might have gotten a hangover from last night because I don't usually drink a lot. I would have stopped after two beers and a shot but Mark pawned his shot off on me too."

"You do remember that we're supposed to go out tonight?" he teased.

"I wasn't drunk!"

"So you remember hooking up?"

"What?" I heard him start laughing. He was kidding. Whew.

"Where did you want to go tonight?" He still sounded amused.

"It's not fancy," I said hesitantly.

"Good. I wear a tie five days a week."

"It's not that far from my apartment and we could walk there if you didn't mind."

"Great, the weather's beautiful."

"It's Middle Eastern food. Is that okay?"

"That's fine."

"You're very easy to get along with outside of court."

"Are you saying that I'm not easy to get along with in court?"

"You can be tough sometimes."

"So can you."

"You're being very easy right now though."

"Maybe I'm hoping you'll be easy later." He laughed and I felt myself start to sweat. "I'm teasing you. I said that I would leave everything up to you and I'm fine with all of your suggestions. It just so happens that I like casual, I like walking and I like Middle Eastern food."

"Okay, well if you like walking we could go for a walk after we ate."

"Sure. Did you have somewhere in particular you wanted to go?"

"Yeah, it's close by though. Either you'll appreciate it as much as I do or you'll think I'm kind of nuts but it would probably be better that you knew that going in."

"What time should I pick you up?" he asked, sounding very amused now.

"How about six o'clock? I live in the Chatham. It's just off of Walnut…"

"I know exactly where it is. I live two blocks away from you."

"Well, that would make a booty call very easy. Oh shit. I said *that* out loud too didn't I?" I heard him laugh really hard. Good, hopefully he thought I was joking.

"Gabrielle?"

"Yes?"

"I also like you." I wanted to throw down my phone, jog the two blocks and throw myself into his arms.

"Yeah, well I like you too even if you do put my clients in jail. See you later Mr. Prosecutor."

"See you later Ms. Saucy Mouth."

We hung up and I collapsed onto the sofa and starting kicking my legs and making a noise so high-pitched that it probably attracted every canine on the block and was picked up by sonar in the Atlantic. Jess, who had tactfully left me alone, came running back in.

"Jesus, Gabrielle! Are you having a seizure?!"

"Please please please can I keep him mom? I promise I'll take care of him! Oh baby, I'll take care of him!"

"Good lord. She's finally gone around the bend. Can I have your Manolos when they come to take you away?"

"Jessica, he's so sexy! He's got such a great sense of humor and he was totally comfortable with me choosing everything. He even said something kinda sorta romantic. I've heard that such men existed but I've never seen one up close."

"Well, we need to make sure we don't frighten him off. We'll approach him very slowly and speak in quiet gentle tones. Put on some nice perfume and let him sniff you."

"God, I hope he doesn't think I'm nuts after tonight."

"Oh don't worry honey. I'm sure that he already knows that you're nuts."

* * *

At five-thirty Jess was sitting on my bed paging through Glamour while I got ready.

"It says that brown eye shadow really makes hazel eyes pop."

"Why would I want my eyes to pop?" I asked, pulling a brush through my hair. I was leaving it down even though it was a warm night because he had seemed to find it so appealing the night before. I figured that if I was willing to shove my feet into high heels every day I had already demonstrated a willingness to undergo a little discomfort in the interest of looking good.

"You know what I mean." Jess was the fashion and beauty expert of the two of us. She always looked great. Of course it didn't hurt that she was gorgeous. She had long auburn hair, big chocolate brown eyes, creamy white skin and seriously dangerous curves. She couldn't look bad if she tried.

"What are you wearing?" I picked up a short cotton skirt and a white scoop neck top.

"I figured this would be casual and comfortable but still show off my girl stuff. And the top makes my boobs look good without making me look like a walking dairy state."

"Good choice. You're going to wear pretty undies aren't you?"

"It's only a first date and he has to leave early."

"Gabrielle!" She sighed in exasperation.

"Okay! Just in case, I'll make sure that I don't wear granny panties."

"Thank you! I talked to Mark today, by the way."

"You did? Did he say anything about last night?"

"Of course! Why do you think I called him? Apparently everybody called him today. Turns out that Mr. Heavy-hitter hasn't actually dated anybody since law school. He's been riding the casual hook-up train for almost two years now." She went back to paging through her magazine.

"He seemed to agree to date fairly easily."

"Like I said last night, he wouldn't have agreed if he didn't want to. He was interested already, but you apparently blew his mind last night when you told him you would make him prove that he could handle your tongue."

"Who *was* that woman?" I asked disbelievingly. Jess put down the magazine and stared at me silently for at least ten seconds. (Did you ever time that? It's longer than you think.) Then she slowly rose to her feet.

"That woman was *you,* Gabrielle. Listen, I have something important to say to you and I need you to hear me. Be confident! You are sexy and he wants you. And it's okay for you to want him back. As long as he treats you with respect you can screw his brains out if you want!"

"You're very wise."

"I know, honey." She patted me on the back.

∾ CHAPTER FIVE ∾

Twenty minutes later I was dressed, perfumed, made-up, brushed, and about to collapse from nervous tension when Braden called from the lobby to tell me he was on his way up. Jess gave me a final once over and nodded her approval.

"Just remember, Gab, he's just as scared of you as you are of him."

"Somehow I doubt that."

The bell rang soon after and all of the oxygen mysteriously left the room. That happened a lot lately. Maybe I should check into a pulmonary specialist too. Jess walked over calmly and swung the door open like the father of a sixteen-year-old girl headed for the Junior Prom. She managed to look both deliriously happy for me and mildly menacing at the same time.

"Mr. Pierce. Won't you come in?" Yeah, that sounded warm and inviting.

"Thank you." He smiled and I saw her soften just a little. "Call me Braden." Had I ever noticed how cultured his voice sounded before? Probably not, since previously I had only heard him argue with me and tease me. He walked into our apartment looking much better than he had a right to, in a pair of loose fitting tan chinos and a white polo shirt. He could have just stepped out of an ad for Ralph Lauren. The Rolex was pretty nice too. And oh, I smelled the spicy-minty. Yum.

"You can call me Jessica," she said, giving him a once over.

"Thanks." He turned in my direction. "You look great," he said, checking me out none too subtly, starting at my Manolos and moving upward. His eyes seemed to linger a couple of extra seconds on my chest. I guess that he agreed with me about the top. Eventually his gaze made it up above my neck. "You always wear your hair tied back in court. I didn't realize that it was that long until last night." He was looking at it like he was picturing doing something naughty with it. Suddenly I could have cared less if my hair felt like a wet blanket on my head later. He had managed to turn me on just by looking at me. This man was much too sexy.

"Thanks. You seem younger when you're not looking so... prosecutorial."

"Well you know, the mantle of authority and all." He grinned.

"Okay kids, don't forget, Braden there has to go to school tomorrow so don't stay out too late."

"Thanks mom." I smiled. Braden held the door for me and I led the way to the elevator. It felt like the air was thick with sexual tension already and we weren't even five minutes into this date.

"It's a perfect night for a walk," he said.

"Good." I smiled with genuine pleasure. "I like walking around the city in the evening. There's always this feeling like something exciting is about to happen."

"Maybe something exciting is about to happen," he said, stepping into the elevator with me and looking directly into my eyes in a way that made me breathe faster. There was definitely an oxygen shortage in this building. The tension started to build even more. He glanced at the emergency stop button like he wanted to push it and then push me up against the wall. I probably only noticed because I was thinking the same thing. Neither one of us pushed the button, though. We reached the ground floor without interruption and the doors slid open, breaking the spell.

"This restaurant is literally like two minutes away, just over on Sansom. It's a little kabob place. The lamb is good if you don't think too much about how cute and cuddly your entrée once was."

"I try not to contemplate what my dinner was like in life."

"Probably wise." I glanced up at him and smiled. "So, you grew up around here?"

"In Bryn Mawr," he replied, naming a town on the Philadelphia Main Line with one of the wealthiest zip codes in the United States.

"Nice neighborhood."

"The Upper East Side of Manhattan isn't too shabby either."

"Been talking to Mark huh? What else did you find out?"

"Your mom is a VP at Goldman Sachs and your father is the CEO of a Fortune 500 company. So, you're a trust fund baby like me but you're an only child. I've got to share my inheritance with my younger brother and sister."

"Well, at least you know I'm probably not after your money."

"Most people highly motivated by money don't become public defenders."

"My parents like to point that out too, but not for the same reason."

"Are you close to your mom and dad?" he asked.

"Yes, very. They've been happily married for twenty-eight years and they're very loving parents. Is your family close?"

"Yes, exceptionally," he answered. "My parents have been happily married for thirty years. And my brother and sister and I are close even though Drew and I rag on each other."

"You went to Georgetown Law and you're twenty-seven like Mark?"

"Right. You went to Penn Law and you're twenty-six?"

"Yep. So now we know the details," I said with a smile.

"Now we know the details," he agreed.

"Ah, here we are," I said as we approached the restaurant. "I warned you that it's not fancy."

"I don't care about fancy as long as it tastes good. I'll try the lamb even though I'm afraid that now I'm going to think about how cute my dinner once was."

"Sorry about that." We went down the steps from the sidewalk to the entrance below and entered into the quaint interior filled with delicious smells and Turkish music. I saw my friend Ahmet rushing to greet us.

"Gabrielle! It's good to see you! Come in! Sit down! Damla will be happy you are here! And you brought someone with you!" He gave me an inquisitive smile.

"I've been telling him how great the food is here."

"Ah, yes thank you!" He beamed. He handed us menus and then hurried off. He was back in a moment with his wife Damla.

"Gabrielle! You are looking so beautiful! And who is your friend?" Damla asked with a huge smile. Damla was so warm she glowed.

"This is Braden. He's a lawyer too."

"And are you on a date?"

"We are actually, yes."

"That *is* good news!" she said, clapping her hands excitedly. Great, even the people at the kabob place were thrilled to see me with a date. "She is very lovely!" Damla said to Braden. "She will have beautiful children someday." I wanted to slide out of my chair and crawl under the table to hide. I started to read the menu with the focus of a Talmudic scholar.

"I haven't had that yogurt soup in a while. That was really good." Thankfully they took the hint.

"I'll send Fatma over to take your order. Have a very nice date!" Damla said sweetly.

"We hope we will see you many times," Ahmet added. They kept smiling and waving as they backed up toward the kitchen. When they got there I saw them peek their heads back out again. They had huge smiles and waves for us. I waved and spoke to Braden as I smiled back at them.

"I helped them with some immigration stuff once. They're very thankful people. And I haven't really dated anyone in a while so I guess they're happy that my attractive ovaries might not go to waste."

"Why haven't you been dating?" he asked.

"My opportunities are mostly for inner-office romances or one night hook-ups with strangers but neither one of those really appeals to me much. So, why have you been... um?"

"Having casual sexual encounters with no emotional investment or commitment?"

"I was just going to say not dating, but okay, if you prefer."

"It's been a while since I've been interested enough to want to know more about a woman than whether she preferred to be on the top or the bottom."

"Oh. Well, I'm flattered, I guess, and for the record, I like both. It just depends on my mood." He grinned and I saw his eyes start to heat up. Fatma came over and took our order. When she left Braden picked up where we left off.

"I should warn you that I'm very out of practice with the dating thing and it might take me a little while to get back into that mindset. For example, although part of me *is* sitting here thinking, wow here's this amazingly smart and sexy woman and I really want to get to know her better, there's still that other part of me that's thinking I want to take her back to my place and bang her until she can't walk straight."

I felt a little lightheaded for a second but then I imagined a little Jess hovering over the table saying "Confidence, Gabrielle! It's okay to *want* to be banged until you can't walk straight, honey!" I wasn't exactly sure why Jess was dressed like Yoda but I was just going to go with it.

"Ah, well. They don't really have to be mutually exclusive goals do they?" I started, and his grin slowly got bigger as his gaze got hotter. I was feeling very baby gazelle-like at the moment.

"Not at all," he said in a low sultry voice.

"Not tonight! I mean, because, well you have to go somewhere tomorrow." I swallowed.

"Okay? So, you *don't* want to hook up with me?" He looked confused. *Oh fuck!* I was totally messing this up! I didn't want him to think that I didn't *want* to!

"I'm not saying that I don't *want* to have sex with you! Believe me! I do! In fact, I want to have hot sweaty monkey sex with you! Okay, maybe that was a bit too candid. I'm just saying that I want it to be different than if you just picked me up in a bar. I wouldn't want you to just leave and thank me on the way out the door. I'm not expecting some kind of huge emotional connection right away. I just want it to be different than going to bed with my vibrator. Do you know what I mean?"

"You have a vibrator?" he asked with a smile and I rolled my eyes. "I'm just kidding! I know what you mean, Gabrielle. Would it shock you if I told you that I felt that way too?"

"You do?"

"I'm sitting here on a date with you, aren't I? I invited you over to my place to spend time with my friends. I invited you to my family's fundraiser at my parents' home. Obviously, I don't view you in the same way as some person I hooked up with at a club last weekend and whose name I forgot. Or never knew. What I meant was that I'm trying to do this right but I'm distracted by how much I want you physically. That's all."

"Oh. Oh!" I smiled. "Well, um, I feel that way too. You distract me a lot. "

"I kind of got that from the hot, sweaty, monkey sex comment."

"Oh Jesus. I really said that, didn't I?" I felt my face getting hot.

"Don't be embarrassed! Weirdly enough, I think that may have been the sexiest thing anyone has ever said to me. And believe me, I would be happy to oblige, but I understand what you're saying about tonight. And I'd like to be able to take my time and not be worried about having to be somewhere. Don't worry, I'm a big boy and I can wait a while. Not a *long* while. I have kind of a strong libido."

"So do I and I don't have much of an outlet for it, so believe me, I don't want to wait a long time either. I've been having X-rated dreams about you for God knows how long. Okay, that's probably too much information too."

"You're a very upfront person." He laughed.

"With you at least, it seems. So anyway! Since that's not in the cards for tonight, maybe we could just focus on getting to know each other better. We did the basic details but we didn't try to figure out if we have similar interests. Besides sex I mean," I said, and he laughed again. "I amuse you, don't I?"

"Yes, very much, and that's one of the things that I like best about you. I'm sorry if this sounds sexist but I find you kind of adorable sometimes."

Our entrees arrived then and we spent the rest of the meal discussing hobbies, books, movies, television shows, our college majors and activities, and our favorite pastimes. (Besides sex.) Amazingly, Braden and I actually had a lot in common. Perhaps the oddest thing we shared was a mutual enjoyment of watching PBS in bed. We wound up talking for hours. By the time we sat sipping our Afghan tea I felt much more comfortable with him, even though I was more attracted to him than ever.

"Well, that was delicious. Excellent choice. So where did you want to take me now?" Immediately, my stomach got a little queasy and it wasn't because of the lamb. Even I had to admit that what I was going to suggest was kind of an eccentric thing to do on a first date — or any date.

"I want to take you to hear one of my favorite musicians."

"Okay, great!" He called Ahmet over with the check. He and Damla effused joyful tidings a bit more and wished us well. I'm not sure, but I think they may have actually blessed us in Turkish. Braden left them a very generous tip and I knew he would now be on their list of VIPs. It was after nine when we finally left.

"We have to go to Suburban Station."

"Suburban Station? Is this musician out of town?

"Nope." I smiled and didn't elaborate. We walked the several blocks to the entrance I was looking for, descended the steps and started walking through the cavernous tunnels leading to the underground regional rail station. As we rounded a bend I heard what I was listening for, a deep rich smoky voice singing the blues and strumming a guitar. It was Stan the bluesman. I started walking faster. Within a couple of minutes we came upon Stan. He was sitting on a couple of milk crates holding his guitar.

"Gabrielle? Is that you?" An elderly voice called out to me. Stan's eyes were going a little in his old age.

"Stan! How are you?" I smiled at him as I walked closer.

"I'm just fine and how about yourself?"

"Great. I brought somebody with me to listen to your music."

"Is this your young man?" Stan looked up at Braden and gave him a big grin.

"This is our first date," I explained. "Braden, this is Stan. He's a genuine bluesman. He knew all the greats; Willie Dixon, Big Boy Crudup, Muddy Waters, T-Bone Walker and he played with quite a few of them."

"Oh hush now," Stan said. "You're gonna make me blush. Tell you what, since this is a special occasion, I'll play you a special song by another fella you may have heard of, Mr. John Lee Hooker."

Stan started to play and I heard the opening chords to *I'm In the Mood*. I started clapping my hands along with him. He was awesome as always, making that guitar sing.

A few other people started to gather and Stan immediately went into two more songs as folks dropped money in his guitar case. When he finished up, a middle-aged guy who had been standing over against a wall approached him.

"I've got to tell you sir, I'm a big-time blues fan and you've got some real talent."

"He certainly does," I said. "This is Stanford Benson you're talking to."

"The Stanford Benson? You're kidding me right?"

"No sir. Stanford Benson from Atlanta Georgia."

"Have you been playing here long?"

"A few months. I've fallen on some hard times, to be honest with you sir. It can be hard for an old bluesman to get gigs these days."

"My name is Ron Baker. I write for the Philadelphia Inquirer and I'd like to write a story about you. I'd also like to introduce you to a friend of mine who owns a little club called the Blue Moon. I think he'd be thrilled to have you play his place."

"Well sir, I would certainly appreciate that," Stan said, his voice cracking a little. I was feeling kind of emotional myself to tell you the truth. I figured it was time for us to make our exit.

"Thanks so much, Stan. That was like the coolest first date song ever."

"Yeah, I agree," Braden said and dropped a hundred bucks in Stan's guitar case on top of the fifty I had slipped in there surreptitiously.

"Thank you! Both of you! I think you must be good luck."

We waved goodbye, and walked in contented silence for a couple of minutes and then Braden turned to me and said, "Well, how about that? Something exciting happened."

"Yeah! No kidding, I really hope Stan gets a regular gig," I said and he gave me a strange look that I couldn't interpret. I figured that he was probably thinking that I was nuts. "Is this the weirdest date you've ever been on?"

"Yeah, probably. And I *like* it, but I do really have to get up early."

"We can just head on back if you want."

"It's not that I want to. It really is only because I have to get up at five and I'll be helping him move." He hesitated and then said, "I could cancel game night tomorrow and just take you out if you wanted. Mark and Adam would understand."

"It's okay. Game night is fine." I looked at him and smiled. "You're going to be tired anyway."

"You're pretty easy to get along with outside of court," he said smiling back.

"Maybe I'm just hoping you'll be easy next Friday night," I teased. His look heated up again.

"I wouldn't worry about that if I were you. I think your chances of getting pretty much any kind of sex you want are exceptionally good." My tummy flipped over.

He walked me to my apartment door but didn't make any move to touch me. He just stood there about three feet away from me waiting to see what I wanted him to do.

"I had a great time tonight," he said, watching me carefully.

"Me too," I said, a little nervous about actually initiating anything.

"Well then, I guess I'll call you tomorrow." He started to turn back toward the elevator.

"Kiss me! Please?" He paused and turned back. "I asked nicely." He smiled and then walked slowly over to me, looking into my eyes as he approached. When he was directly in front of me he leaned down to kiss me slowly and gently on the lips. My heart was pounding so hard I thought he must be able to hear it. I had just witnessed a famous bluesman playing a private dedication to me in a train station but not even that seemed as unbelievable as the fact that this man who I had wanted for months was actually kissing me. He started to move away and I threw my arms around his neck and pulled him back. He kissed me harder then and I opened my mouth to invite him in. Within minutes I had the door pressed up against my back and Braden pressed up against my front and his tongue was confidently stroking mine and exploring my mouth sensuously. His hands were under my shirt, against my bare skin, exploring my ribcage sensuously too. Sensuous exploration seemed to be a strength of his and I felt that this was a very good sign.

I was getting a little crazed out there in the hallway, to be truthful. I could feel his erection pressing up against me and I was starting to squirm shamelessly against him. Just the thought that I could get him into that condition was blowing my mind. It was a little scary that a simple goodnight kiss from this guy was driving me into such a state of hyper-arousal so quickly. Even though I felt hot and flushed I still had goose bumps everywhere. It was like my body didn't know what in the hell to do with this much stimulation so it just threw everything it had at it.

His hands started to explore higher and his fingers grazed the bottoms of my breasts and then gently traced the outline of my nipples through the soft fabric of my bra. I'm sure they weren't difficult to find, since they were so hard that they ached. I became vaguely aware of a quiet moaning sound and realized that it was me. My self-control was almost at the breaking point and I was getting close to telling him that we could always sleep in next weekend when I heard Jessica on the other side of the door.

"Hey, Gabrielle? I really hope that's you moaning out there. Are you planning to have sex in the hall? Don't forget that Kaylee next door is only fourteen." Braden and I flew apart and I straightened out my clothing while I caught my breath and cleared my throat.

"I'm just saying goodnight. I'll be right in," I called out.

"Goodnight," he said, sounding a little out of breath himself. "I'll call you tomorrow." He gave me a sexy grin and headed for the elevator without objection or complaint. I ducked into my apartment and went off to my room to break out my all-time favorite online purchase.

❧ CHAPTER SIX ❧

The next day when Braden called he told me that he was running late and he asked me to come by at about six-thirty. Since we were just hanging out at his place I dressed casually in cut-offs and my "Brainy Is the New Sexy" tee-shirt.

"You're sure you want to go drink beer and eat pizza with Adam and Mark?"

"I'm sure that I want to go and do anything with Braden."

"Do you even know how to play baseball?"

"Basically. You hit the ball and run around the bases and the other team tries to stop you. How hard can it be? I don't completely understand football either and I watch the Harvard-Yale game."

"You really have it bad for this guy. I can't imagine you doing this for anyone else."

"I have court early tomorrow and so I probably won't be home late."

He greeted me at his apartment door, looking very cute in faded jeans, an old gray tee-shirt with Phillies written on it and bare feet. His hair looked slightly damp. He smiled when he saw my shirt and then his eyes traveled down my legs.

"Come in and make yourself comfortable. You're welcome to take off your shoes, or any article of clothing that you like, for that matter." He gave me a smile that made my tummy feel all fluttery. I slipped off my shoes and left them by the door. His apartment had an open layout with beautiful dark hardwood floors. Straight in front of me there were floor to ceiling windows along one exterior wall that presented a spectacular view of the Square and the buildings beyond. To my left was a modern kitchen and dining area and to my right a large flat screen TV was mounted on the interior wall and surrounded by an arrangement of a black leather sofa and matching loveseats. There were also lots of books and bookshelves everywhere. I loved books. I also loved people who loved books. This too, was a very good sign.

"This is really nice, Braden. I like the way that it's so open but it still feels cozy."

"Thanks." He looked genuinely pleased with the compliment.

"So I guess Adam and Mark aren't here yet?" I wandered over to the window to check out the view and I imagined how the buildings in the distance looked lit up after dark. It must be beautiful. I was a city girl.

"They usually come at about seven," he said walking up behind me. "I wanted to have a chance to spend at least a little time with you alone. This was the best I could do. I didn't get home until six myself and I wanted to at least shower."

I turned around and put my arms around his hips. "I don't know. I think I might like you a little sweaty," I teased. It's amazing how brave six months of celibacy and a very sexy guy could make me.

"Well, I'm looking forward to getting sweaty with you."

I started feeling warm and my skin felt tingly. I bit down on my bottom lip and his eyes seemed drawn to it. He traced it with the pad of his thumb and then he bent his head down and kissed me, biting it himself and tugging it into his mouth. He sucked on it lightly before deepening the kiss and slowly rubbing his tongue up against mine. I began to shiver a little and when he moved away from my mouth and started trailing kisses down my neck my legs got shaky.

"Uh, Braden," I said a little breathlessly.

"Mm?" he replied, tugging my earlobe into his mouth and sucking on it. *Jesus that felt good!*

"I think I may need to sit down."

"Sure," he said, looking a bit concerned. I'm sure my eyes were probably glazed over and my face was flushed. I probably looked drugged. He took my hand and led me over to the sofa where I plunked myself down less than gracefully.

"Are you feeling okay?"

"More than okay — I was feeling so good that I was afraid I might hit the floor," I said throatily, and a big beautiful grin slowly took the place of the worried look. He sat down beside me and picked right up where he had left off, returning his attention to my very lucky earlobe. I ran my fingers through his hair enjoying how warm and soft it felt even slightly damp. Actually, he was warm all over, but his hair was probably the only soft part of him. I ran my other hand over his back, and lordy, those muscles were tight. I breathed in his spicy scent and I *felt* drugged too to be honest. I was high on Braden.

My hands weren't the only ones that were busy. His had started out on my back but then one hand had worked its way to my front and up under my tee-shirt. He reached into my bra this time, cupped my breast and circled my very attentive nipple with his thumb. I whimpered a little and arched my back, pushing against him hard. He stopped kissing me for a moment and gave me that blue flame look.

"They're going to be here soon." His voice was a little husky. "We don't have a lot of time and I don't want to drive both of us crazy, but, you know the other night when you took your jacket off at the pub?" I nodded. "I couldn't help but notice you have really gorgeous ti... uh, breasts. Could I, um? Could I maybe just..." He had a sexy, almost boyish, smile on his face. I nodded again and I noticed that he was breathing quickly and looking just a little flushed himself. He held my gaze but reached behind me and unhooked my bra. Then he gently eased my shirt up. I realized at that moment that there was a fairly good chance that Braden was a boob man. His gaze dropped and he let out a low groan. Yep – boob man.

"Beautiful." And then a slightly shaky breath. "Must touch." He swallowed hard and reached out to cup and caress my breasts, lightly pinching my nipples and making me moan and push myself against him some more. *Christ*, I was totally shameless with him! "Perfect," he said in a low thick voice almost to himself. Oh my God. I was so turned on that I was starting to tremble. He gently pushed me down onto my back, leaned over me and lowered his head. I felt his tongue graze one very hard nipple…

… When Adam and Mark rang up from the lobby. That had to have been the quickest half hour of my entire life. I let my head fall back against a pillow, stared at the ceiling for a second and, I'll admit it, I said a *really* bad word. Inner-Gabrielle also kicked the wall a few times. I looked back at him and despite startled amusement at my colorful choice of expletive (recall that I spend my days interviewing guys in jail), I could see from the expression on his face his self-control was getting a work-out. I wasn't the only one in the room craving some hot sweaty monkey sex.

"I'm sorry," he said. He sounded apologetic and looked frustrated.

"It's okay." I sat up and fixed my clothes while he had them buzzed in. When he was done I looked at him and smiled. "Don't worry. We'll have the opportunity to get seriously freaky soon." I know — I'm just so wonderfully warm and romantic sometimes. A sweet talker like me should write for Hallmark.

"I'll make sure it was worth waiting for," he said, giving me a slightly wicked look and went off to splash cold water on his face. I could have benefitted from being hosed down.

* * *

Not long after, Mark and Adam were at the door and Braden invited them in. They obviously didn't see me standing off to the side behind them. Ask me how I figured that out.

"Braden looks happy." Mark smiled. "Everybody'll be getting deals tomorrow. Stole a car and committed sixty-three moving violations during a high speed chase? No problem. Just don't do it again."

"So did Harvard take Yale or did Harvard go down?" Adam asked.

"More importantly did Yale go down? We want to hear how you handled her tongue," Mark said lasciviously. I suppose that I could have gotten all offended by this but, come on, it wasn't like Jess and I didn't dish details too, and I mentioned that I spend time with guys in jail, right? I just rolled my eyes.

"Don't you think you should at least say hi to her first?" Braden asked.

"Oh fuck!" Mark spun around. "Hi, Gabrielle! How are you doing?" Adam just cracked up.

We were waiting for the pizza and sitting in front of the TV drinking beer while some kind of pregame show was on when Mark brought up a different subject.

"So how about that article in the Times today that mentioned Gabrielle's dad?"

"I didn't read the Times today. Just the Inquirer," I said.

"I was busy moving Drew all day. I didn't get a chance to read anything," Braden added.

"Does your father know that you're dating Gabrielle?" Adam asked and I immediately started to get worried. Braden looked at him warily.

"I told my parents that I just started dating somebody and that I was bringing her to the fundraiser, that's all."

"My dad's not in jail or anything?" Images of Ivan Boesky and Michael Milken floated through my head and I started to panic.

"Nothing like that!" Mark assured me. "You have the Times?" he asked Braden. Braden got up and brought it in, handing it over to him. He paged through until he found what he was looking for. "It's called *The New Kingmakers* and it's a piece about a small group of CEOs who aren't really well known but who supposedly have a lot of influence. The article said that these guys all have been showing interest in supporting centrist politicians – almost like they had a plan. We just thought you'd be interested since Gab's dad is one of the CEOs mentioned and your dad is, you know, a centrist politician?"

"My dad lives in New York. Why would he get involved in a Pennsylvania Senatorial election?"

"The article was hinting about their ability to put somebody in the White House," Adam replied. Great. This was starting to sound like some weird conspiracy theory.

"And they have a "plan." Isn't that special? You know, I have some footage of an alien autopsy you guys should check out," I said sarcastically, and Braden snorted with amusement.

"Switching sides already." Adam shook his head.

"Hey, it's the New York Times, not the National Enquirer," Mark shot back. "I just figured that Senator Pierce might be interested in knowing that his son is dating the Kingmaker's daughter."

"My dad does things strictly by the book," I said. "He wouldn't make a bed without asking three people to advise him, two people to draft proposals and someone to provide catering. He's not sitting in some smoky back room plotting the future of the country."

"Can I see the article?" Braden asked. Mark passed it over and Braden took a few minutes to read it.

"My dad would probably just find it an amusing coincidence. For the record, he's not the pawn of any secret cadre of businessmen with moderate political views." He winked at me and my tummy fluttered again. Ha! I was on the teasing end for a change and Braden was on *my* side! I loved it!

"I think you guys should take a road trip to Roswell," I joked.

"Maybe you can prove that Elvis is still alive and break the Da Vinci Code on the way," he added and I giggled. Mark and Adam gave each other a look.

"I think it's just the two of us now, Adam," Mark said.

"Want to lay some cash on how long he has?" Adam asked.

"Six months," Mark answered.

"Until engagement or actual marriage?"

"Just until engagement. You've got to give him some time to get past denial and make it to acceptance."

"Nah. What are you, blind? This is only their second date and he may not even have banged her yet. He's going down like the Hindenburg this time, man. I say engaged in three, married in six." Adam smiled and sipped his beer "It was a good run though, Brade." He lifted his beer in a toast.

"You're nuts!" Mark replied. "I say, you've got to give him some time to get *her* under control. I think she's more dangerous than people realize. Engaged in six, married in twelve."

"You're on. I'll take that action for a Benjamin," Adam said and wrote something down on a scrap of paper and stuck it in his wallet.

"Isn't betting illegal in the Commonwealth of Pennsylvania outside of licensed venues?" I asked Braden with a smile.

"We might have to make a citizen's arrest," he smiled back.

The pizza arrived and I have to admit that watching the game was actually kind of interesting. I wanted to demonstrate that I was interested in learning more about the things Braden liked, so I asked questions and made a few observations – although admittedly, some of them may have been a little… odd. I even found myself cheering at various times. Once it was at the wrong time, but Braden cleared that up. Several times I caught him watching me and smiling as I stared at the screen, my brows furrowed in concentration. I definitely amused him.

When the game was over, I helped him to clean up and he seemed to like watching me do that too. In fact, he seemed almost fascinated by watching me do the dishes and put them away for some reason. I had a feeling that my shorts were probably riding up every time I reached for the top cupboards. Mark offered to walk me two blocks back to my building before driving home. Before I left Braden gave me a sweet goodbye kiss which, of course, led Adam and Mark to both tell us how disturbingly cute we were and led Adam to inform Mark that he should be prepared to pay up.

~ CHAPTER SEVEN ~

IN THE COURT OF COMMON PLEAS OF PHILADELPHIA COUNTY, PENNSYLVANIA

Monday

<u>Commonwealth v. Sanchez</u>

Braden was questioning the witness, Mr. Lao, owner of a corner market that my client had held up. I won't even say "allegedly" held up because I was quickly discovering that there was pretty much no doubt whatsoever that my client was guilty. Mr. Lao was a small, highly agitated man who spoke with a heavy accent and gestured a lot with his hands. His message, nevertheless, was coming across loud and clear. We were screwed.

"So Mr. Lao, it's your testimony that the defendant, Mr. Sanchez, held you up at gunpoint and asked you to open your cash drawer. What happened then?" (My client claimed that this was all a big misunderstanding, incidentally.)

"He say 'not enough money' and he look mad. Then he tie me up with tape and I sit behind counter." Yeah, kind of hard to see how this could have been a misunderstanding.

"And what did Mr. Sanchez do then?"

"He work register. Wait on customer. Take money." I forced myself not to roll my eyes. Inner-Gabrielle was slapping my client upside the head.

"Wait a minute!" Judge Channing cut in incredulously. "Did you just say that *he* worked the register?!" I sighed. *Why did I always get these cases?*

"Yes. He wait on customer. Make change," Mr. Lao answered.

"How long did he do this?" Braden asked, glancing at me. *Here it comes. Are you ready for it?*

"Eight hour." *Cue confetti!*

"He worked a full shift?!" Judge Channing cut in again. I saw Braden cover his mouth and turn toward the prosecution table to fumble with some paper. *Yeah, laugh it up, pretty boy.*

"Yes. He good worker." Braden coughed.

"No further questions Your Honor."

"Ms. Ginsberg!" Judge Channing looked at me dubiously.

"Mr. Lao," I said rising to my feet. "English is not your first language, is it?"

"No."

"And Mr. Sanchez spoke with an accent. True?" (Not like tying him up hadn't given him a hint to my client's intentions.)

"Yes. He have accent."

"Thank you. No more questions." I sat down.

"Any redirect?"

"Just one question, Your Honor," Braden replied. "Mr. Lao, did you understand everything that Mr. Sanchez said to you?"

"He say give me all your money or I shoot you. You see when you look at security camera video." *Yep. We were screwed.* Inner-Gabrielle started filing her nails. This one was over.

"No further questions."

"I'm assuming there's no argument, Ms. Ginsberg?" Judge Channing asked, giving me a look that clearly said that there had damned well better not be any. I tapped my pen against my legal pad as if I were actually giving it careful consideration and making a strategic decision to hold off. I wasn't fooling anyone. I had nothing.

"No, Your Honor, however, we hope to discuss the possibility of a plea bargain with the Commonwealth."

"Obviously. All charges held for trial. Schedule it." He banged his gavel. That, thankfully, was the last case of the day. Braden brought me the order and Mr. Sanchez, the industrious armed robber, was led away.

"No deal."

"What? What do you mean no deal?"

"Gabrielle, the man worked the counter for eight hours with the owner tied up behind him. It's all on video. I would have to try *really hard* to lose this case at trial."

"You want to waste your time trying this? What is it you think I would say to the twelve jurors who gave up their day for that great example of the criminal justice system in action?"

"Maybe you could put on your 'everybody has a right to a trial' defense."

"You know, I'm going to win with that one someday, baby. You had just better watch out."

"Look, I won't object to him pleading guilty."

"With no agreement? How kind of you! Well, at least people won't question whether I'm trading sexual favors for deals."

"Wait a minute! You never said that was on the table!" he joked.

"I may have no other choice. He worked the freaking cash register for eight hours to get more money! On camera! C'mon, big boy. I'll let you cuff me for plea to unlawful restraint with a two year cap." I winked.

"Pack up your stuff and come with me," he said, shaking his head and packing up his own files. I packed up all of my files and followed him out of the courtroom. I saw that we were headed toward the onsite DA's offices where prosecutors prepared witnesses and negotiated plea bargains. We went in and he led me to an open interview room, shutting the door behind us. I figured that he had taken pity on me and would throw some kind of bone.

"So, you want to discuss a deal after all?" I asked seriously.

"I'll think about it, but don't expect it to be generous, and I won't offer anything if the victim objects."

"Okay?" I said, feeling a little confused. "I guess I can understand that. So why did you want to come here?"

"Because I want to kiss that saucy mouth."

"Oh," I said, surprised, and felt goose bumps form on my arms. We were at work. This was... different. He walked over and stood right in front of me. I could feel heat radiating from his body and, God, he smelled good. He grabbed my chin and tipped my head back. Then he looked intently into my eyes for a second, leaned down, and I could feel his warm breath and sense his lips about to brush mine, when he pulled back, teasing me. I opened my eyes again, unsure what to do and afraid to move. I was about to start panting and a small whimper escaped my throat.

It seemed to fire him up and his mouth came down on mine hard and took total possession of it. So far he had been a slow, sensuous kisser but today he was more greedy and demanding, almost dominating, and I'm not ashamed to tell you that I liked it! He reached inside my suit jacket and ran his fingers lightly along my back, sending shivers up and down my spine and I felt my lower regions heating up and liquefying. After melting my panties for a few minutes he pulled back.

"I have a confession. I tend to get a lot of adrenaline flowing in court," he said in a husky voice. "When I'm in court with you, I also tend to get a lot of testosterone flowing. The combination fires up my libido like you wouldn't believe."

"I should argue with you more often," I replied a little breathlessly.

"You argue with me all the time. We're lawyers. And you've been driving me crazy for quite a while now. If we hadn't started dating I probably would have banged half the women in this courthouse."

"I thought that you had banged half the women in this courthouse."

"Okay, the other half."

"You know, I think I'm happy that I'm a lawyer. And, believe me, I don't say that a lot."

"Nobody says that a lot. I really need to have some hot sweaty monkey sex with you on Friday. And when I say "some" I mean hours' worth. I'm talking getting seriously freaky until we pass out."

"That's the best offer you've made me all day. You know that if I wind up trying this dumbass case, I'm going to make you use that adrenaline and testosterone to service me all night."

"Well then, we'll definitely need to sleep in the next day. Now I have to get out of here before *I* hit the floor... with you under me."

Tuesday

<u>Commonwealth v. Murphy</u>

My client, Ms. Brandy Murphy, had elected to go non-jury for her simple assault trial. That meant that the judge would determine whether or not she was guilty of assaulting her boyfriend Mr. Vinnie Virillo, who was presently testifying for the Commonwealth. The fates were smiling down on Ms. Murphy. That morning Judge Channing had awoken with a case of the runs, and sitting in for him was Judge Anita Blasko, President of the Women's Bar Association. The courtroom also happened to be packed with women who had dated at least one Vinnie Virillo in their lives.

"Mr. Virillo, can you please describe for the judge what led to the police arriving at your house on April sixteenth of this year?" Braden asked the witness.

"I was in bed with my girlfriend and she started beating on me, so I got up and ran, and she ran after me and the neighbor called the cops."

"Let's go back, you were in bed with your girlfriend and what specifically happened?" More like what *hadn't* happened, I thought cynically. I tried to keep my expression neutral even though Mr. Virillo had the same effect on my stomach as mixing a few gin martinis, a bottle of red wine, some orange Gatorade and a Twinkie. Don't ask how I know that.

"We were having sex, you know? I got off, but she didn't, and she was really pissed, sorry, mad, because I ain't been trying too hard lately if you know what I mean." Many women sitting in the courtroom waiting for cases knew what he meant, because I heard some angry female grumbling coming from behind me.

"Are you saying that she became angry because you reached orgasm before she did?" Let me just take a moment here to give myself some credit and point out as an aside that I have some pretty mad concentration skills, because hearing Braden Pierce say the word "orgasm" was almost enough to make me actually have one... okay, back to business.

"Not *before* I did!" My client got up from the defense table and yelled at Braden. "That selfish bastard don't care if I ever do!" One of the spectators tossed out a, "you tell 'em, honey!"

"Ms. Murphy!" I whispered harshly, all but forcing her to sit down. "You can't do that. You're just going to hurt your case."

"Ms. Murphy!" Judge Blasko cautioned. "Listen to your lawyer and remain calm for your own good. And I'll need everyone in the courtroom to remain quiet, please." Ms. Murphy was mad and I didn't blame her. Luckily, Judge Blasko looked like she didn't either.

"So, Mr. Virillo," Braden continued, "when you say she beat you, what do you mean?"

"She whacked me in the chest."

"Was it a hard whack...Uh, that is, did she strike you with force?" Braden glanced at me and actually looked embarrassed. I could tell that he hated this case.

"Well, really it was more like a push. I went flying off of her and I wasn't sticking around to find out what else she would do. She was really pissed, man. Sorry – mad."

"And you said she ran after you?" There was more mumbling from the female part of the crowd and Judge Blasko shot them a warning look.

"Yeah! I headed for the door and she threw my clothes after me. The old lady who lives next door was outside and she got all worked up because I was naked, you know? So I told her, hey, lady, my crazy ass girlfriend is gonna beat the crap outta me and she called the cops on her."

"No further questions." Braden sat down with a look of relief.

"Ms. Ginsberg, cross." Judge Blasko gave me a look that made me think that she was hoping I would kick this guy in the wack. I was happy to oblige. Mr. Virillo was goin' down, possibly for the first time in his sorry life. I stood up and advanced on him confidently. He seemed to shrink back.

"Mr. Virillo, you didn't sustain any injuries, did you?" I asked.

"Nah. I was too fast for her." He started to laugh at his own stupid joke but I cut off his mirth with a quick follow-up question. I stood directly in front of him now and stared at him hard as I watched him squirm. I got the feeling that he wasn't used to women standing up to him. In fact, I suspected that was part of the reason that we were there.

"She shoved you so hard that you quote "flew off of her" unquote but you didn't have a single mark on you?"

"Objection. Argumentative." Braden still had to do his job even if he hated the case.

"Overruled. Answer the question." I got the feeling that the judge really wanted to say, "answer the question asshole." It must be hard to be a judge sometimes.

"I meant I got up fast and ran because I knew she wanted to beat the crap outta me." I walked over to the defense table and made a show of picking up the file and looking it over.

"There's nothing in your statement to the police that indicates that she threatened you, is there?"

"No. I mean she didn't have to say it."

"You've never called the police before, have you?"

"No, but there's always a first…" I cut him off.

"You made a comment to her before she allegedly shoved you, didn't you?"

"I think I may have said, 'better luck next time, babe' or something like that but I was kidding around, you know?"

There were actually some boos from the spectator section and a voice called out, "You're lucky you weren't with me, baby, or this would have been a murder trial!"

"I want order in this courtroom!" Judge Blasko banged her gavel. I glanced over at Braden. He was barely hiding his disgust for the "victim" in his case and he looked like he wanted to leave.

"After you said, 'better luck next time babe,' she said 'get off of me, you loser.' Correct?"

"Something like that."

"You're six feet two inches and weight two hundred and twenty pounds, right?"

"Yeah."

"She's five foot two and weighs one ten, right?"

"Sounds right."

"It doesn't say here that she was armed, does it?"

"She wasn't, but she threw stuff at me." He was starting to sound like a petulant child.

"She threw your clothes *out the door,* correct?"

"But *I* was out the door so it was the same thing." He looked like he wanted to stick his tongue out at me.

"And when your elderly neighbor threatened to call the police because you were outside unclothed and yelling obscenities yourself *that* was when you claimed to be in fear for your safety, right?"

"Yeah." Mr. Virillo gave me a mean look and sat there sulking. Inner-Gabrielle would have liked to have assaulted him for real. I suspected that most of the courtroom, including the judge and the prosecutor would have happily helped. I had accomplished what I set out to do and Mr. Virillo wasn't laughing now. He was starting to look worried and I didn't blame him. He might need a police escort to get out of this courtroom.

"No further questions." I sat back down. Ms. Murphy looked triumphant.

"Redirect?"

"No, Your Honor." Braden wasn't stupid "The Commonwealth rests."

"The Defense rests, Your Honor, and we'll waive argument unless the court deems it necessary."

"The Commonwealth waives argument and stands on the evidence as presented," Braden added. He was so sexy when he was being all prosecutorial even in dumbass cases like this one. Judge Blasko deliberated for five minutes and returned a verdict of not guilty. I had won a trial! In case you didn't know this, that didn't happen all that much for public defenders, even really experienced ones. And even better than winning, my client was actually innocent! That happened even less! Ms. Murphy thanked me and left with her head held high, to the vocal support of several women in the courtroom. Mr. Virillo attached himself to a deputy and slunk out. Braden came over to the defense table.

"Was it a hard whack?" I asked with amusement.

"Come and talk to me. Please?"

"Oh, poor Mr. Pierce," I said with a smirk.

"Maybe you can comfort me. Oh wait, I meant not *confront* me," he teased, and I felt my cheeks heat up. He was much too good at teasing me.

"Fine, I'll come talk to you but you had better not leave before I'm finished."

"Oh, don't worry!" he said with a laugh.

I grabbed my stuff and stood closely beside him, (I wasn't taking any chances with this crowd), as we walked out together and headed for the same interview room we had gone to the day before.

"I know we've only had a couple of dates, and so we haven't really gotten very far with the physical side of our relationship yet," he said as soon as the door was closed behind us, "but *please* fucking tell me that you realize that I wasn't excusing his performance. I wish that she *had* beaten him!"

"If you say so," I teased. "I don't know though, sometimes I think you guys all stick together."

"Oh come on! I wanted to apologize to every woman in that courtroom and then I wanted to grab you and take you back to my place and make you come like ten times."

"Oh *my*! You're much more 'virile – o' than I realized."

"Oh, that was bad." He winced.

"I'm sorry. I couldn't help myself. I've been dying to say it." I gave him a lascivious look. "Feel free to do that on Friday by the way. In fact, maybe I'll just add that to the list of things that I want to do, since it's my turn to choose." He was looking at me like maybe he wasn't going to wait until Friday.

"Just for the record, Harvard desperately wants to go down at this moment and there are only two things stopping me from just locking the door right now. One, that I don't want either one of us to ever associate sexual arousal with Vinnie Virillo, and two, I'm not really sure that it does lock."

"Ooh. I thought that I was excited just because I won a trial and exonerated an innocent woman, but after hearing that, I'm actually tingling."

"It's the adrenaline," he said with a suggestive look. "Maybe I'll have to let you win more often."

"You didn't *let* me win and it's more than adrenaline!" I laughed.

"I'm only kidding." He grinned. "I want to kiss you again, in lots of places, but I don't think I should. I'm pretty tingly too and I sense my good judgment rapidly going straight to hell."

"Adrenaline?"

"And testosterone." His eyes roamed over my body and came to rest on the top button of my blouse. "Shit! I'm so turned on right now. The fact that it's after that case is almost enough to make me seek counseling."

I let my eyes roam a little too and I could actually *see* how turned on he was. Oh my! I hadn't even touched him. He was a healthy boy. "Okay," I said throatily. "I'm feeling *too* tingly now. I need to go or I'm going to start begging you to do some really naughty things and I don't want to wake up with you *here* tomorrow morning." He took a deep breath and he was looking kind of flushed. I probably looked like I just ran ten miles.

"Yeah, we need to go. Now," he said clearing his throat and raking his fingers through his hair. He pulled his suit jacket closed and buttoned it. Then he took out some files to strategically carry in front of him. As we walked out together I wondered if we would really make it to Friday.

Wednesday

Commonwealth v. McBride

"I'm sorry Your Honor, but I just don't see how a Taco Bell burrito can be considered a deadly weapon," I said in exasperation.

"Perhaps Ms. Ginsberg hasn't eaten at Taco Bell lately," Braden responded.

"I don't know Mr. Pierce. I think I'm actually with Ms. Ginsberg on this one," Judge Channing replied. "Okay, I'm going to dismiss the aggravated assault and bind this over for trial as a simple assault." He banged his gavel and I returned to counsel table. Braden came over with the judge's order a moment later.

"Aggravated assault? With a burrito?"

"It was worth a try," he smiled. "You could have pleaded it down. I would have offered you a good deal. And I personally think that Taco Bell food should be outlawed anyway."

"So you had an agenda."

"Mr. Pierce, call the next case," Judge Channing barked.

"Commonwealth vs. McBride," Braden called out and a tired-looking woman accompanied by a clearly irate man approached Braden. Another man, nervously fidgeting with his tie walked over to me, his slightly wacky-looking girlfriend trailing behind him.

"Who are all of these people?" the judge asked.

"Your Honor, this is the victim, Ms. Parker and her boyfriend Mr. Connolly, who was a witness," Braden answered.

"And this is the defendant, of course, Mr. McBride, and his girlfriend Ms. Rodriguez who is a witness for the defense," I explained.

"A defense witness. Oh goody," Judge Channing said. "Before we get too out of hand here, why don't you summarize the Commonwealth's case, Mr. Pierce?"

"Your Honor, the Commonwealth will demonstrate that on May 11th of this year the victim, Ms. Parker was riding a city bus with her boyfriend, Mr. Connolly, when she felt her, uh, behind being grabbed. When she turned around she saw that it was the defendant, Mr. McBride who had engaged in said grabbing. Mr. Connolly had witnessed the action and the two males engaged in a verbal altercation. Mr. McBride is charged with indecent assault."

"And you have a defense, Ms. Ginsberg?"

"I do, Your Honor."

"And that would be?"

"Mistaken identity."

"Mistaken identity. Of course." Judge Channing didn't look pleased. "Wayne!" he yelled to his deputy. "Get me some Alka Seltzer!"

"Be right back, Your Honor," Wayne said, scurrying off. Braden and I each presented our witnesses. His side basically just said the same thing he had.

My side's testimony consisted of Ms. Rodriguez, affirming that she and my client were a very playful couple, and that he frequently grabbed her behind in public. Further, she was standing directly next to Ms. Parker on the very crowded bus. So crowded, that it would be difficult to tell one behind from another. She also pointed out that as soon as he had recognized his mistake, Mr. McBride had apologized profusely to Ms. Parker, but that Mr. Connolly had become quite hostile. In fact, Ms. Parker had seemed inclined to accept the apology, but Mr. Connolly would not let it go.

"And your argument is, Ms. Ginsberg?" the judge asked when all testimony was complete.

"That first and foremost my client lacked criminal intent, but that this case is also ridiculous. Seriously, Your Honor, is this a worthy investment of the resources of the Commonwealth of Pennsylvania and the time of the Court of Common Pleas of Philadelphia? My client grabbed the wrong behind on a crowded bus and apologized to owner of said behind. The DA's office wants to have him labeled as a sex offender! Although Mr. Connolly is angry, it doesn't even seem like Ms. Parker wants to prosecute this case."

"Objection, Your Honor!" Braden said, flashing me a warning look.

"Sustained. However, and I can't believe I'm going to say this twice in the same day, I think Ms. Ginsberg has a point, Mr. Pierce. This was a quick grab as I understand it? Not a prolonged fondle? And he immediately apologized. His girlfriend isn't even mad at him. That should tell you something. Can't we just resolve this?"

"Judge!" Mr. Connolly jumped in. "He grabbed my girlfriend's ass! Wouldn't you be mad if some pervert did that to your girlfriend?"

"Well... err, that's not relevant, Mr. Connolly," the judge answered.

"How about you?!" He demanded, turning to Braden.

"Well, frankly..." he began, but stopped as soon as he saw my glare. "I'm not permitted to testify."

"Any guy would be mad!" Mr. Connolly shouted. "You can't just go around grabbing women's asses on the bus!"

"It was a mistake and he apologized, Your Honor," I repeated emphatically.

"Perhaps if Mr. McBride had also apologized to Mr. Connolly," Braden suggested.

"To him?" I asked indignantly. "It was her a... behind and he apologized to her!"

"Mr. Connolly happens to have exclusive access to that behind," Braden continued.

"Exclusive access?! What is she, an easement?"

"ENOUGH!" Judge Channing had finally reached his limit and slammed down his gavel. "Mr. Connolly, if Mr. McBride apologizes to you would you let it go?"

"Yeah, I guess. Just don't let it happen again!"

"Hey man, I'm really sorry! Hell, I would be mad if somebody grabbed her ass too," he said gesturing toward Ms. Rodriguez.

"Yeah, okay," Mr. Connolly answered as the four of them walked off.

"Case dismissed," the judge said and banged his gavel again. That was the last case of the day and Braden and I both packed up our things to go.

"Perhaps we could have a little chat?" I asked with a smile.

"Sure."

"How about my office this time? It's closer," I answered. Public defenders had an onsite office just like prosecutors did. It was the place that we used to interview clients and witnesses. Because it was the end of the day it was practically empty. I went straight to one of the interview rooms and shut the door behind me.

"A burrito as a deadly weapon? A mistaken fanny grabber as a sex offender?"

"There's a lot of pressure right now at my office to push things through. I threw out all of the higher charges on that case! It would have been resolved before trial."

"I know, but these are people's lives, Braden! Those stupid schmucks had to miss work to come here. There are so many serious cases out there, involving seriously bad people. Why are you guys wasting time with this garbage?"

"I don't like it either! I have to do my job, though, just like you have to do your job when you tell a jury that it's reasonable to believe that a normal person throws a wine and cheese party in his pants!"

I tried not to laugh. Really, I did. I fought it for as long as I could and then I finally gave up and dissolved into the kind of laughter that makes you double over and pee your pants — which thankfully, I didn't do. Braden started to laugh with me and the two of us could barely breathe after a couple of minutes.

"So if we were on a date," I gasped, "and someone mistakenly grabbed my ass on a bus, would you prosecute him as a sex offender?"

"You really think," he gasped, wiping his eyes, "that I would take you on a date on a bus?" He almost choked, he was laughing so hard, and I lost it all over again. It took at least five minutes for the two of us to really calm down. My stomach ached and tears were streaming down my face.

"That felt really good." He smiled.

"Oh my God, yes! I needed to release some tension *so* badly!" I agreed. I saw his eyes darken and his gaze heat up and I breathed in deeply. That hot Braden sex look did me in every time. He smiled seductively and walked toward me slowly. "Braden, we're in a public place." I laughed nervously as I backed up. "Where we work." He kept coming and soon I felt the wall up against my back. "And I know *that* door doesn't lock," I said in a shaky voice.

"Hmm," he said, reaching around me and gently kneading my bottom. "So, would this be a quick grab or prolonged fondle I wonder?" he whispered. "And while we're at it, do I have exclusive access to your ass, Gabrielle?" he asked as he lowered his mouth toward mine.

"Of course you…" I murmured just before he kissed me. The tension and the adrenaline had been building all week and like someone had opened a floodgate we just let ourselves go wild. He pinned me against the wall with his hips as I ground my own hips into him like a wanton hussy. Our tongues were engaged in a battle of a whole different kind now. I wrapped one leg around him to give me better friction and he reached for the hem of my skirt and began to push it up as I reached for his belt. I got it open quickly, even though I couldn't see what I was doing and we were writhing around against each other. It was amazing how good my fine motor skills were when I was highly motivated. *Holy shit*, we were actually going to get seriously freaky right there and then. I would probably get aroused every time I looked at that wall. That could be awkward, considering that I came in here to negotiate plea bargains.

I was wearing thigh-high stockings and panties, (I don't have the coordination to deal with pantyhose before I've had my morning coffee.) He pushed the edge of my panties aside and I felt his fingers slide in and begin stroking my clit. He broke the kiss, breathing hard.

"Jesus, Gabrielle. You're so wet," he said hoarsely. I slipped my hand into his trousers and under the waistband of his underwear.

"I believe that I have your attention too," I said, now officially panting. I couldn't see what was down there but I could certainly feel it. Trust me. It was hard to miss. No pun intended. I gripped him and slid my hand along his length from base to tip. It was quite a journey. He groaned and whispered in my ear.

"Oh that's it, baby. I need to be inside you right now. I'm going to nail you right up against this fucking wall." Suddenly someone knocked on the fucking *door* and we froze.

"Yes?" I called out, trying to make my voice sound normal.

"Gabrielle, they need you back at the main office."

"Tell them I'll be right there," I called out, praying that she wouldn't open the door.

"Okay." Footsteps disappeared down the hallway. We both let out a sigh of relief. After a few seconds of panting and letting my heart leave my throat and return to my chest cavity he stepped back.

"It's for the best," he said huskily. "I say I want to be able to take my time with you and then I shove you up against a wall in a public defender interview room after a fanny grabber case."

"What, that's not romantic enough for you?" I laughed, still sounding kind of out of breath.

"Besides, we would have had to figure out something else anyway because I don't have a condom with me. I'm not *that* well prepared for court," he said sounding amused, as he refastened his belt.

THE LAW OF ATTRACTION

"I'm on the pill," I said and I saw him hesitate. "And I'm healthy," I added. He still didn't say anything. "Of course I would understand if you wanted some verification."

"I trust you. If anything, I think I should show you verification that I'm healthy – which I am. I get tested regularly and I've always used a condom." I nodded and then that sunk in.

"Always? As in you've never not used one?"

"Never," he answered. "With my ex-girlfriends it was more about making sure that they never got pregnant. I figured that if I didn't plan to marry them I should do my share to make sure that I never knocked them up."

"Oh, well, I'm fine with that. It's no problem."

"Not so fast." He started to pace. I think he did that when he was mulling something over. I was starting to get to know his body language well. "There's no reason to think your pill wouldn't be effective and I'm a twenty-seven-year-old attorney now, so even if it wasn't I could handle it."

I wasn't sure that I knew what he meant by "handle it" but I had never forgotten to take it, even when I didn't technically need it, since it made my monthly visitor so much easier, so I wasn't worried about it not working. Finally he seemed to come to a conclusion. "I think that I would like to try just relying on that, your pill I mean, if you're okay with that."

"I'm okay with that. Thanks for trusting me. I trust you too. I'm afraid that we'll have to continue this pre-sex talk at another time, though, because if I don't get back to my office the entire city will come to a halt – at least that's what they've trained me to believe."

Thursday

<u>Commonwealth v. Garcia</u>

I could feel that my face was flushed and my pulse was racing. I knew that my eyes were bright and flashing with passion. I was so turned on I was almost shaking. I knew the look Braden was giving me, like blue heat, it was a look that said that he wanted me. Right

here and right now. I stepped toward him and he stepped toward me…
and then both of us realized that the other one wasn't backing up and
that we were now literally toe to toe and practically on top of each
other. We both stepped back and started circling – actually circling –
like boxers in the ring.

"The knife was found among Mr. Garcia's possessions while he
was sleeping in Fairmount Park. This case falls under the Open Fields
Doctrine outlined in Oliver v. United States and the line of cases that
interpret it." Braden's voice sounded low and tense.

"It was found in a paper bag that belonged to him. He had a
Reasonable Expectation of Privacy in that bag. It's controlled by Katz
v. United States," and the cases that interpret it," I shot back at him.

"Okay! I've heard enough argument and I have your briefs on the
issue." Judge Channing looked vaguely uncomfortable. He was
probably able to guess that there was more being suppressed here than
evidence. "Let's take a break. We'll reconvene in fifteen minutes." He
banged his gavel and headed for his chambers. Braden raked his
fingers through his hair and began to pace. I went to the defense table
to catch my breath.

"I feel like I need a cigarette," Adam said. He looked flushed.

"Yeah, that was like watching porn," Jess added. Braden and
Adam looked at her. "I imagine."

"If you don't bang her soon, you two are going to wind up in the
Supreme Court," Adam joked.

"Or in jail," Jess added.

"Braden, do you want to discuss that…" I said a little desperately.
We only had fifteen minutes but I really didn't feel like it was a
choice at that point.

Apparently, he didn't either.

"Yes," he said, before I even finished making something up for us
to supposedly discuss. Grabbing my hand, he pulled me out of the
courtroom and headed for the DA's interview rooms.

"My office is closer," I said breathlessly.

"Our doors lock. I checked," he said letting go of my hand as we almost sprinted down the hall. We made it to the DA's office and burst into the waiting area... just to find all of the interview rooms occupied. *Shit! Shit! Shit!* We stood waiting impatiently as a MUZAC version of Karma Chameleon quietly played in the background. I checked my watch. We had twelve minutes. A door opened and a prosecutor and a public defender, still discussing something, began to vacate a room. I saw the fifty-something assistant district attorney who had prosecuted Mr. Harris, the shoplifter, stand and turn in that direction. Before he could take a step, Braden climbed *over* a coffee table and dove toward the door. The ADA and PD who were leaving gave him a startled look.

"Hey, Rob. How's it going?" Braden asked with a smile.

"Great, Braden. You in a hurry?"

"Yes! Actually, kind of an urgent matter. You don't mind do you, Gerald?" he called out to the older prosecutor.

"Go right ahead. I can wait," he said looking a little confused. I smiled and waved.

"Ms. Ginsberg?" Braden called me, trying to sound nonchalant.

"Hello Mike," I greeted the PD as I rushed toward the room.

"Gabrielle. You didn't bring any files with you?"

"Didn't need any," I said with a bright smile. "I've got it all up here." I tapped my forehead and dashed into the interview room. Braden closed the door behind us and locked it. He quickly checked his watch, as he took his jacket off and threw it on the desk.

"We have ten minutes. I think that manually is our best bet." He actually picked me up and sat me down on the desk in the room, pushing my skirt up and my legs apart as I got his trousers open. His mouth was on mine in a second and we were practically devouring each other, we were kissing so wildly. He pushed my panties aside and slid two fingers up inside me, circling my clit with his thumb as I writhed against his hand. I reached in and freed him, gripping and stroking his impressive erection. I still hadn't gotten a visual of the Harvard endowment yet but I knew it was big.

I broke our kiss to gulp some air and then attacked his neck, biting and licking and kissing him while building the rhythm of my strokes. I added my other hand to gently cup his balls.

"Yes or no?" I panted.

"Yes," he groaned. "Squeeze a little but be careful." I did what he asked and his breathing became ragged. His fingers slid in and out of me while he kept the pressure on my clit continuously, and I panted and tried not to moan. I had to bury my mouth against his neck to keep myself quiet. In case you were unaware, trying to come in a public place in ten minutes is not exactly an easy feat for a woman. I knew that I would have to work to pull this one off.

I tried to relax my body and just let my orgasm build. Luckily, he had very skilled fingers. If anyone could get me there, he could. I felt myself getting closer and I just allowed the sensations to wash over me, emptying my mind of everything and just focusing on the intensely pleasurable feeling between my legs. Braden was breathing very heavily and I knew that he could probably come right then but that he was waiting for me. I just needed to… let… go.

I gasped and my inner muscles clenched and pulsed as a tremor passed through my body. As soon as he sensed me coming he groaned and came in my hand. Thank God there was a box of tissues on that desk too. We stood there panting for a moment and then he kissed me lightly on the lips.

"I needed that," he said, as his breathing returned to normal.

"Me too." We managed to clean up enough to make it to the restroom in the lobby with a minute to spare, and we were just walking in the courtroom door when the judge took the bench. Both of us were noticeably calmer and more relaxed. Judge Channing wasn't ready to rule on the motion yet so we just picked up where we had left off and finished our cases. Afterward, we all packed up our stuff and got ready to go.

"So, did you two have a productive case conference?" Adam asked with a smile.

"They must have, judging by how happy they looked when they got back," Jess commented. A deputy came into the courtroom and called out.

"We need a PD to talk to a guy in lock up! A Mr." he checked the file, "DeWayne Johnson."

"Oh I know that case," Adam said. "That's the gentleman from the North Philly "social club" charged with triple homicide."

"I'll take it," I said.

"Hold on!" Braden stopped me. "You can't go have a chat with a gang banger in lock up."

"Why not?"

"He's violent."

"That's probably why he's charged with triple homicide, Braden. Although I will point out that he's innocent until proven guilty even if he is a gangsta."

"There must be a male PD around."

"I've interviewed violent males before and this guy's just a shooter anyway. I feel reasonably confident that they took the gun away from him when they arrested him."

"Yeah, but they'll lock you in with him. By the time they opened the door he could hurt you."

"Well they're not going to let him out to come see me. Where do you think I meet my clients? Starbucks?"

"I don't know why, I guess I just never thought about *you* going to do that kind of stuff. I thought your office would only send guys or at least not twenty-six-year-old women. It's a serious case and they should have a senior defender in there anyway."

"I'll just see what he needs and then if I can't or shouldn't handle it I'll get help, but I do this all the time. Half of the lawyers in my office are female and better to send a twenty-six-year-old than a sixty-year-old. Besides, my job is no more dangerous than yours is. You go out to actual crime scenes and you're the dude trying to put the bad guys away."

"I guess so." He didn't look happy about it though. "I'm going to call you tonight."

"To assure yourself that I made it out alive?"

"I want to talk to you about something and also continue our conversation from the other day."

* * *

That night at nine o'clock I was sitting in bed drinking herbal tea and watching Antiques Roadshow just like most twenty-six-year-olds, (okay, not really), when Braden called.

"Mr. Pierce."

"Ms. Ginsberg. I have a different kind of privacy issue to discuss with you. I know that tomorrow is supposed to be your choice but my parents want us to spend the weekend. Is that too weird for you? I know we just started dating and we're planning to get freaky tomorrow, so if it's too weird, just tell me."

"Are your parents going to be in the room when we get freaky?"

"They likely won't even be in the house. They usually go out Friday nights after dinner. My younger brother and sister do too and I'm sure they'll invite us along but I would rather stay in and have hot, sweaty monkey sex with you."

"You're sure that they want me to come too? Maybe they just want to spend time with you before the fundraiser thing."

"I think that they *especially* want you to come. Have I mentioned that they think twenty-seven is a good age to start thinking about settling down? Like I said, if this is too much pressure after two dates, then I completely understand. They're just extremely excited that I'm having a relationship of more than a couple of hours in duration. It's been a while."

"I'm okay with it, I guess, if you are. I'm sometimes a bit awkward around people I don't know well yet, but I clean up pretty well and I could probably make myself presentable."

"My brother Drew is much more socially awkward than you are."

"Thanks." I laughed. "He and I will probably get along well."

"I'm sure he'll *want* to get along well with you. He's a twenty-three-year-old player."

"You must be his hero."

"I will be after he meets you. I'll tell my mom it's okay then, and that you can just stay with me. I'm sorry that this isn't exactly the sexiest location for us to finally get to sleep together."

"Braden, we made each other come in an interview room at the courthouse today."

"That's a good point." He laughed. "That was also pretty impressive teamwork if I must say so myself. Are you in bed?"

"Yeah, I'm watching Antiques Roadshow."

"Me too. So now we can say that we've watched TV in bed together."

"When Mark and Adam ask?" There was silence on the other end. "Hello? Are you still there?"

"Yeah, I was just thinking about you being in bed with me. Today was just a stop gap. I need tomorrow night to get here quickly. Under other circumstances it might actually make *me* a little uncomfortable to get to know you biblically for the first time in my parents' house, but I'm desperate. I'm starting to get really distracted and not always at convenient times. So should we finish the pre-sex talk so that we don't have to worry about it later?"

"Sure," I answered.

"Do you have a favorite position?"

"Whichever one I'm in at the moment. How about you?"

"All of them. How many sexual partners have you had?"

"Six, which includes the first one, even though that was a onetime encounter."

"Your first time was a one night stand?"

"He wasn't just some guy I met at a frat party. He was a friend. I thought he was more than that but he was too happy being a player."

"How old were you?"

"Eighteen. I was a freshman at Yale and he was a sophomore. It's weird, you remind me a little bit of him. You're not going to sleep with me and then decide that we should just be friends, are you?"

"No. I always make it very clear upfront if I'm only interested in a one-night encounter and I don't tend to wind up being friends with the women I have them with."

"How old were you?"

"Sixteen, but my girlfriend was eighteen."

"You gave it up for a cougar," I teased.

"Why do I remind you of him?" he said, going back to the other topic. He seemed very interested in this.

"I don't know. He was tall and exceptionally good-looking like you. He sounded very well educated and upper class. He was very popular and he hooked up a lot. He was planning to go to law school. You're different in a lot of ways though too. You're much funnier and you and I have many more interests in common. He was very much a nineteen-year-old. You just hang out with guys who act like they're nineteen."

"He should have made things clear before he slept with you."

"I should have, too. In his defense, I don't think he knew that I was a virgin and I don't think he planned it. It just kind of happened. Besides, was it really surprising that a popular nineteen-year-old didn't want to get too tied down? I should have brought it up beforehand like I did with you."

"Yeah, by the time you got to me you were a crack negotiator. Good thing that Jessica was right and I wanted to agree with everything you asked for."

"Well, I wanted to agree to hook up with you. So you'll be lucky number seven."

"I promise that you'll get lucky. I'm going to let you go now so that you can rest up. I'm going to have some adrenaline and some testosterone flowing tomorrow."

"Sleep well."

"We'll both sleep better tomorrow night."

THE LAW OF ATTRACTION

Friday

<u>Commonwealth v. Franklin</u>

"Your Honor, my client has no criminal record. The marijuana in this case was for personal use and represented a lapse in judgment, nothing more. We would like to work out a settlement with the District Attorney's Office in an effort to avoid prosecution."

"Mr. Pierce?" Judge Channing asked.

"Normally that wouldn't be a problem Your Honor, but there was just so much marijuana involved in this case – nearly a pound." Braden doubled checked his notes and glanced at my client.

"But, there were no packaging materials, no cutting materials, no large sums of money, no weapons, nothing to indicate that my client was dealing, so regardless of the amount, the evidence points to personal use."

Judge Channing turned to my client with a withering look. "Ms. Franklin, how old are you?"

"Eighty-two in July, Judge, and still as lively as ever." She smiled.

"Obviously," he said scathingly. "And all of this marijuana was for you alone?"

"Well, it was my whole stash, honey," she answered earnestly. I winced a little.

"Ms. Ginsberg has explained that you can't do this anymore?"

"Yes." She sighed heavily. "It's not worth the trouble. I'm going back to whiskey."

"That's good. I mean, well. That's... acceptable. Okay, I'm going to advise the District Attorney's office to work out an agreement for community service."

"Understood, Your Honor," Braden replied.

Ms. Franklin wobbled off as I returned to counsel table. Braden walked over to hand me the order.

"Seems like a fun gal," he said.

"I'll trade you sexual favors for the old lady's freedom," I joked quietly.

"You're on."

"Mr. Pierce! Call the next case," Judge Channing bellowed.

"Commonwealth v. Wagner!" Braden called. My client, dressed in a hat with ear-flaps and a tee-shirt with a picture of a smiling donkey and a caption that read, "I Lost my Ass in Las Vegas" walked forward. It boggled my mind that this morning when he had gone through his closet *that* had jumped out at him as the most appropriate thing to wear to court.

"What's this about?" Judge Channing asked, giving my client an irritated look.

"Your Honor," Braden began, the Commonwealth will establish that on April 14th of this year Mr. Scott Wagner stopped Mr. Franklin Jordan with what turned out to be a toy gun, and demanded that he drive him around from ATM machine to ATM machine as he withdrew money from his *own* account. He's charged with carjacking."

"I'm asking for a psychiatric evaluation, Your Honor, and I request that my client remain out on bail."

"Granted! Court adjourned. Get me out of here." Judge Channing got up and left without saying goodbye. I was pretty sure that he was getting close to retirement.

Braden turned to me with a smile. That smile always caused my tummy to flip flop and it probably would even if we were together until I was Ms. Franklin's age.

"I'm going to drop these files off and then I'm going back to my place to finish packing, and look forward to having carnal knowledge of you tonight."

"I like a man with goals." We packed up our files.

"I'll finally know what it feels like to go au natural," he said with a wicked smile.

"Come as you are," I joked.

"Oh, that was *really* bad!" We grabbed our briefcases and headed out of the courtroom and toward the elevators.

We discussed some details about the day's cases on the elevator ride down and then said goodbye at the door to the criminal courts building as we headed off to our respective offices. I could swear I heard him whistling as he walked away. Even though I was a bit less obvious about it, I too was quite happy at the thought of once again entering the world of the sexually active. The fact that I would be making my re-entry with Braden was still pretty amazing to me. This man had starred in nearly all of the recent fantasies that accompanied those very special "private" moments alone in my room at night with my battery-operated friend.

∽ CHAPTER EIGHT ∽

I got back to my office and filed my paperwork. Jess wasn't back yet. My phone buzzed and I saw my dad's number. I had spoken to my mom earlier in the week, so I knew that he had been briefed.

"So, honey, how'd you meet this guy? In court?"

"Yeah. We're always in front of the same judge. I was interested in him for a while, and Jess kept saying that she thought he liked me too, so one night when I saw him out I flirted with him."

"*You* flirted with *him*?" He sounded dubious.

"Yeah, I flirted. I can flirt. I may not do it a lot, but I'm capable."

"Hey, I'm not complaining. I was starting to worry that you were going to become one of those ladies with all the cats. I'm glad you found somebody you like. I like his dad's politics too by the way. He's a smart guy. Of course I can't tell anybody that after that piece in the paper or somebody might read too much into it and harass you or something."

"What do you mean?"

"Thanks to my friends at the Times, the extremists think I'm trying to control the government and the conspiracy nuts think that I already control the government. Now my daughter's dating a senator's son. Who knows what they'll come up with?"

"I don't care what they say. I don't take dating advice from conspiracy nuts and extremists."

"Just be careful, sweetheart and if anybody bothers you let me know. I'm not exactly strapped for cash. I could arrange for you to have some security, or at least a very good alarm system. If nothing else I'll buy you a nice dog."

"I appreciate it, but I'm more worried about saying something stupid when I meet his family than I am about some guy who thinks he saw Jim Morrison working at Wendy's."

"Hey, don't you be nervous. Anybody would be lucky to have you."

"Thanks, Dad."

"Your mom and I would be really happy if it worked out. At least we would know that this guy wasn't after your money. He could probably even help you figure out what to do with it."

"Good. Maybe you could worry a little less then. I love you. Tell Ma I said, "hi.""

"Okay sweetheart, I love you too. Have fun with the guy you picked up."

* * *

At five-thirty on the dot I was stowing my overnight bag and a garment bag in the trunk of Braden's BMW. Even with rush-hour traffic it wouldn't be very long until we reached the Pierce home in the suburbs. Braden was still in a very good mood and I sensed that it wasn't just because he would be getting lucky later. I suspected that he was genuinely happy to see his family. Hopefully, that meant that he had very nice parents. He did say that his family was exceptionally close. I also hoped that he was right about them not minding if we shared a room.

"So, did your ex-girlfriends share a room with you?"

"I've never invited any of them to stay with my family. I should warn you that my parents are probably going to find it significant that I invited you, and they may throw out a few hints."

"Believe me, you haven't experienced hinting until you've met Ben and Judy Ginsberg."

"Oh yeah?" He glanced at me again with an amused look.

"Don't be surprised if you go to shake my dad's hand and he gives you a stack of college brochures for our future children."

"He doesn't own a shotgun or anything, does he?" Braden joked.

"Are you kidding me? My father considers spicy food to be a deadly weapon. He probably would have backed you in that burrito case. Besides, he's a businessman. He just destroys people financially."

"Well, that's a relief."

"To tell you the truth my father is my hero. I've always said that he's like the most romantic guy in the universe because he comes from a pretty impressive family but he married my mom even though her family is completely nuts."

"He must love her."

"Yeah he does, and she loves him." I smiled.

"I'd like to meet them."

"I'll introduce you to them. It's just the rest of my relatives that I'll have to hide from you."

"I think that you'll like my parents. They're nice people and they love each other a lot too."

"Thanks for introducing me to them. That's nice."

"I apologize in advance for everything that comes out of my brother's mouth."

"Ha! You should meet my bubbe! That's my grandmother. She's the most offensive person I know."

* * *

It wasn't much longer before we left the highway and started driving along more country-like roads, peppered with gorgeous homes. Eventually we pulled into a long drive and approached a Georgian-style house with a gray stone facade and white trim. My family's brownstone on the Upper East Side was stylish, but this place was beautiful. It looked very spacious and I guessed that it had at least five or six bedrooms.

As we got out of the car a group of people came out to meet us. They all immediately headed straight for Braden and then there was a lot of hugging going on. Even though Braden wasn't far away from here, they were, obviously, a close family. There was certainly no question that they were related. This was one attractive group of tall blonde people. Braden's father was handsome and distinguished-looking, the gold streaks in his hair mixed with gray. He didn't have the aggressively friendly demeanor that a lot of politicians have, but rather, he seemed laid back and genuinely warm. Braden's mother was beautiful. She had dark blonde hair and the same blue eyes that Braden had. Eyes, which at the moment were fixed on me, and thankfully, looked friendly.

"You must be Gabrielle," she said in a soft voice. "Oh my! You're gorgeous." She gave me a warm smile. "I'm Claire and we're so happy you're here." She came over and pulled me into a friendly hug. These were very huggy people.

"I guess you figured out that that's my mom and that's my dad. This is my brother, Drew and my sister, Beth." Beth looked like a younger version of Claire and Drew looked like a younger version of Braden, who looked like a younger version of his dad.

"Wow," Drew said. "She's hot." Braden turned and glared at him. "What? Mom said she was gorgeous!"

"It's great to meet you," Beth broke in, and came over to hug me too.

"We're very pleased to have you, Gabrielle," Braden's dad said, hugging me of course. "I'm Tyler." Wow. I got to call Senator Pierce Tyler.

"Thanks for inviting me. It was very thoughtful of you."

"They were thrilled to hear you were coming!" Drew offered. "They're hoping Braden will finally settle down."

"Drew," Tyler said in a warning tone.

"What did I say now?" Drew asked, sounding exasperated. He started walking toward me when Braden stopped him.

"Where do you think you're going?"

"Everybody else got to hug her."

"You already said hello."

"Actually, if you'll recall, I said that she was hot and you got all huffy."

"Drew, please help me with their bags," Tyler said, intervening. "Braden, why don't you help us while Mom and Beth make Gabrielle comfortable and get to know her better?"

"You need both of us for that? Maybe I want to get to know her better too." His father and Braden both gave him a stern look. I was definitely starting to understand what Braden had said about Drew.

I followed Claire and Beth into the marble-floored entry and off to one of the dark paneled doors down a hallway to the side of a large staircase. It turned out to be a parlor with wide windows overlooking the rear lawn. The room was done in a combination of burgundy and cream, and although it was very tasteful, it also looked warm and inviting. There was a fireplace and above it hung a picture of a blonde man dressed in colonial garb. Yep, the Pierces had been here for a while.

"Please sit down and make yourself comfortable," Claire said with a smile.

I sat down on a love-seat while Claire and Beth took the one across from me. We chatted for a bit and I filled them in on more details about my family and my life. I learned that Beth was twenty-five and working in the education department of the Philadelphia Museum of Art and that Drew was a law student at Georgetown, just like Braden had been. Being in the middle, Beth was close to both of her brothers. She assured me that even though Braden and Drew bickered, they were close despite the four year age difference. Claire shared that she spent most of her time involved in charity work, and in running their family foundation. I had a feeling that being a senator's wife also came with its share of responsibilities.

"So did you and Braden meet in court?" Claire asked.

"Yes, he and I have been assigned cases in front of the same judge frequently."

"Is he a good lawyer?" Beth asked.

"Yes, he's a very good lawyer." Beth and Claire smiled at each other and I realized that they were proud, which I found very cute.

"Is he as good a boyfriend as he is a lawyer?" Beth asked.

"We just started dating but so far he's been really thoughtful and easy-going. He's said some really sweet things too."

"Braden?!" Beth laughed and glanced at her mom who was smiling happily.

Just then we heard the men returning from upstairs and Claire let everyone know that it was time to head in for dinner. We entered a formal dining room with a table beautifully prepared. We had all settled in and a housekeeper had come out with a soup course when Drew spoke up.

"So you two are sleeping together?" Beth dropped her spoon and Claire nearly choked on the water she was sipping.

"Drew!" All of the Pierces said in unison.

"What? I just meant are they sharing a room. Is it a secret or something?"

"What it is, is none of your business," Braden said testily.

"I was just asking!" He ate a spoonful of his soup. "I was wondering…"

"The answer is no," Tyler added.

"Why not?"

"Because your brother is twenty-seven and an attorney and you're twenty-three and a law student," his father replied.

"And what? I have to make you worry that I'll never get married before you'll let me bring a girl home with me?"

"You can bring a girl home," Braden answered. "You just can't sleep with her."

"Okay Braden!" Tyler warned. "Please remember that you *are* twenty-seven."

"Seriously, guys, this is not even close to polite conversation," Beth chimed in. I actually found the conversation rather amusing, truthfully. Drew kind of cracked me up. Talk turned to the fundraiser, though, and we continued with that as the soup was cleared and dinner was served.

The conversation then turned to what everyone's plans were for the evening. Drew and Beth had planned to go out to a club with a group of mutual friends and Tyler and Claire were planning to go out and catch a movie. Braden and I were invited along with both groups but he politely declined on our behalf, citing a stressful week and our desire to rest up before the fundraiser the next day. Drew snorted derisively and Beth kicked him under the table none too subtly.

By dessert I was starting to nervously anticipate the evening ahead. The fact that Braden had been running his fingers along my inner thigh for several minutes didn't exactly help me to calm down. It was already past seven-thirty. It couldn't be long before the others left. When we were finished with our dessert and coffee Drew and Beth went off to get ready and Claire and Tyler retired to the family room, where Braden and I joined them. I was being quieter than usual, but so far during this visit, I hadn't done anything awkward and the Pierces were so nice that I had started to relax with them.

"You know, Braden, there will likely be a lot of familiar faces there tomorrow and I'm not sure you'll be thrilled to see all of them," Claire said. "Marla might possibly be there for example."

"Oh great!" He cringed and turned to me. "Marla's a shallow, narcissistic harpy who I used to date years ago. She still can't believe that I broke up with her."

"Can't believe it as in 'how could he have done that?' or can't believe it as in she thinks you're still her boyfriend?" I asked a little nervously.

"She doesn't think I'm still her boyfriend, but she refuses to believe that anybody wouldn't *want* to be her boyfriend, including me." I could tell that I was just going to love Marla.

"Cameron will be there for sure," Tyler added.

"Terrific." He turned to me again. "Cameron's my cousin. Marla cheated on me with him. I should probably be thankful since I wanted an excuse to break up with her anyway, but I wasn't in on the plan, you know?"

"It was so long ago, Braden. I wish that the two of you would just put it behind you," Claire said.

"Yeah, we'll see. I do think that maybe I'll have a little chat with him. There's something I'd like to ask him about."

"The Masons will likely be there with Felicity," she went on.

"The Masons want to marry their daughter off to me." Braden explained. "The mother, Mrs. Mason, is a snob with the warmth of a glacier and her daughter, Felicity, reminds me of Wednesday Addams but more Goth. I think the father might be a hologram."

"And will you be marrying the lovely Felicity?"

"I would be more likely to marry Cameron."

"Cole Stephenson will be there of course," Tyler noted, looking uncomfortable.

"We need to steer clear of him for sure," Braden said, giving me a disgusted look. "He's a state representative and a complete political animal. He would sell his soul to get elected to a federal congressional seat. He's also a social climber and a lecher. His eyes won't leave your cleavage."

"This sounds like a fun party."

"Most of the folks who'll be there will be quite nice," Claire said in an apologetic tone.

"I'll just smile and nod a lot," I replied

"Braden should do that more often. We're hoping you'll be a good influence," Claire said to me.

"Maybe I'll be a bad influence," Braden said, smiling at me in a way that made me glance at my watch. It was almost eight-thirty already. Claire noticed my gesture and quickly checked her own watch.

"We'd better get going, Tyler. I don't want to miss the beginning of the movie."

Claire and Tyler wished us a good night and excused themselves. As soon as they were gone Braden turned to me with a naughty smile.

Without a word he pulled me onto his lap and began nuzzling my neck. I nuzzled him back and we worked our way to each other's mouths and started kissing. Just as our tongues were becoming deliciously entwined I heard Drew.

"Christ, Braden, can't you even wait until we leave the house?"

"Braden's head fell back onto the top of the sofa in exasperation. I slid off of his lap and felt myself blushing as I tactfully retreated to my own seat and straightened out the skirt of my short summer dress.

"How many rooms are in this fucking house, Drew, and you have to be in this one right now?"

"Just be thankful that we're all going out so you can "rest" in privacy." He made the little air quotes to make it clear that he didn't think we would be resting.

"You didn't have to go out," I said, feeling embarrassed. Had the Pierces planned their social outings around us having sex?

"Don't listen to him!" Braden said. "They go out all the time on Friday nights when they're here."

"I'm sorry, Gabrielle," Drew laughed. "I'm just giving Braden a hard time." He sat down in a chair next to us and sipped a Coke.

"He's just jealous."

"Damn right I'm jealous. You get to sleep with your girlfriend tonight and I'm going out with my sister. There would be something wrong with me if I weren't jealous, dude."

"Stop thinking about my sex life."

"Just make sure you don't remind me of it later. Don't forget that my room is right next to yours and the walls are thin."

"Didn't you have to be somewhere?"

"In case you're wondering, Theresa left for the night already and Mom and Dad left for the movies. They'll probably be back by midnight. Beth and I are leaving in about five minutes. I'm not sure what time we'll be home though."

"Thanks for the update," Braden said dryly.

"Just trying to be helpful." Drew grinned.

"Perhaps we'll see you out," Braden said getting up and walking over to the door. Drew got up and walked out to the entry where Beth was already waiting.

"Have a good night," Beth said with a smile and a wave.

"Enjoy your rest," Drew said, mimicking her gesture and singsong voice.

As soon as the door closed I started to walk toward Braden but he held up a hand, signaling me to wait. A minute later Drew came back in.

"What?" He laughed. "I forgot my phone!" He walked over to a writing table where a cell phone was lying next to a large vase of flowers. "Don't worry, Braden. I'm really leaving now. You can rest in every room in the house if you want." He left again and Braden walked over to the window and watched them pull away. Then he turned toward me with a very happy smile. He walked over and took my hand and led me upstairs.

❦ CHAPTER NINE ❦

When we got to the top of the stairs we walked down a long hallway and Braden stopped in front of a door on the left. He opened it and stepped aside for me to enter, coming in behind me. He walked over to turn on a bedside lamp and then turned the overhead light off, making it much more intimate. He went over to his music player, found something on his iPod, and seconds later I heard BB King singing the sexy blues song *Need Your Love So Bad.* He walked slowly toward me, staring into my eyes with a positively sinful look. I swallowed hard and took a deep breath.

"Do you know how much I want you, Gabrielle?" he asked softly when he reached me. My legs felt like they were going to give out and I wasn't sure that I saw consciousness in my immediate future. I was already too aroused to be nervous anymore, so I freed my inner hussy. (Note, I said hussy.)

"Show me," I whispered.

He put his hands on my hips and pulled me tightly against him. I immediately knew how much. The answer was pressing into my lower abdomen. He leaned down and kissed me almost ravenously, his tongue exploring everywhere and rubbing up against mine sensuously. I felt a little overpowered by it but I liked it too. His lips moved away from my mouth and toward my ear. "Does that give you a better idea?" he whispered seductively.

"It gives me lots of ideas. What are you going to do about it?" My inner hussy had obviously decided that she liked being freed.

"Saucy wench." He smiled wickedly. "I may have to spank you." He sank down to kneel at my feet, removing my shoes and tossing them aside. Then he ran his hands up my bare legs and under my skirt, letting his fingers slide into my panties, and pushing them down over my hips. They dropped to the floor and I stepped out of them and kicked them aside. Fixing me with that hot look of his he reached around behind me, unzipped my dress and unhooked my bra. In one easy move they both hit the floor. If there were an Olympic category for undressing women he would be a serious contender for the gold. He had some mad skills. There were a few drunken nights in college when I could have really used his help. I just watched in lust-dazed fascination as he stepped back and starting at my feet let his eyes slowly trail up my bare body.

"You're beautiful everywhere, Gabrielle," he said huskily. "Undress me."

My hands were shaking but I managed to slide them up under his tee-shirt and ease it up. Being taller than me he helped out a little. When it dropped to the floor I nearly joined it. *Good lord!*

I had never seen a body like that. All of his muscles were well-defined. He was the first guy I had ever been with who had a six-pack that didn't say Budweiser on it. I swallowed and let out a slightly ragged breath as I looked up and saw he was smiling at me with amusement.

"You're so... oh my God." Seven years of higher education and that was the best I could come up with.

"I take it you like my body, too?"

"You can take whatever you want looking like that, mister."

I made my now really shaky hands move to his pants and I opened the button and pulled down the zipper, easing them over his hips. They fell to the floor and he stepped out of them. Then he kicked off his own shoes and pulled off his own socks, which was just as well. Socks really aren't all that sexy, and it got us to the main event that much faster. All that was left was a pair of blue striped boxers. I had a feeling he was a boxers guy. I sucked in a deep breath and looked up into his eyes. Then I eased them off (having previously learned that yanking could be a dangerous thing when it came to aroused men and underwear) and he stepped out of them, holding my gaze. I looked down and for the first time actually *saw* what I had been working in those interview rooms in the courthouse. My eyes grew wide as my mouth popped open. *Holy freaking moly!* Harvard really was well endowed!

Standing there in all of his naked glory he looked so damned good I could have sold tickets.

And there were plenty of sexy, appreciative, erotic, even romantic, things I could have said at that moment, but instead I looked him deeply in the crotch and said, "I'm not sure that's going to fit." *Huh?* His brain wasn't running on a full blood supply either, so it took a moment for that comment to sink in. No pun intended. When it did he sounded very clearly amused.

"Don't worry, baby. We'll make sure it fits." He backed me up until my knees hit the edge of the bed. Then he sat me down, pushed my back down flat, knelt on the floor in front of me, and hooked my knees over his shoulders. *Christ on a cracker!* Harvard was going down.

He nibbled and kissed and licked his way up my right thigh, or maybe my left, I wasn't exactly coherent at the moment. Then he ran out of leg. His tongue entered me. I entered orbit. And I didn't exactly go quietly. (You think those rockets were loud?) He held me down while my hips bucked and I moaned loudly. Then like he was lapping up a melting ice cream cone he slowly dragged his tongue higher and suddenly I could feel every nerve ending in my entire body light up.

While his mouth worked me into a frenzy with little strokes and licks and circles, the volume of my appreciation continued to rise. His fingers slipped inside me and his lips covered my clit. When he actually started to suck, I started to scream. Personally, I was glad that Drew had reviewed the family itinerary because at that point even the neighbors knew his name. I let go of the blankets that I had in a death grip and buried my hands in his hair, still trying to ride his mouth and hand, completely delirious with pleasure. I swear to God I don't think I could have told you my full name at that point. I was as close to really and truly passing out as I had ever gotten in my life.

He paused for a minute, sounding a little out of breath. "Gabrielle, baby, you're going to come. Do you want to finish this way or with my cock inside you?"

"Yes please," I moaned. I felt him smile against me and start to go back to making me crazy when his question finally made it into space, where my brain was still floating around. "Inside me! I want your cock inside me! Please!" I gasped desperately. He gave a happy little growl and then he crawled up onto the bed and pulled me along with him as he sat up straight with his back braced up against the headboard.

"Come and sit on my lap," he said. Now, technically, people had been saying that to me since I was a child, but trust me, nobody else has said it quite like *that*. Inner-Gabrielle sang the Hallelujah chorus. He didn't have to ask twice. I crawled over and straddled him and he pulled me up onto my knees and buried his face against my breasts, latching on to my nipple and sucking vigorously on one side and then switching to the other. I could only whimper and moan at that point. My legs trembled so hard that I had to brace my arms on his shoulders so that I wouldn't collapse as he positioned himself at my entrance.

"Look at me, Gabrielle," he demanded. And I fixed my eyes on him dazedly. He gave me the hottest Braden sex look I had ever seen. "Let's see if it fits now, baby," he said in a voice that sounded like he was barely holding on to his self-control. His hands grabbed my hips and pushed me down as he slid slowly inside me inch by inch. Needless to say, it fit perfectly. He was buried in me up to the hilt and we just stared at one another in stunned silence for a second.

"Oh my God!" He finally gasped and his voice was strained. "I can't believe how good you feel. I think I want to live here." He seemed to be enjoying his new experience.

I was incapable of producing anything coherent at the moment so rather than throwing out some witty banter in response I said something like "Ohgaahaad" instead. Feel free to quote me.

He bent his knees, held my hips and started to move under me, thrusting upward, sliding me up and down on his cock in smooth strokes, pulling my hips slightly forward so that my clit was coming into direct contact with his pubic bone every time I took all of him. I saw all kinds of bright colored lights flashing in front of my eyes. I was either more sexually stimulated than I had ever been in my life or the police were parked on his lawn — a realistic possibility, with all the screaming I had been doing. Vaguely I remembered that I was on top and I should probably contribute something to the effort. I started moving up and down under my own power, slowly at first and gradually picking up speed.

"Oh Gabrielle," he groaned. "That's it, baby. Just like that. Oh yes! Oh fuck! You feel so good." I felt myself rapidly climbing upward toward an amazing orgasm. "Come on, baby," he urged. "Give it to me." I finally arrived at the summit, celebrated madly, and promptly fell over the edge of the cliff before I could even plant a flag. My body shook and he, along with everyone else within a mile radius, got to hear me scream his name again one last time. Wow, he even knew when I was going to come. Such a smart guy. I collapsed against him, shaking and bathed in sweat and he hugged me tightly and stroked my hair. Such a sweet guy too. I wanted to nominate him for something. Take that Vinnie Virillo. That's how a real man does it.

When I was able to stop gasping for air and some oxygen returned to my brain, I became aware of the fact that he was still very hard and still buried deep inside me. It would be impolite to just leave him like that. Besides, I was never one to waste. There were people going to bed horny all over the world that night.

"So what do you want to do now, Harvard?" I asked shakily. He smiled at me with a dazed look and kissed me lustily. Then he smacked me playfully on the ass.

"Get up, saucy wench and grab onto the headboard." My stomach did a flip flop. That kind of sexy should come with a warning label. I got up and facing the wall, grabbed onto the headboard as instructed. He knelt behind me and pulled my hips back further so I was leaning over a little more. Then he nudged my knees further apart and with one hand cupping my breast and one hand stroking my clit he leaned over me and began kissing my neck as he positioned himself at my entrance again. When he pushed into me, I moaned and pushed back against him. He began rolling his hips and built up into a steady rhythm, and after some indeterminate amount of time, (What do you think, I was checking my watch?), I felt myself about to come again. He was still multitasking impressively, rolling and fondling and stroking and kissing, when he whispered in my ear.

"Oh baby. Your pussy feels so fucking good. I almost can't take it."

And that was the moment when I discovered that having Braden Pierce talk dirty to me during sex was enough to drive me out of my freaking mind. I completely lost control again as my muscles clenched and I trembled and moaned. When the last wave of sensation had passed he urged me down on to my back and he crawled on top of me, bracing himself above me with his arms. He leaned down and kissed me deeply and then he eased into me again. I groaned and he started moving, slowly at first and then faster and faster. I just wrapped my legs around his waist and held on for the ride. I watched him above me with fascination; his eyes were dark, his pupils dilated, skin flushed, hair damp, a sheen of sweat covering him. He was breathtaking.

"Gabrielle!" he bit out in a hoarse voice and suddenly he groaned and went still, I felt him shudder and then he collapsed on me. I took his weight for a few seconds but he quickly rolled onto his back and pulled me onto his chest. I heard his heart hammering beneath me as his breathing gradually slowed down. "So good," he said, sounding stunned.

"Well, you were right. It fit." I panted. I decided that I really liked my inner hussy.

"So good," he said again. "No words." Our breathing gradually began to return to normal.

"Wow, we've been having sex for almost an hour," I said, finally glancing at my watch. I was still wearing my watch? Jesus, I really was a lawyer.

"That means we still have two more hours before my parents get home."

"What are you, seventeen?"

"I can go again after I recover. Believe me, it won't be a problem. Gabrielle, I have never experienced anything in my entire life that has felt that good."

"Me neither. Braden, that was incredible. It's never ever been like that before."

We cuddled up with each other, nuzzled and petted, and gave each other sweet little kisses everywhere. Then our cuddling turned to fondling and soon Braden was very skillfully employing his oral skills again as I informed him loudly over and over that his tongue was the Eighth Wonder of the World. I finished that way that time but like the Energizer Bunny Braden just kept going, burying his face gleefully between my breasts and licking, biting and sucking at will.

Faster than you could say, "Harvard takes Yale" we were going at it full throttle again. This time around we didn't confine ourselves to bed. We explored the floor, an armchair and ultimately his desk. After all, it had worked well in the interview room. It worked even better with me lying back and him leaning over me which placed him at an incredibly intense angle and created wonderful friction right where I needed it. We definitely had a winner, folks. I was becoming very fond of desks in general, and I'll tell you, that desk was one quality piece of craftsmanship. The wall it was slamming into, however, may have sustained some damage.

My voice was a bit hoarse from all the screaming I had done earlier, but the desk sex was just so inspiring that I managed to loudly express myself vocally one last time. If I'm not mistaken, I believe that I begged Braden not to stop, told him that I loved how big he was and I had never felt so full, let him know I had never been with anyone who had ever fucked me so well, and then made it abundantly clear that I was coming. Now, I may not have all of that exactly right. I was, after all, a bit distracted. Of course, there was someone else who could verify the accuracy of my recollection if necessary. (As I found out later.)

We were collapsed in an exhausted heap, panting back in bed and close to passing out when we heard Claire and Tyler arrive and call out that they were home. Braden kissed me and smiled.

"Need to "rest" for real now," he said sounding like he was half asleep already.

"Night," I replied and although I'm not sure, obviously, I think I was unconscious before I got to the last "t."

∽ CHAPTER TEN ∽

I woke up the next morning with a feeling of contentment I hadn't experienced in... Well, okay, ever. Contentment has never really been my middle name. My middle name was actually Sara but it should have been angst.

I moved to stretch and my arm smacked into something warm and hard. I opened my eyes and saw a beautiful blonde guy staring down at me. A second later it sunk into my sleep-addled brain, the beautiful blonde guy was mine. It wasn't a dream. Thank God.

"How long have you been awake?" I asked.

"Not long."

"And what are you doing?"

"Watching you sleep, and thinking."

"Thinking about what?'

"How I've never wanted to just watch a woman sleep before."

"Well, I am very good at it. I've been doing it my whole life." He smiled and tickled my ribs, which of course made me squeal and rub against all of his warmness and hardness. And trust me, there was plenty of hardness. Hmm. We would need to make sure we didn't waste that either.

"In the past I would just be at home alone thinking 'wow, I got laid really well last night'," he continued. "But with you, I'm thinking, 'She's so beautiful. I want to wake up with her every morning. And wow, I got laid really well last night'."

"I like sleeping with you too. You're very warm and cuddly." I snuggled up closer to him. "And I've got to tell you again, that was the best sex I've ever had in my life. Let's have lots and lots of sex. In fact, let's have as much sex as possible."

"That works for me. I'm going to need to be hittin' that on a regular basis. I'm not kidding you, Gabrielle, that was the best sex I've ever had too, and frankly, I've had *a whole lot* of sex." He smiled. "I can't believe that I found someone who I'm so compatible with."

"We are pretty compatible aren't we? And not just in bed either."

"No! On the floor and in the chair and especially on the desk." I sat up and gave him a slightly indignant look and he started laughing. He loved teasing me so much. He started tracing a finger along my abdomen and my nerve endings lit up like a cell phone grid of Manhattan. Then he was cupping my breast and making those delicious little circles around my nipple with his thumb again.

"You may have to carry me downstairs," I panted as he started nibbling at my neck.

"That's okay. It will give Drew great joy to be able to make rude comments," he said, climbing over me and leaning down to kiss me slowly and thoroughly. I ran my hands along his back. His body felt so good that I wanted to keep touching him forever. Except that probably wouldn't go over too well in court. He sat back, grabbed my ankles and rested them on his shoulders, leaning over and sliding into me deeply. "Oh yeah, baby! I remember *this* place," he sighed and groaned. "I'm not hurting you am I?" he asked, breathing heavily.

"No, it's wonderful," I gasped. "I must have a big vagina or something."

"Not big." He laughed. "Just accommodating. You're really tight. Ah, fuck! *Really* tight. I love it when you do that."

"Lots of walking – good muscle tone."

He adjusted his angle and unbelievably it felt even deeper. "Tell me if it's too much like this."

"Not too much. Fits fine," I bit out. "You like au natural?" I moaned.

"You must be kidding. The other way is great. But compared to this… like taking a shower in socks." His breath was coming in short rasps and a sheen of sweat had formed on his skin.

"I like that I'm the first." I lifted my hips up to meet him as he slid in and out of me, and grabbed on to his beautiful tight ass.

"Me too. And it's very primal. Like claiming your mate. Marking your territory. Male thing you know?" He had that wonderfully dazed look on his face.

"Mm, I like being claimed. Oh yeah, that's so deep. It feels so good."

"Can't talk much more. No blood left in brain."

From that point on I just enjoyed watching him watching our bodies join as he thrust into me slowly and deeply, pulling back so far that he almost pulled out and then pushing back in until I had taken every inch of him. He seemed fascinated, almost hypnotized by it and I loved seeing him experience so much pleasure. It still blew my mind that it was my body bringing it to him. Then finally he reached down between us and started stroking my clit, and all the blood left my brain too.

I felt a deep intense orgasm building and I just relaxed and let it happen. An incredibly powerful sensation washed over me and my inner muscles clamped down in the most deliciously gut-wrenching way. Braden started to move faster and faster, pounding into me in such a good way, and within a couple of minutes I felt him go still and then shudder, his breathing audible and ragged.

"Oh, Gabrielle!" He groaned. "I come so hard with you."

We rested in each other's arms for a while, cuddling and canoodling lazily, and then he suggested we go grab a shower. While in the shower he grabbed me again. While I was able to walk downstairs under my own power, we didn't make it there for another hour. Believe me, there's nothing like starting out your day with a highly motivated, very physically fit guy in his mid-twenties.

* * *

We got downstairs just before noon and while we had clearly missed breakfast, at least we had a good shot at lunch. Thank God. I was famished. Braden really knew how to work up an appetite. One thing that seemed different this morning, in addition to a very good ache between my legs, was that he seemed to want to be in physical contact with me at all times.

He was continuously touching, holding, stroking and caressing me. We sat for a while with his parents in the parlor while they relayed the plot of the legal thriller they had seen the night before and quizzed us on how realistic it was. All the while Braden held me close to him and played with my hair. Then we wandered into the family room where Beth and Drew were hanging out and listening to music.

"Hey big guy," Drew said, and something in his voice made Braden's gaze fly to him. I really should have picked up on that, in retrospect.

Beth told us funny stories about their evening out while Braden held my hand, rubbed my leg, massaged my shoulders and so on. Personally, I loved it. He could touch me as much as he wanted. Finally, Drew said something, though, of course.

"What is it you believe will happen if you actually stop touching Gabrielle for a minute, Braden?" He was watching Braden's fingers as they stroked the inside of my knee and he almost looked a little flushed.

"I like touching her. Mind your own business."

"Oh I know that you like touching her, Braden." He and Braden shared a look that seemed to convey some kind of silent communication. Inner-Gabrielle decided that willful ignorance was sometimes the best choice. "From the way you're looking at her, I assume that you'll be ready for a "nap" soon," he said. Drew loved those little finger air quotes. Beth was looking both amused and highly embarrassed as she got up and told us she was going to check on lunch.

"I'll need some food first. "Napping" requires energy," Braden said quietly, making little finger air quotes of his own.

"You're definitely a big eater. In fact you're a wonder. Some of us managed to get out of bed long enough to eat *breakfast*," Drew went on undeterred.

"And some of us were "otherwise occupied.""

"You must be hungry too, Gabrielle. Even if you were *completely full* last night I'm sure you've worked up an appetite by now," Drew said, smiling in a flirty way and giving me a look that suddenly almost erased the four year age difference between him and Braden. Wow, they could have been twins. Hey wait, I knew that look… Inner-Gabrielle decided that denial was also a very convenient tool. The look that Braden was giving his brother seemed to hover between panicked and homicidal.

"Why don't we have a little chat later, Drew?" Braden asked with a smile.

"Love to," Drew answered, looking not unlike the Cheshire Cat in Alice in Wonderland. Just then Claire appeared at the door.

"Lunch is ready, everyone." She smiled. "Let's go in."

We got up and Braden continued to hold my hand as we walked to the dining room. When we sat down his hand found a comfortable resting place on my thigh. There was more chat about the movie and the club that Beth and Drew had visited, but he and I were distracted by other things, like smiling stupidly at each other. Eventually it was Drew again who broke into our happy little reverie.

Yo! Braden, dude! Mom's talking to you! Stop falling in love for a minute and pay attention."

"Yes?" Braden asked a little tersely.

"I was just letting you know that you'll need to be ready and downstairs by five. And I wanted to let Gabrielle know that we have a hair stylist and a make-up person coming if she'd like to borrow them."

"Thanks," I said with a smile. Claire was so nice.

"Fine. Hey Dad?" Braden said to Tyler. "I was wondering if maybe I could talk to you about something later." Tyler immediately appeared attentive.

"Why can't you talk to him now?" Drew asked.

"I have some questions I want to ask him."

"Don't you think you should have asked him about that last night?" Drew smiled.

"Drew!" Tyler looked at his younger son menacingly. "That would be fine, Braden. Why don't we take a walk after lunch?"

"Gabrielle!" Claire said, smiling brightly. "We should talk more and I would love to show you some baby pictures of Braden." Drew looked at his mother curiously and then turned to his sister.

"Uh oh, you don't think he got her..." he began quietly to Beth.

"They've only been dating for a week. Didn't Dad have that talk with *you*?" Beth cut him off, whispering through clenched teeth with a smile.

When lunch ended Braden reluctantly took his hand off of me and followed his father out of the room. Claire led me back to the parlor as Beth and Drew headed off in their own directions.

"Bye, Gabrielle," Drew called out with a smile. He was being very exceptionally friendly this morning. Inner-Gabrielle decided that sometimes it was best not to contemplate things too deeply. I made myself comfortable while she settled in and fixed me with a warm happy maternal gaze.

"So Gabrielle, Braden is obviously quite smitten with you. We've never seen him act like this before."

"Oh." I smiled. "Well, I'm quite smitten with him too," I said, a little surprised.

"Let me get those photos. Braden was such a cute little boy." She got up and walked over to a bookshelf, taking down a thick leather-bound album. For the next forty-five minutes I looked at pictures of the most adorable tow-headed, precocious child I had ever seen in my life, taking his first steps, winning little league awards, earning first place in a spelling bee, starring as Ebenezer Scrooge in the church Christmas play, riding his big boy bike, splitting the atom and conquering small nations.

I felt like a chocolate bar sitting in the sun, all sweet and gooey. I was a goner. I was going to have to marry this guy someday because there was no way I was letting him go. Unless, you know, he really wanted to. Go, that is. I wasn't going to get all Glenn Close in Fatal Attraction and start playing the soundtrack to Madame Butterfly a thousand times and boiling people's bunnies, but I digress…

He and his dad came back in and both of them looked relaxed and happy. I wondered what it was that they had talked about. Braden offered me a tour of the place and I accepted. After seeing adorable little boy Braden I was eager to be touching my big boy Braden again. He seemed to share in that sentiment as he was at my side like a heat-seeking missile.

It was a beautiful, warm, clear day and outside I could see that a huge tent had been set up on the rear lawn. We exited through the French doors at the rear of the house and descended a flight of stairs that led down to a swimming pool and a Jacuzzi. A small pool house stood off to the side not very far from the tent. We walked down and checked out the progress that workers were making with setting up for the fundraiser. Everything looked lovely. Who knew you could do this with a tent? I wished that I could have brought these people with me when I was a Girl Scout forced to participate in *Survivor: Camp Louisa in the Catskills.*

I saw that a stage had been set up. They would be having an auction that evening and a band would be playing later. I thought that it might turn out to be a fun evening. We strolled back out and across the grounds and then circled around to the front of the house again. Braden gave me a tour of that too. It was really a beautiful home. In addition to the parlor, family room and dining room I had seen, there was a huge kitchen and a cozy library on the first floor. The basement held a work-out room and a game room that had a full private bar and opened out onto a patio by the pool. As I had guessed there were six bedrooms upstairs. The whole place was beautifully decorated with classic pieces and obvious good taste but it still managed to create a warm atmosphere that felt like a family home.

"It's getting late," he pointed out. "How long will it take you to get ready?"

"Probably no more than an hour. I wanted to get your opinion about whether I should wear my jewelry though. You said that this was formal but I don't want to look like I'm trying too hard."

"What kind of jewelry did you bring?" He was giving me a curious look.

"My good stuff," I replied and he looked amused.

"I'm sure it's fine but I'll give you my opinion if you want it."

We went upstairs to his room. Now, in the daylight, when not distracted by other things, I saw that his walls were covered with framed photos of the Harvard rowing team, along with plenty of awards and even a set of oars. Braden really liked boats. I would have to remember that. I went over to my bag and removed the box to a lovely necklace that my mom and dad had given me.

"This was my graduation gift from my parents when I finished law school." I held it up to show him. I glanced up and saw that he looked a little surprised.

"Are those diamonds?"

"Aren't they pretty?" I loved seeing the stones sparkle in the light.

"They're beautiful. You just tossed them in your overnight bag and brought them along?"

"Yeah, why?"

"Just asking." He gave me a look I couldn't interpret. "Do your parents worry about you a lot?" he asked out of the blue.

"Yeah, as a matter of fact they do," I admitted. "Why?"

"Just wondering. Why don't we take a trip to New York soon?"

"Maybe my parents should come to Philly. I told you that I have some rather eccentric relatives? Like my bubbe for instance. That's my grandmother. She's kind of…blunt."

"She'll get along well with Drew."

"My cousin Rachel, is a bit bitter about her divorce. She's thirty-two and sleeps with guys in their early twenties."

"She'll get along *really* well with Drew."

"And there's my uncle Ira, the King of Dry Cleaning. And my Aunt Ruth. She's something like Fran Drescher, but with a more nasal voice and heavier New York accent."

"Everybody has embarrassing relatives. You should meet my cousin Derek, the Larry Flint of the Main Line. Actually, on second thought, you shouldn't meet my cousin Derek. Ever."

"Braden, you're going to meet these people and never want to even consider having children with me. I need to wait until you're madly in love with me before I inflict my family upon you."

"Gabrielle, don't worry so much." He laughed. "I don't care if you have eccentric relatives. I'm dating, and potentially breeding with you, not them."

"Okay, okay we'll take a trip to New York soon but don't say I didn't warn you. Going back to my original question though, is the necklace too much?"

"No. It'll be fine. It's very beautiful and tasteful. Just like you." He smiled, walked over and cupped my face in his hands, leaning down to kiss me gently. I heard a knock at the door and Beth called out.

"Gabrielle? I'm sorry to bother you but the hairdresser and the cosmetologist are ready for you now."

"Go ahead," Braden encouraged me. "I'll get dressed while you go see them."

"Okay, I'll be right there," I called out. I quickly undressed and found my robe. I wrapped it around myself and I went out and followed Beth down the hall to her room. The stylist and the make-up professional worked on me for about half an hour and I had to admit that the results were very nice. My hair was piled on top of my head with loose tendrils flowing down and I had the "smoky eyes" that Jessica was always talking about. When I got back to Braden's room he was in his bathroom and I stepped into my evening gown. Occasionally, I did splurge, and I had known from the minute that I had seen this dress that I had to have it. It was a shimmery light beige color with strips of fitted silk charmeuse making up the bodice and a flowing chiffon skirt. It was so soft that it felt almost sensual against my bare skin.

"Will you zip me, Braden?" I called out. He walked out of the bathroom and my mouth went dry. He was wearing a tux and he looked drop-dead gorgeous. This man was born to dress in formal wear. His eyes roamed over me from head to toe appreciatively.

"You look so beautiful." He walked over to where I was standing and eased my zipper up slowly. Then as he helped me to fasten the clasp on my necklace there was another knock on the door.

"Yo Braden! Mom and Dad want to know if you're ready," Drew yelled.

"We're not deaf," Braden said swinging the door open.

"I thought you might be "otherwise occupied." He snickered. Then he caught sight of me. "Whoa! Gabrielle, you look smokin' hot in that dress, baby."

"Did you just call her baby? Do that again and I'll hurt you. Badly. Now stop ogling her," Braden said, pushing Drew back into the hall. "We'll be down in a minute." There was some grumbling as Drew left.

"He's right though. You do look smokin' hot in that dress, baby and I'm allowed to ogle you,"

Braden said, smiling and kissing my hand.

✑ CHAPTER ELEVEN ✑

He held onto it as we headed downstairs, where the rest of his family was waiting in the family room with a guy named Alan, who was Tyler's press aid. Apparently, there were journalists from Main Line Today, Philadelphia Magazine, Vanity Fair, the Philadelphia Inquirer and a few other smaller papers waiting to ask some questions and snap some photos. I guess that happened when your dad was a Senator and you had a party.

We went into the parlor where the journalists and photographers were waiting. Braden hovered next to me protectively, keeping his arm around my waist. At first the questions were all about the foundation and the work that it did but then out of left field came a question from the journalist from the Vanity Fair.

"Ms. Ginsberg, aren't you the daughter of Ben Ginsberg, the CEO recently mentioned in the Times?" I saw the other magazine journalists perk up and pay attention. The newspaper people didn't look as interested. Even other reporters probably found that article a little out there.

"Yes, he's my father," I answered before Alan jumped in.

"The Senator hasn't had the opportunity to meet Gabrielle's parents yet."

"Does your dad like Senator Pierce's politics?" the guy from Main Line Today asked.

"Well actually..."

"I don't think that Mr. Ginsberg has made any official endorsement or statement on the matter," Alan answered for me in political speak.

"Off the record then," a woman from Philadelphia Magazine chimed in. "Might this be the joining of a political dynasty and a business empire?"

"Empire?" My dad had an empire? First he was a kingmaker, now he was an actual emperor. Did these people *know* my dad? He could barely match his socks without my mother's help. Now my grandfather, he was more of an emperor. He was probably up in heaven financing major expansion as we spoke.

"Now, now," Alan laughed. "Don't you think that's putting a little pressure on the kids?"

"*Their* kids would be among the wealthiest people in the country," said the journalist from Vanity Fair. Did my parents have *that* much money? But they were so... average. Jesus, I really should have taken the money lectures more seriously.

"Gabrielle, is your father hoping to see you married to the son of a president?" asked the guy from Main Line Today. Was he kidding? My dad would be happy if I just didn't become a crazy cat lady. This whole conversation was surreal. Alan looked like he was about to stroke out.

"Okay folks, we've got to wrap this up," he said with a smile and a slight twitch. Why did I get the feeling that nobody had mentioned it to Alan that Braden was dating a kingmaker's daughter? They snapped some last minute pictures and I smiled dutifully, wondering if I would become one of Braden's Google Girls now. At least I would add some variety.

We headed down to the tent. The Pierces would stand in a reception line as guests arrived and I was left to my own devices, to a certain extent at least. Alan was hovering around to make sure that none of the journalists tried to corner me and I recognized the fact that the private security team members were watching me along with the Pierce's. That was nice of them. I guess they figured Braden's dad would be rather annoyed if the only woman his son had shown an interest in actually dating in two years got knocked off at his own party.

I stood off to the side and watched the guests arrive and mingle. They were mostly who I thought of as "the beautiful people" although clearly not all of them were actually beautiful. I needn't have worried about wearing my good jewelry or felt self-conscious about the fact that my dress cost as much as some of my clients made in a month. In this crowd I blended. The reception line was just starting to wind down when I heard a familiar voice from the past say my name. I froze. It couldn't be. There was no way. I had to be mistaken. I steeled myself, fixed a smile on my face and turned to face him.

* * *

"Cam? Wow, how are you?" I tried to sound cool and collected but my voice came out cracking and unnaturally high. I sounded like a boy going through puberty.

"Gabrielle. It *is* you. I thought it was, but you look sort of different."

"Well, it's been a long time. We were in college then. A lot's happened. I graduated and went on to law school. I passed the bar and now I've been practicing law for two years. I'm sure I look a bit different. I am different. Really different — in lots of ways. I mean how could I possibly be the same? Who's the same after eight years? Wow. Can you believe that it's been eight years?" The words came tumbling out in a continuous stream. I was speaking so quickly I could barely understand myself. He seemed kind of confused but he had obviously latched onto the word "law."

"I'm an attorney too. At Findlay Clay," he said naming one of the most prestigious firms in town. No wonder we had never run into each other. That legal world was as far away from mine as one could get. Suddenly, the name of the firm clicked.

"Is the Clay...?"

"My father... and my grandfather... and my great-grandfather. Where do you work?"

"I'm a public defender," I said almost defiantly. Inner-Gabrielle was jumping up and down and screaming "Oh shit! Oh shit! Oh shit!" like some foul-mouthed rhesus monkey.

"That's so interesting!" *Huh?* He actually sounded like he meant it. Yeah, it's interesting. He should meet freaking Tiny.

Just then Braden walked up behind me and put his arm around me possessively. "I see you've met my cousin Cameron." Oh *fuck*! You just had to know *that* was coming. (By the way, I sometimes swear a lot when I'm stressed.) No wonder he reminded me of him! How could I have not seen the similarities? Stupid! Stupid! Stupid! I was filled with tension and I noticed that Cam had tensed up too. Great, and I really didn't mean that.

"I knew Gabrielle back in college." Now I felt Braden tense up. This was getting better by the moment. Everybody was tense in the tents. (I also make stupid jokes when I'm stressed. Okay – I do that normally too.) "We were friends." That was all he said, although he looked at me intently. He wasn't going to humiliate me. Thank God for small miracles. "So the two of are you dating?" he asked.

"Yes," Braden answered. "Exclusively."

"I see. Well, you're a lucky guy. Gabrielle is incredibly nice, and thoughtful, and sweet, and pure ..." He flinched as soon he realized his mistake. "Hearted. Pure hearted. And although she didn't realize it, I wasn't good enough to be her... friend."

"No doubt," Braden said cynically. I needed a drink. Or several. Why couldn't somebody win a fucking trial now?

"Well, so anyway, as I was pointing out to Cam... eron. It's been *eight years*." I said significantly to Braden. "That's a very long time and much has *changed*."

"Yeah — you're even more beautiful than you were then," Cam said with a smile. Mr. Charming. I wanted to beat him senseless.

"Well, that's because I'm happy. Very happy. I'm finally dating the guy who I've wanted for the past six months." I looked up at Braden with an adoring smile.

"Six months? Really?" Braden asked. That seemed to mollify him a little.

"I take it that you haven't been interested in me for as long?"

"Oh, I've been picturing you naked since about three seconds after I met you, but I'm a guy and you're hot."

"Well, I'm libidinous and you're hot too." He was looking significantly more cheerful now.

"I'm glad you're happy now, Gabrielle. I want you to be happy. That's all I ever wanted." He sure had a funny way of showing it.

"Well, thank you. I want me to be happy too." I smiled.

"Maybe we could be friends again," he suggested.

"Didn't he suggest being friends once before?" Braden asked. "Well at least he can only take your virginity and then blow you off once." Well. If there had been any doubt that Braden had figured it out, that pretty much dispelled it.

"Gabrielle!" Cameron sounded like he was in actual physical pain.

"Braden!" I just sounded pissed.

"What?" Suddenly the resemblance between Braden and Drew was uncanny.

"Gabrielle, I never meant for that to happen. I didn't even know." He looked ill.

"I figured that out, Cam. Look, it was a long time ago and we're all grown up people now." I gave Braden a warning glance. "Let's just forget it and move on." I realized at that moment that I did really want to move on. I had been thinking about something that had happened when I was eighteen for long enough.

"*Can* we be friends again?" he asked, sounding very earnest.

"You want to be friends? Sure. We can be friends and I'm hoping that the two of you will also try to get along."

"Why not? It's not the first time he's slept with my girlfriend."

"Braden!" I glared at him and then what he had said sunk in. "Wait, am I your girlfriend?"

"Do you want to be my girlfriend?"

"Well, yeah."

"Then you're my girlfriend. And I know that you deserve better than me too, but I don't care, because I'm selfish and I want you."

"Okay, since he's my friend and you're my boyfriend I want you to call a truce. That means no more snark, Braden."

"I thought you liked my sharp tongue." He gave me a wicked look that made my tummy flutter.

"You have no idea how much I like your tongue, Braden; there aren't words to describe how much I like it, just primal noises, but I want to try to put all of this shit behind us, so work with me here."

"Fine. Peace, Cameron. And thanks for giving me an excuse to break up with the harpy."

"Peace, Braden. No problem. She's here by the way."

"I don't suppose you'd be willing to distract..."

"Are you nuts?! I'm surprised my dick didn't freeze off the first time." I saw the two of them exchange amused looks. That was progress. Sort of. "So is this a bad time to tell you that the reason I thought it was interesting that you're a public defender was that my firm is sending me to the Defender Association to learn how to do pro bono cases for them?" He looked at me with a smile.

"What?"

"My firm..." *Oh Jesus.* That's just what we needed, an associate from a big white shoe firm coming in to organize financial portfolios for drug dealers.

"Oh you're going to *love* that, Cameron!" Braden laughed. "Just wait until you meet your new clients. Why don't you tell him about Mr. Sanchez, Gabrielle? He was interested in making money."

"I've been bored lately and I thought it would be kind of exciting," Cam said naively and Braden laughed harder. This was going to be a bloodbath.

"Okay, Cameron. If you manage to make it through this I'll consider that you've done penance and I'll never mention the harpy to you again." Braden smiled.

"It's a deal!" Cam looked genuinely happy. He had been waiting a long time to be forgiven.

"If you want you can shadow my friend Jess and me," I offered. What the hell. Maybe it would help us all get past the awkwardness. "We're usually in the same courtroom with Braden and his friend Adam."

"Really? Well, maybe they'll let me." He seemed really happy. He'd been waiting a long time for me to forgive him too. "Looking forward to it! I'm going to go say hi to Aunt Claire and Uncle Tyler."

We said goodbye and when he had left Braden turned to me.

"I had a feeling it might possibly be Cameron you were with. People have always said we look and sound alike. He's the right age and he went to Yale and to law school."

"I honestly didn't know, Braden. It was so long ago and he was younger. I swear that my being attracted to you has absolutely nothing to do with him. He was cute and I was eighteen. You get me big-girl excited." I reached up and ran my finger along his jawline.

"Oh really?" He smiled.

"Really," I said suggestively.

"Well, maybe we can..."

∽ CHAPTER TWELVE ∾

He never got to finish that sentence because a platinum blonde in a Valentino dress that probably cost enough to support a village in the Third World for a year, came charging up, and standing directly in front of me as if I weren't there, proceeded to try to start a conversation with Braden. If you could call it that.

"Braden! There you are. I've been looking all over for you."

"Why? I have nothing to say to you. I had nothing to say to you when I was dating you."

"Oh for Christ's sake! Get over it already. I'm getting tired of your dramatics."

"What the fuck are you talking about?" he demanded. I had backed up by this point and circled around to Braden's side. Obviously this was Braden's ex, the lovely Marla.

"Cut the bullshit. If you want to start thinking about running for office you're going to need the right wife and lucky for you, I'm still available."

"You're out of your mind! I would never marry *you*. I don't even like you."

"My family has money and influence. We don't have to like each other. We don't even have to fuck each other although you had no problem fucking me before."

"I was nineteen! I had no problem fucking anybody!"

"Yeah, okay, whatever. If you're not careful you're going to lose me."

"Lose you? I can't get rid of you! You can't seem to get it through that empty, deluded, narcissistic head of yours that I have no interest in you. And why would you think I was interested in politics either?"

"Why else would you want to work for the DA? It's not like they pay anything."

"I have a trust fund. I could work for free if I wanted. How did you even get on the guest list?"

"By agreeing to donate a grand to your family's fucking foundation."

"Well Marla, thanks for the donation but I have a real girlfriend now, who I actually like."

I must confess that up until then I had been feeling mighty awkward just standing there listening to this conversation while both of them completely ignored me. As soon as Braden made that little revelation, though, Marla seemed to notice me for the first time.

"Her?" she asked disdainfully, looking me up and down. "This mousy girl in the fake jewelry and the Carolina Herrera knock-off?"

"Hey! This is a Carlos Miele original and this is a diamond necklace from Harry Winston. You're one to talk about fake with your bleach blonde hair, your spray tan and your plastic tits, lady."

"Did you hear that, Braden?!" Marla screeched.

"Yes, I did," he answered with obvious amusement. "You tell her, baby." He leaned down and kissed me. "Now Marla, I think it's best that you left. You've wasted more than a thousand dollars' worth of my time and patience." He signaled one of the security team and explained that Marla had overstayed her welcome. We walked off as she was being hustled toward the drive complaining loudly and threatening to sue.

"She's a real sweetie." I smiled.

"Yeah, she's a charmer. I must have been insane. Oh shit," he said looking up and trying a bit too late, apparently, to steer us in the other direction. I followed his gaze and saw a man who appeared to be somewhere in his late thirties or possibly early forties. He had "pretty boy" looks and blindingly white teeth with an expression that reminded me somehow of the Big Bad Wolf. (The better to eat you with, my dear!) Not far behind him was a woman who looked like she might be in her mid-forties. She might have been considered quite attractive if she just didn't look so... mean. She had black hair streaked with iron gray and a cruel expression on her thin lips. She looked like someone who would have blended in well at a witch burning. They were closing in on us rapidly. Bringing up the rear were a painfully skinny and anemic-looking older man who might have been forty... or fifty... or sixty, and a sullen young woman with jet black hair and lily white skin. She was dressed all in black, including her lipstick. Those two looked like they would have preferred to have headed in the other direction, or anywhere else for that matter, other than after the first two.

"Braden! How the hell are ya?!" said the guy with the teeth, grabbing Braden's hand and pumping it up and down almost frantically. He looked like a demented Ken doll.

"You're looking quite dashing tonight, Braden," said the cold-looking woman in an even colder voice. "Isn't he, Felicity?" she asked the sullen young woman. I had never seen a more inappropriately named person in my life. She would have made Wednesday Addams look like Doris Day.

"Yes, mother," Felicity answered without even glancing in Braden's direction. The skinny older man said nothing. I almost didn't see him standing there for a moment. He blended in so well with the white tent wall.

"And you must be the fabulous Gabrielle Ginsberg," Mr. Teeth, who I suspected was Cole Stephenson, the lecherous politician, went on, while speaking directly to my boobs. *Fabulous?*

"Gabrielle," Braden said, pulling me closer to him, "these are the Masons and this is..."

"Cole Stephenson at your service," Mr. Teeth said, nodding like a bobble-head doll and giving me a cheesy smile and the two-handed finger point that announced he was a wild and crazy guy. "And *this* is the kingmaker's daughter." He grinned like he had just said something witty.

Mrs. Mason, in contrast, was looking at me like she wanted to kick me. Or damn me to Hell. Felicity was looking at me too, but I couldn't really interpret her expression. At least it didn't seem to involve wrath. Actually, she might have been admiring my necklace. I suspected that the blank expression on her face was as close as she came to expressing approval, or joy, or happiness, or anything. Mr. Mason said nothing and did nothing. I got the feeling he said and did nothing a lot. Maybe he really was a hologram.

"Ginsberg?" Mrs. Mason said in a way that made it sound like she was saying, 'root rot,' or 'genital warts'. "I don't believe I'm familiar with that name."

"Well, there was a famous poet, Allen Ginsberg, and there's a Supreme Court Justice, Ruth Bader Ginsburg. No relation."

"Gabrielle's father is a real mover and shaker in the Big Apple," Cole put in and winked at me. I cringed. He reminded me of a used car salesman — who moonlighted as a pornographer. "We're lucky to have someone with her obvious sophistication joining our little circle of country bumpkins." His gaze was traveling up and down my body like he was a starving dog eyeing up a side of beef. Even though he was creeping me out, I almost laughed out loud when he called me sophisticated and the Pierces bumpkins.

"New York, hmm." Apparently Mrs. Mason didn't approve of New Yorkers. "I'm sure she's very sophisticated." I was pretty sure that she had just called me a tramp. I didn't want to contemplate what else she might be thinking, as it would probably have been offensive on so many different levels.

I saw Beth gesturing to us in the background and I nudged Braden and let him know.

"Oh sorry to run!" he said, not looking sorry at all. "But my sister needs us." He pulled me off quickly and we headed for the stage. When we got there Beth let Braden know that she was going to need some extra help for the upcoming auction. He hesitated.

"I don't know if I want to leave you alone with these people," he said to me.

"I don't blame you, Braden," Beth said, glancing at Cole and cringing herself. I think Cole made a lot of people cringe. "Gabrielle, you could help me out by bringing these lists up to the house and putting them on the desk in the library. If you don't mind, that is. It's just busy work, but it would get you out of here, and it really would be doing me a favor. They have important information on them and I don't want them to get lost."

"Sure, no problem." I took the papers from her and set out for the house. When I got there I found it bustling with various catering, decorating and entertainment people. I dropped the papers off and headed back toward the tent.

Halfway there I was cornered by Cole Stephenson. "So, Gabrielle, this thing with Braden's not serious is it? I mean he's a bit of a ladies' man you know?" I couldn't believe this guy's nerve.

"Well now he's one lady's man," I said as I tried to walk around him.

"Well, if it doesn't work out, I'd like a shot at you." A shot at me? "You know, there are some people who think I might make it to the White House someday; so you could say I'm looking for my First Lady." He gave me a toothy grin. Or perhaps I should say he gave my boobs a toothy grin. I felt like I needed to bathe.

"As enticing as that sounds, I'm afraid I'm not interested." Once again I tried to do an end run around him but he was quick with evasive maneuvers. We looked like we were doing some kind of strange dance.

"Hey there, I hope I didn't offend you! I just meant that you're one little girl who shouldn't go to waste. With your connections and money," he glanced at my necklace, "and my political savvy, the sky's the limit, babe."

"I'm very happy with Braden."

"For now, but he doesn't always appreciate beautiful women like I do. I would treat you like a princess. Just keep it in mind." I wouldn't be able to forget it if I tried. I would probably have nightmares about it. Then out of nowhere a very unlikely cavalry arrived.

"Ms. Ginsberg. I wonder if you can help me. I have a legal question," Felicity Mason said. Great. I hated giving out free legal advice at parties, but at that moment, I would have drafted her will in crayon on a cocktail napkin to get away from Cole.

"Sure! Call me Gabrielle. Let's walk and talk." We escaped from the Big Bad Wolf. When we were several feet away I asked her what I could help her with.

"Nothing. I just wanted to help you get away from him. He's an asshole."

"Ah, so it's not just me who thinks so."

"No. Everybody thinks so, but only some people say so. He's got his uses for some."

"I see." I didn't really, but I didn't know what else to say.

"You should watch out for him, and he's not the only one. Marla's not as stupid as she seems and my…"

"Gabrielle, over here!" I heard Braden call out as we approached the tent. I thanked Felicity for her help and I walked up to Braden and tucked myself up close to him.

"I ran into Cole."

"What did he want?"

"He wanted to tell me that you're a ladies' man and so if it doesn't work out he wanted a shot at me because he might be in the market for a future First Lady."

"I'll kill him."

"He's not worth it. He's a complete fool, Braden. It's kind of scary that people elected him."

"I think that there are about ten people who live in his district, and nine of them are related to him."

"That would explain it, although I wouldn't be surprised to hear that it was a close race."

I had a few more close encounters of the annoying kind with Mrs. Mason as the night wore on. I kept feeling like someone was watching me, someone other than the security people. On more than one occasion I caught her sneering at me like I had just popped out of a cake with tassels on my tits. Seriously! What had I ever done to this woman?

∽ CHAPTER THIRTEEN ∽

Dinner was a big hit and the auction went even better than expected, raising plenty of money for the foundation. I had even dug into my trust fund a little and purchased a weekend getaway to the Finger Lakes in July that included a stay at a Bed and Breakfast and tickets to the wine festival.

"So, want to share a bed and some wine with me in the Finger Lakes?" I asked Braden.

"Absolutely. Right now, though, I'd like to take a trip with you to the pool house. I was thinking that maybe you might like to have a little rendezvous with me there and we could see if I could get you big-girl excited."

"In the pool house?" I giggled like a schoolgirl.

"There's a massage table there that I'd like to introduce you to." He smiled a very sexy smile and my tummy completely flipped over.

"But there are people wandering around all over the place and it's so close to here."

"So, we'll have to be quiet and quick. I won't go Vinnie Virillo on you though. I promise."

"Okay!" I smiled in anticipation and he took my hand as we slipped out the side of the tent. It was a bit after eight o'clock and just starting to get a little darker but we could still see very clearly. We passed people coming and going and I heard laughter and conversation from various directions.

When we got to the pool house Braden gave a surreptitious look around and quickly found the key and unlocked the door. It was kind of dark inside but there was enough light coming through the windows so that I could see well when my eyes adjusted. I followed him into a small room occupied by a massage table and shelves stacked with towels and various bottles of scented oils and creams.

He pulled me into his arms and started kissing me eagerly, doing all of those wonderful things he did with his tongue. I'm telling you, that tongue could win awards. I moaned quietly as his hands ran all over my body. Those hands were pretty talented too. He broke the kiss and whispered in my ear.

"Take your panties off."

"I'm not wearing any. I like the way this dress feels against my bare skin." At first he looked a little stunned. Then I saw his gaze heat up and a cocky grin formed on his beautiful lips.

"Bend over and grab the edge of the table," he ordered in a low thick voice. I did what he asked and he pushed my skirt up around my waist, pulled my hips back a little and then smacked me hard on the ass. Ooh! I felt his fingers glide across my entrance and then backtrack to start massaging the back door if you know what I mean.

"Braden?" I asked a little nervously.

"Don't worry. Not tonight. Just testing the waters," he said, sounding amused. His fingers slid forward again. "You're so wet," he said, stroking me broadly up and down. He traced a path up to my now throbbing clit. "And swollen." Then two fingers slid up inside me. "And ready. That's my baby." I heard him unzip and felt him position himself behind me and then he grabbed my hips and thrust into me deeply as I gasped and arched my back. One hand slid inside the bodice of my dress and cupped my breast, pinching my nipple kind of hard. He was being a little rougher but I didn't mind. The other returned to stroke my clit relentlessly, never taking away the pressure. Then he began his hip roll and I entered a state of complete sexual euphoria. The feeling was so good and so intense I almost couldn't stand it. Or stand for that matter. My legs were starting to shake and I hoped that they didn't give out. He kissed my neck and bit my earlobe as I whimpered and tried to swallow my moans. After several minutes of blowing my mind he started talking.

"You feel so good, baby," he whispered in my ear and I immediately felt myself start climbing. "So hot and so wet." My muscles tensed up. "Oh, that's right, baby. So tight. I love it when you grab my cock like that," he ground out and I was right on the edge. "Gabrielle, this is the sweetest pussy I've ever had." Okay, that was it! Folks, we had a winner! I cried out (I couldn't help it!) and my muscles clenched hard, pulsing rhythmically as my body trembled. He stayed with me until I rode out the final waves and then his hands returned to my hips and he grabbed on and slammed into me hard and fast until I felt him freeze and hold me tight against him. He let out a low groan and a ragged breath. "Oh Fuck!"

Hot damn! That was some good sexing! We stood still for a few minutes just catching our breath and then he turned me around and kissed me deeply and tenderly.

"There's a bathroom over there if you need it," he said quietly as he zipped up. I looked up and immediately became alert. "What is it?"

"I thought I saw something by the window but it was probably nothing."

"Are you sure?"

"Pretty sure. If someone were there people would notice and wonder why he was peeping in the window of the pool house, right?"

"You're probably right. We had better get back though."

"Thank you for the rendezvous." I smiled. "It was fun."

"Believe me, Gabrielle. You don't have to thank me."

I popped into the bathroom and tidied up. When I came back out he had an almost proud look on his face.

"Feeling kind of possessive huh?"

"I guess it's a male thing."

"Consider my girl parts to be officially your territory."

When we went back to the tent the band had taken the stage and people were dancing to old songs. I saw Beth, Drew and, Cameron, sitting off to the side. Beth waved us over and we went and sat down with them. Drew was looking smug; Beth was looking happy and Cam was looking… well, drunk, to be perfectly honest.

"Mom's calling me over, I'll be right back," Beth said, getting up and rushing off.

"So, Gabrielle, what do you think of the pool house?" Drew asked with a knowing smile. Braden and I both looked at him with surprise.

"What, are you stalking us?" he asked. "You need to get some more hobbies."

"And you two need to learn how to sneak off better. You guys just casually strolled off with half the party watching. Here's a hint big brother, nobody thought you were planning to go swimming."

"Were you selling tickets for a place at the window?"

"No, but I should have thought of that!" Drew laughed.

"I thought I really did see somebody by one of the windows," Cam slurred. "But I've been seeing a lot of weird shit since I had that last rum punch."

"Are you okay, Cam?" I asked with a bit of concern. Cameron was looking a little green.

"Me? Oh, yes." He sat up straighter. "I've just been having a few… dozen cocktails."

"All of the mothers with unmarried socialite daughters have been stalking him." Drew grinned. "Mrs. Mason has even decided that Cam might be a good alternative to Braden for Felicity's hand in marriage."

"Lucky you," Braden teased.

"I talked to her before and she actually seems like a pretty nice person," I said. "If you had those parents you would probably dress in black and look sullen too."

"You're so nice, Gabrielle," Cam rambled with a slightly glassy look in his eyes. "You were always so nice to everybody. You knew all the homeless people's names."

"So, you guys planning to hook up anywhere else tonight?" Drew asked. "I think there's some space on the dance floor." Braden glared at him.

"Hey! If you were dating her you'd be hittin' that shit every chance you had too and you know it. Gabrielle is very hot and she's got an amazing..." Cameron said somewhat incoherently to Drew. Okay, time to get out of there!

"May I have this dance?" I interrupted quickly, turning to Braden. He smiled and stood up to escort me to the floor. Even though he had been feeling the need to claim his mate and mark his territory in the pool house he was being very sweet and gentle now. We laughed a little and smiled stupidly at each other a whole lot, dancing to *Blue Moon* and *Dream a Little Dream of Me*. Who knew that romance could be so great? Well, pretty much everybody but me until now I guess. Claire and Tyler looked completely in love, staring into one another's eyes.

The evening had been a great success. (Luckily, Cam had ridden with relatives and so he wasn't driving.) When things finally wound down we headed back up to the house. Braden's family and I all had some tea in the kitchen and we traded stories about the evening for a while. Despite a rocky start, it had turned out to be one of the best Saturday nights I had spent in a very long time. Okay, it was one of the best ever, although there had been that trip to Disneyworld when I was six. It was nearly 3a.m. when we all finally headed up to bed and now that the adrenaline was gone I was starting to feel very tired. We wished everyone goodnight and went into Braden's room.

"Now that I can finally get you out of that dress, I think I may be too tired to do anything about it," he said, walking over to me and helping me with my zipper and my necklace.

"We already had a rendezvous, Iron Man. I'm tired too. How about if we just cuddle and see how we feel in the morning?"

"Sounds good." We both set about getting undressed and ready for bed. It took me a while to wash off the make-up and brush out my hair and when I left the bathroom I saw that Braden was sitting in bed reading and waiting for me. I just stood there and stared for a minute.

"What?" he asked, looking up with a smile.

"I was just thinking what a nice sight it is to see you reading in bed."

"It's a nice sight to see you doing anything in bed." He pulled back the covers invitingly and I came over and snuggled in. He put down his book and turned out the light, pulling me into his arms.

"I told your mom that I was quite smitten with you."

"Well, I told my dad I was quite smitten with you. That's what I was talking to him about after lunch."

"I wondered what you were talking about."

"I just had some relationship questions. I trust his judgment. My parents are very happy together."

"My parents are too and they still flirt with each other even after all the years of marriage."

"I'd really like to meet them."

"How about next weekend?"

"You're on." I could tell even without being able to see him that he was smiling.

CHAPTER FOURTEEN

Everyone was late getting downstairs the next morning and we all met for brunch in the dining room. Afterward, we packed up our stuff and got ready to go. Even though we were only a half an hour away, everyone was hugging and promising to call and visit and e-mail. Beth and Claire made me promise to have lunch and go shopping with them too. I could see how happy that made Braden. In the car ride on the way home he had a contented smile on his face.

"Are you and Jessica just going to hang out tonight?"

"Yeah, she'll be curious to hear about the weekend." And personally, I wanted to gush about Braden and his family and talk to her about moronic Marla, creepy Cole and mean Mrs. Mason. As far as Cam went, I figured I would just mention the coincidence that an old college friend of mine was Braden's cousin, and mention that he might be shadowing us sometime in the future.

"I'm going to do the usual Sunday night hang out thing with Mark and Adam."

I wondered if he talked to Adam and Mark the way that I talked to Jess. Probably not. There would probably be a few suggestive jokes and then they would eat pizza, drink beer and watch sports. That seemed to be their pattern. Braden brought me back to my apartment and helped me with my bags, giving me a warm kiss goodbye and telling me he would call me later to say goodnight. As I walked in the front door Jess came hurtling at me like a human cannonball.

"Was it good?" she demanded in between bites of the Haagen-Dazs she was holding.

"The weekend? Yeah, it was fun," I answered with a smile. She gave me a "don't fuck around with me" look.

"And how was the sex?"

"That was amazing." She followed me into my room and sat on my bed while I unpacked. She listened avidly while I gave her the basic run down as she made appreciative noises and comments. She actually blushed a little when I told her about the pool house. I don't think she realized that Braden could be such a naughty boy. I also told her all about the rest of the weekend, from Drew's funny comments to Cole's obnoxious ones. We spent the better part of the evening giggling and laughing and between the two of us we polished off all of the Rocky Road.

Monday came and went without much fanfare. I visited clients at the jail and caught up on paperwork. Braden made a goodnight call and I was already looking forward to seeing him again. Tuesday morning Jess and I arrived at work as usual, coffee in hand, and we were just sitting down at our desks to start preparing cases for court the next day when Chief Deputy Public Defender, Chuck Collins stopped by our office with Cam in tow. His request had been granted. He would be shadowing Jess and I and sharing our office space for the next few weeks. Jess seemed perfectly happy with that and I suspected that the fact that Cam was a really cute and sexy guy made this assignment a little less burdensome.

Before long Cam and Jess were laughing together, which I took as a good sign. I had been so engrossed in my work I hadn't even heard what they were talking about.

"Any interesting cases tomorrow?" I asked, wondering what was so funny.

"Nothing spectacular. How about on your list?"

"I've got a pretty good one. A guilty plea — Mr. Maximillian Davis. I'm not going to spoil it for you though." I smiled. The hours went by quickly and we made plans to go out to lunch with Braden, who stopped by at noon. The four of us headed for Reading Terminal Market, chatting on the way.

"So Cameron, give investment advice to any felons yet?" Braden asked with a smirk.

"Not yet but I've got definite ideas for expanding their portfolios."

"Well, I'm sure it will be an interesting experience for you. I hope you'll get to be there when we do Mr. Davis' guilty plea tomorrow."

"We get all the good ones, don't we?"

"Uh, hello? I get my share of good ones too," Jess chimed in.

"I hope that you two will let Cameron share in the fun." Braden smiled.

"Can't wait," Cam replied, grinning the grin of the blissfully unaware.

When we arrived, we browsed the various stalls for something good to eat and when we had all picked up our lunches we found a place to sit and dug in.

"So you and Gabrielle were friends in college?" Jess asked Cam.

"Yeah, we were in the same lit class and she obviously got it. I obviously didn't, so I asked her to help me study."

"And it had nothing to do with the fact that she was hot," Braden said dryly.

"Braden!" I rolled my eyes.

"It had something to do with the fact that she was hot," he said with a laugh and I almost choked on my curry. "But it had more to do with the fact that she was so smart."

"So you thought she was hot and smart?" Jess asked.

"And funny and very nice," Cam added, glancing at me and smiling but nevertheless looking a little uncomfortable. He turned his focus to his Pad Thai.

"So how come you never asked her out?" Jess asked. Oh my God! I was going to kill her.

Cam hesitated. "Well, I was kind of a serial dater, and besides, when we first met she was dating somebody. Jonathan Parker, right?" he asked me. "It's weird but for some reason, I always thought he was gay."

"He, uh, well," I coughed. "He was. That is, he discovered that he was. Gay, I mean," I said and Cam almost spit out the Coke he was drinking.

"Discovered that he was gay? He didn't know that already?"

"People don't always realize that right away. Do they?"

"I'm not sure, but I think that most people realize it on some level, although maybe they haven't come to terms with it," he answered tactfully.

"How long did you date a gay man?" Jess cut in.

"Just a couple of months."

"And it never occurred to you?" she asked incredulously.

"Well, I'll admit that I thought it was odd that he was so shy, you know, about physical contact. I didn't really bring it up though because I didn't want to pressure him."

"So you never had any physical side to your relationship?"

"We were affectionate. We held hands and hugged. He put his arm around me and we gave each other little cheek kisses. At the time I had hardly any sexual experience at all so I was pretty naïve." I saw Cam look away uncomfortably. Braden wasn't looking terribly comfortable either.

"And what did you do on your dates?" she wanted to know.

"Hung out and watched movies, went out dancing. Stuff like that."

"Honey, are you sure you were dating? I mean it sounds to me like you were his hag," Jess said sounding bewildered. I saw Cam and Braden glance at each other and struggle valiantly not to laugh. They were barely holding on there. At least they were kind of bonding.

"I think we were dating. I have to admit that I wasn't really surprised when he told me he was gay, but I assumed it was something he had just figured out. I didn't want to push him to discuss it, in case he wasn't ready." Suddenly it sunk in. "Oh my God. I had an imaginary boyfriend."

That one was just too much. They lost it. Those two bastards totally cracked up! Cam turned his head and Braden covered his face with his hands but they couldn't hide the way their shoulders silently shook. Finally, they pulled it together.

"Just for the record, *we're* really dating," Braden said, catching his breath, which almost started Cam off on another laughing fit.

"I'm glad that you two find this so amusing." I calmly went on eating my lunch. I was actually thankful for their little laughing fit because it had allowed Cam to avoid answering Jess's question. I really didn't want to discuss it at the moment.

We finished up our lunch and Braden kissed me goodbye and whispered in my ear that we would have a private lunch soon. Then he returned to his office and we returned to ours. We worked on through the afternoon and finally at the end of the day, we said goodbye to Cam, and Jess and I headed home. When we got there I stopped at our box to pick up the mail and we went upstairs.

⌒ CHAPTER FIFTEEN ⌒

We walked in and I was going to toss the mail on the entry table, but something caught my eye; peeking out of the pile was an envelope that was addressed to me in sloppy handwriting that I didn't recognize. There was no return address. What the hell? I stood there and stared, starting to feel a little apprehensive for some reason.

"Jess," I called.

"What's the matter?" she asked, coming over to me.

"It's nothing big. Just that there's a letter addressed to me and it doesn't have a return address. I don't recognize the writing."

I ripped it open carefully and removed a note from inside. Jess leaned over to read it along with me. There was a single sheet of plain white paper on which someone had written a short message in the same sloppy script. It said, *"You should not be with him. End it now before you get hurt."*

"Who do you think wrote this?" she asked, sounding shocked.

"Well, Marla seems like she may not have both oars in the water and she's certainly nasty enough. She's also fixated on getting Braden back."

"Okay, there's a good possibility," Jess agreed.

"Cole was creepy and he was definitely hitting on me. He kept saying that if it didn't work with Braden I should consider dating him. This letter is so ambiguous. It's hard to tell if the writer is warning me off for my own good or threatening me."

"That's a good point. He could be trying to get you away from Braden. I'd say that's another good suspect."

"Then there's Mrs. Mason, who was giving me dirty looks all evening. She wants Braden for her daughter but I could also tell she just didn't like me in general. I think she saw me as this interloper in her elite little Main Line WASP community."

"She did sound pretty evil. It might not be anybody who was at the fundraiser though. There are a lot of strange people out there. Remember that article in the Times you told me about — the one that sounded like a conspiracy theory? What if it's someone who buys into that stuff?"

"The gossipy magazines that covered the fundraiser in detail haven't come out yet and I don't think that the coverage in the papers was very specific. That was really all about the Foundation. So it's not really public knowledge that we're even dating. It's just a hunch, but I feel like it was one of those three."

"Maybe you should report it to the police."

"Not yet. I can't mention that I suspect anybody."

"Why not?"

"I can't go around accusing a state representative of doing something like this without any proof, and I think that the Masons are big financial supporters of the Pierce family foundation. I don't want to risk alienating them based on some dirty looks. As for Marla, her family is wealthy and well-connected and I don't want anyone to get sued. "

"Fine, but you should still tell the police. Maybe you should tell your dad, too."

"It would just worry him and he would want to buy us a Pit Bull or hire me a bodyguard or something. My parents worry about me enough. Actually, I have something else in mind, but I would need your help."

"Uh oh. I don't like the sound of this already."

"Remember I had that forgery trial, the one where I had to hire a handwriting expert?"

"Yeah?"

"Well, I still have his contact information. I think that I should hire him to compare the handwriting in this note to samples that I get from all three of the people I mentioned."

"And just how are you going to get them to give you handwriting samples, Nancy Drew?"

"I'm going to follow them until an opportunity presents itself, but I need your help because they've all seen me but they don't know you."

"We can't just follow people around indefinitely. Do these people even live around here?"

"I think that they all live near the Pierces but I'll verify it," I said, going over to my laptop. I did a quick search and discovered that Cole's district was just outside the city and that he had a place there and in Harrisburg, the state capital. Marla had a townhouse in the city and the Masons lived within a few miles of Braden's parents.

"Marla's right here in the city. It would be easiest to start with her and the most likely time for her to go out would be on a Friday or Saturday night."

"So what are you going to tell Braden? I can't take you to meet my parents because I want to follow your ex-girlfriend around?"

"No. We're going to need extra help."

"You *are* going to tell Braden about the letter though, aren't you?"

"Not yet. He's just like my dad. He'll get all worried and uber protective. He might get himself in trouble by going after one or even all three of the people who I suspect. He might even suspect Cam of being jealous or something and I don't think it was him." Suddenly it dawned on me. "That's it! Cameron can help us."

"But Marla knows him too. Maybe we should ask Mark."

"Mark would tell Braden. He'll be with you, who Marla doesn't know, and she won't be expecting to see him. Even if he did run into her though, big deal. He could just say he was on a date."

"What makes you think he'll agree to spend his weekends following Marla?"

"I think that he's bored. That's why criminal law sounds exciting to him. Did you get his number?" I asked.

"I did," she said a little sheepishly. "Just in case something happened, you know?"

"What, like the courtroom burned down or something?" I teased.

"Something like that." She fished her phone out of her purse.

"Call him and ask him if it's too late to invite him to dinner with us. You can tell him we need to talk to him."

When she hung up she said that although he sounded surprised, he would be happy to join us. He had a place in Society Hill, another Center City neighborhood which was very near here. I was surprised I hadn't run into him somewhere sooner. We ordered from a local Chinese place and I ran out to pick it up. By the time I got back Cam had arrived and he and Jess were laughing and talking animatedly. I set the table and we sat down to eat.

"So, Jessica says that there's something you want to talk to me about?"

"Yeah, I got this letter today," I said, showing it to him.

"Who would send something like this?"

"I have a hunch that it was either Marla, Cole, or possibly Mrs. Mason."

"Well, any of them would be capable of it, but couldn't it be anybody?" I explained my reasoning to him and he saw my point. Next I outlined my plan.

"So you would want Jessica and me just to follow her?"

"I was thinking that maybe you could at least find out what places she tends to go to. Then maybe we could come up with a plan for getting the sample. This would be just sort of an information gathering phase. What do you think?"

"I think it sounds kind of interesting — sort of James Bond." He laughed. "You're going to tell Braden though, right?"

"Not right away. I'm afraid he'll get worried and upset and have one or more of them investigated and that could have all kinds of ramifications. I'm not telling my dad either or we'll have more alarms in this place than Fort Knox before you know it."

"I don't know if I feel good about doing anything behind Braden's back," Cam said significantly.

"I promise I'll tell him. I'm just hoping to have a little something to go on first. I really don't want to worry him and I honestly don't feel like I'm in any danger. Public defenders and prosecutors get harassing letters sometimes. I think this is just like that."

"Well, I guess it's not like I'm sneaking around with you. More like I'm sneaking around with your roommate." He smiled. "Okay team, I'm in!"

"Great! Okay, I have the address of Marla's townhouse. I say that this Friday you two just see if you can figure out what kinds of places she goes to. Maybe it will give us an idea."

"You're going to see your parents?" Cam asked.

"Yeah, Braden and I will leave for New York by train on Friday after work, so you guys will be on your own, but call me anytime. If I don't answer right away I'll call you back as soon as I can."

We finished dinner and Cam hung out for a while longer before heading back to his place. When he was gone Jess turned to me and I had a feeling I was about to be cross-examined.

"Okay, what's the deal?"

"What's the deal with what?"

"The whole story with you and Cameron and Braden. I get the feeling there's more there than you've shared so far." Jess was very observant. It was hard to get anything past her.

"Let's go get comfortable," I said, heading for the living room and sinking into my favorite armchair. "Cam and I were friends in college and I had a big crush on him. We wound up hooking up one night and I wanted it to be more but he didn't."

"Oh wow. You're kidding." I could that she genuinely sympathized.

"And he and Braden had some tension because back when Braden was dating Marla, Cam hooked up with her too."

"Oh my God! He sounds like he was a total ass!"

"It's weird but I don't think he was. I know it sounds naïve, but I honestly think he's basically a nice guy and that there were reasons for all of his screw-ups. I think that he felt really bad about them for a long time."

"You always give people the benefit of the doubt."

"Maybe someday I'll get the full explanation. I really do think that there is one."

"So do you think that you'll all be able to get along now that you're dating Braden?"

"I think so. I hope so. It was a long time ago and I like the present a lot better than the past. Now I'm going to go relax and watch PBS. There's a special on about the Bill of Rights tonight."

"You wild woman. Forgive me if I don't join you."

"Don't forget to stick around for Mr. Davis' plea tomorrow. I think you'll be more entertained by that.

∽ CHAPTER SIXTEEN ∾

IN THE COURT OF COMMON PLEAS OF PHILADELPHIA COUNTY, PENNSYLVANIA

Commonwealth v. Davis

"You understand the charges that you're pleading guilty to, Mr. Davis? And you understand that you have a right to a trial?" Judge Channing asked.

"Yes sir," Mr. Davis answered.

"Okay, summarize the facts, Mr. Pierce." Inner-Gabrielle rolled her eyes.

"On May fourteenth of this year in the County of Philadelphia, the defendant, Mr. Maximillian Davis, aged seventy-five, was in operation of a vehicle traveling southbound on Broad Street within the city limits. Several motorists called nine-one-one to notify authorities that a vehicle matching the description of Mr. Davis' was driving erratically. Officer Brian Picton of the Philadelphia Police Department got behind Mr. Davis in his patrol vehicle and witnessed Mr. Davis swerve across lanes, hit several parked vehicles and twice drive up on the sidewalk. Mr. Davis did eventually pull over and Officer Picton placed him under arrest. When questioned at the station, after having been advised of his rights and having waived counsel, he explained that he was making, and I quote, 'a booty call.' He further explained that at his age, when the mood strikes he needs to, quote, 'be quick about it' unquote. He is charged with ten counts of driving on the wrong side of the road, four counts of hit and run, four counts of damaging parked vehicles, and two counts of reckless endangerment."

"A booty call, Mr. Davis?" Judge Channing asked in a disgusted tone.

"I've got needs just like you, sir. I just don't have the staying power I used to."

"Ms. Ginsberg?" Judge Channing said, giving my client a look that most people reserved for gum that they found stuck to their shoes.

"Mr. Davis has no criminal record. He was gainfully employed with the erectric – electric! He was employed with the *electric* company for over fifty years. Furthermore, he's an upstanding member of his community." Oh my God. Did I just say that? I saw Braden trying to maintain a straight face. I provided this man with a great deal of mirth. In fact, I filled his life with laughter.

"He was so concerned about remaining upstanding that he could have killed someone from his community," the judge responded acidly. Braden was now biting down on his lip to avoid laughing. I glanced behind me and saw Mark, Jess and Cameron also trying to maintain their composure. Have you ever noticed how everything seems so much funnier when you're not allowed to laugh? Well, court is like that a lot. Adam looked like he wasn't going to make it.

"He deeply regrets what happened, Your Honor, and assures you that it will never happen again."

"Well, the bad driving part anyway!" Mr. Davis offered.

"Thank you for clarifying that," the judge retorted sarcastically. "There's an agreement with the District Attorney's Office I take it?"

"Yes, Your Honor," Braden answered. "The Commonwealth has no objection to a sentence of six months of probation and restitution for the damaged vehicles."

"The court accepts the plea. Mr. Maximillian Davis, you have indicated that you understand the charges and are entering a plea of guilty. I hereby sentence you to six months of probation and restitution for any damage that the owners of the vehicles in question can substantiate. Off the record please." The court reporter stopped typing. "Viagra, Mr. Davis. Viagra!" He banged his gavel just because he could.

"Yes, sir. Thanks, judge! See you later cutie." Mr. Davis smiled and winked at me flirtatiously before going off to report to the probation department.

Braden and I were done for the morning and we packed up our files. We had all decided to go out to lunch. Braden officially introduced Cam to Adam and Mark and we all headed for Reading Terminal Market again. When we sat down to eat Mark got the ball rolling.

"So Cameron, I hope you were paying attention to how Gabrielle handled that."

"The erectric company!" Adam laughed.

"Oh my God. I can't believe I said that," I mumbled.

"He's an upstanding member of the community," Braden added. "That was great too."

"You liked that huh?" I smiled.

"See what you have to look forward to, Cameron?" Mark asked. "One day you too can represent horny senior citizens while attempting to sound dignified."

"Too bad he wasn't around for that case with the nuns," Adam said to Jess.

"I would have been happy to hand that one off to you," she told Cam.

"I should introduce Mr. Davis to Ms. Franklin," I told Braden.

"That would be some hot date." He laughed. "They could head down to the senior center, get high and get laid." Hearing Braden say "get laid" reminded me of the conversation we had recently shared lying naked in bed together just before I had gotten laid very well. It made me feel flushed and sent a jolt of heat to my girl parts. "What?" he asked me quietly. I guess I wasn't exactly hard to read.

"Nothing," I said, feeling my face getting even hotter.

"I think Gabrielle wants you to talk dirty to her," Mark teased.

"Braden's going to be making a booty call later," Adam chimed in. "Just make sure you obey the traffic laws on the way."

Braden looked at me and smiled. He knew perfectly well that I liked it when he talked dirty to me. He probably just hadn't realized that even saying "get laid" could turn me on when it was him saying it. "You want me to make a booty call later?"

"You're welcome to call on my booty if you want," I said, examining my spring rolls with intense interest and feeling like if I blushed any more I would start to glow.

"If you're going to talk dirty, though, just make sure you do it quietly," Jess teased Braden. "Let me remind you again that there's a minor who lives next door."

"Again?" Mark asked with an inquisitive smile.

"According to Drew, Gabrielle's the one you should be warning," Cameron added. *Et tu Cameron? Wait a minute!*

"What do you mean?" I asked, suddenly feeling very worried. I saw Braden shaking his head at Cameron but it was obviously too late. "What does he mean?" I asked Braden. When confronted with the obvious, not even willful ignorance and denial are enough.

"Uh oh Braden," Adam laughed.

"Braden?" I was getting really worried.

"Uh, Drew and Beth got home a little earlier than we thought." He looked a little worried himself, but I had a feeling that he was worrying because he thought that I might have a heart attack. "Beth stayed downstairs to wait for my parents," he continued. "Drew went up to bed though."

"I didn't hear…" Suddenly my spring roll didn't look very appetizing. "He didn't tease you about it," I said weakly.

"Yes, he did. You just didn't really notice because he was doing it subtly and I suspect that you didn't want to know. He teased me about it quite openly when we talked alone later though," he said gently.

"How do you know he wasn't making it up?"

"He asked me where I got my desk and if I needed help repairing the wall."

"I see."

"Your desk huh?" Adam said, glancing at Mark.

"Don't worry about it, Gabrielle." Braden said, rubbing my back. "He's got some pretty wild roommates. He probably hears that all the time."

"And he was only teasing about everybody seeing you guys go into the pool house. He was one of the only people who noticed," Cameron put in. I think he was trying to be helpful.

"In the pool house too, huh? Did you guys even make it to the fundraiser?" Adam asked.

"That was during the fundraiser," Cameron explained.

"*During* the fundraiser?" Mark laughed. "Wow, you two are like bunny rabbits."

"Okay, okay. You're going to traumatize her," Jess warned. "Honey, it's no big deal. So you had a good time with your boyfriend in bed, and on a desk, and in a pool house, and maybe you screamed his name a few times and his little brother heard..." She stopped and looked at me. "This isn't helping is it?" I shook my head. "So anyway, I'll bet your parents are excited that you're coming to visit," she said, nibbling on a French fry. It took me a minute to switch gears mentally but I managed it.

"Uh, yes. Yes, they are. They're excited about meeting Braden too," I answered, thankful for the change in subject.

"They are?" He looked happy.

"Yes, they are. Don't forget, though, that I warned you about Bubbe."

* * *

That afternoon went quickly as I prepared my cases for the next day. They were pretty unexciting, just some drug dealers, check forgers, purse snatchers, and the usual. There were no burrito assault cases or geriatric booty callers. Cam worked with Jess again and they were laughing and talking like old friends.

"So what are you ladies doing for dinner?" Cam asked.

"I think I'm just going to grab something and take it home with me," I answered.

"I don't have any plans," Jess said.

"Well, Maybe you and I could go out and get a bite," Cam suggested.

"Sure," she said. "Maybe we could go out for a drink afterward." Out of the corner of my eye I saw Jess point to me surreptitiously and mouth "booty call" and giggle quietly. I was so glad that people were so up-to-date with the intimate details of my sex life.

"Sounds great," Cam said with slightly unnatural-sounding enthusiasm.

They worked until six and then left together. I put in another half hour and then left, picked up some deli, and went home. I had eaten and washed up by eight and there was no sign of Jess. My cell started ringing and I saw it was Braden, calling earlier than usual. I felt a little nervous anticipation as I answered.

"Hey handsome."

"Still want me to come calling?"

"I would love to be called on. Jess is out with Cameron."

"I'll be there in ten minutes."

He was there in five. I opened the door to let him in and noticed that he was dressed casually in jeans and a tee-shirt but he had a suit bag with him.

"Planning to spend the night?"

"Planning to kick me out of bed?" He came over, leaned down and gave me a deliciously minty, yet wonderfully hot kiss.

"Mm. You're always welcome in my bed."

"Good. Let's go there now and make good use of our privacy while it lasts."

"She could be back anytime. I'm not making any noise tonight."

"Oh, I'll bet I can get you to make some noise." He smiled wickedly.

"Oh really?" I started backing up toward my bedroom.

"Oh really. Besides, I'm not going to be quiet tonight. I'm going to whisper all kinds of dirty things in your ear." I swallowed hard and felt myself start to sweat. I *so* wanted him to whisper dirty things in my ear.

"Come and get me," I said in my best saucy voice and then I turned and hurried into my room.

~ CHAPTER SEVENTEEN ~

As soon as the door was closed behind us he was all over me and I was loving it. He practically threw me down on the bed and he had me naked in under a minute. Before I could even say, 'You're so good at this,' he had himself naked too and he was crawling toward me, pausing to run his tongue around my belly button a few times and then lick his way up to my breasts. *Oh lord!* He was so good at that too. He began circling one nipple with his tongue and then dragged it into his mouth and started sucking vigorously. My hips came off the bed so hard and fast that I almost threw him off but he managed to stay with me. If he ever wanted to give up law he might have a career in rodeo.

"Oh God yes!" I moaned loudly and I felt him smile. So much for not making any noise. He worked on the other breast for a while as I contributed by writhing around, moaning, raking my nails on his back and grabbing his hair. Hey, I was happy to do my part. We were both being rather unruly tonight.

"Promise me," I panted, "you'll tell me if you hear Jess come home."

"I promise," he murmured, leaving my breast and nibbling a trail over my collarbone and up along my neck. Then bracing himself over me on his forearms, and using his hips to create all kinds of delightful friction between us, he started to whisper the most wonderfully dirty things in my ear. I won't go into everything that he said, but by the time he got to "and then I'm going to fuck you hard until you scream my name", I had pretty much lost all semblance of self-control.

He was a man of his word too. He did everything that he promised he would. First he was on top, and then I was on top, and then he was behind me holding onto my hair and playfully slapping my ass in the "naughty but not really painful" way — not in the "I'm going to put a ball-gag in your mouth and suspend you from the ceiling" way. This was the first time we had ever had sex this rowdy together. In fact, this was the first time I had ever had sex this rowdy at all. I'm telling you, this wasn't your grandmother's booty call. Unless, of course, your grandmother was a sex-crazed hussy like me. I don't know what exactly had gotten into us, but for some reason we were just both in the mood to be wicked and wild.

We were also loud. The first time we had been together the sounds of my pleasure had probably echoed throughout the second floor of the Pierce home but tonight Braden was almost as noisy as I was. There were plenty of gasps, moans and groans and he was also still saying very dirty things to me, and no longer in a whisper. Luckily, I knew that the Evans family from next door, along with their fourteen-year-old daughter Kaylee, was off visiting relatives in Martha's Vineyard. It really was best that Kaylee was in another state that evening.

Finally the big moment arrived and I felt my muscles contract and my body shake. I believe I said something like, "Oh yes! Braden, I'm coming!" If I got that wrong, though, you could perhaps ask Jess, who was apparently walking in the front door at just that moment. Braden also managed to contribute a quote or two a few seconds later. I believe his exact words were "Oh fuck! Gabrielle!" accompanied by a groan.

As we lay there panting in a sweaty mass of tangled limbs I listened as Jess flipped some music on and cleared her throat loudly. Luckily I was too physically drained to work up the energy to be mortified. Besides, I think that I was getting used to people knowing what Braden and I did in bed.

"Uh Gabrielle?" Braden said, breathing heavily.

"Yes?" I managed.

"I think Jessica is home."

"Thanks."

When we recovered we decided to cuddle up in bed and watch PBS. At about eleven we went into my bathroom and we got ready to go to bed with plans to actually sleep. It was a nicely domestic contrast to the earlier part of the evening and we snuggled in together contentedly.

"So, I guess that we can add Jess to the list of people who know how good our sex life is," I said with resignation. It was possible that Kaylee knew how good our sex life was all the way out in Martha's Vineyard.

"Don't be embarrassed, Gabrielle. I loved it and what we say to each other in bed is about us, not about anybody else. Unless my parents are right outside. That thought kind of freaks me out a little for some reason."

"That's understandable. Nobody wants to associate their parents with sex. Did you like it better because we were being so wild?"

"I liked it differently. I like it every way with you though. I wouldn't change anything." I leaned in and kissed him very tenderly.

"I'm really nuts about you, Braden."

"You're nuts all right." He laughed. My mouth dropped open with indignation. "I'm just kidding, baby," he said pulling me to him for another sweet kiss. "I feel the same way about you." We held each other very tightly for a few minutes and then fell asleep like that.

* * *

The alarm went off at seven and Braden and I pulled ourselves out of bed. It was still very nice waking up with him but not nearly as much fun as being able to sleep in. Damn job. Why couldn't we just be independently wealthy? Well, technically, I guess we were. So why were we getting up again? The image of a certain blonde socialite with no apparent skills popped into my head. Okay, that was why.

"Coffee," I muttered.

"Coffee," he agreed.

We threw on some clothes and wandered toward the kitchen. Jessica was there already looking all bright and cheerful. God, I hated morning people.

"Morning Gab. Hello Braden," she said cheerfully.

"Good morning," Braden mumbled. I said something like "gemnneg."

"Help yourself to some coffee. You're in the office all day, Gab?"

"Uh huh. I was thinking that if I get enough done I might try to do some research and figure out how we might get those samples we discussed."

"Ah, good idea. The plan at the moment seems kind of abstract."

"I'll figure it out."

"Is there more?" Braden asked, peering soulfully into his now empty coffee cup. What, had he inhaled it?

"God, we're like addicts," I replied.

"I wish they made a caffeine IV," he said.

"I just drink it for the taste," Jess said brightly. Two pairs of tired unamused eyes turned on her. "Just sayin'."

* * *

We all got ready for work and walked in together, stopping to pick up bagels and muffins on the way. We said goodbye to Braden as he headed toward his office and we headed toward ours.

"Sorry if we were kind of loud last night," I said sheepishly.

"I only caught the end. I was walking in during the big finish."

"I've never been like this before. I'm like a shameless harlot with him."

"In other words you have a good sex life."

"How did dinner and drinks go?" I asked as we crossed Market Street avoiding random taxis and bicyclists who were obviously out for blood. I could navigate city traffic on autopilot.

"It was fun," she replied as we made it to the sidewalk on the opposite side of the street and navigated around the line at a food cart that was blocking most of the sidewalk. Ah, the intricacies of urban pedestrian travel.

"Just fun? No spicy hot sexual chemistry?"

"I don't think he's interested in me."

"It's probably like when I didn't think that Braden was interested in me."

"Uh no." She laughed. "No offense, but you're one of those people who's so smart that you're oblivious, like professors who walk into walls. I, on the other hand, am very good at reading the signals that guys put out. Cam and I get along great, and I'm happy to have him as a friend, but that's probably all that it will be, at the moment at least."

"That's so surprising."

"Not really. I think he's attracted to you. In fact, I think that he always has been. Maybe he just didn't realize how much back when you were in college." We steered around a group of pigeons surrounding a pretzel like they were having a meeting about it, and narrowly avoided a dog walker accompanied by the entire AKC Kennel Club.

"But he knows that Braden and I are together."

"That doesn't mean he can control how he feels. I'm sure he'll work through it eventually, though, so I wouldn't worry about it." We finally arrived at our building and took the elevator to our floor. Cam was there waiting in our office.

"We brought you breakfast," I said, dropping a blueberry muffin on his desk.

"Thanks!" he smiled at me brightly. "So, did Braden come visit you last night?" he asked nonchalantly. Now that Jess had been planting ideas in my head again I was watching his reactions. He and Braden had just made up after eight years on tension. I wanted to make sure that the truce lasted.

"Yep. We watched NOVA .We're both PBS addicts."

"Such a wild and crazy couple," Jess teased. And she knew how wild and crazy we could be.

"Braden was always into that stuff. He's a closet intellectual. He probably should have been an academic." He had a little stack of files on his desk that he was going through – a baby public defender pile. I remembered those days.

"Me too," I said. "Oh well, too late now."

"You could still do something different," Jess chimed in. "Maybe you could work for some kind of historical group or museum. They need lawyers, don't they?" She started digging through the newly arrived grown-up public defender pile of files next to her desk that looked like if it fell it could crush a village.

"I'm fine doing this for now. At least I feel like I'm helping people and occasionally I even get a client who's innocent. I told you about Ms. Murphy didn't I?"

"Gabrielle Ginsberg, champion of falsely accused sexually frustrated women."

"I should put that on my business card." A pile of files arrived for me too. So nice that nobody wanted me to feel left out. The one I needed was, of course, on the bottom of the pile.

We worked on preparing our cases that morning and Jess took Cam with her to watch parole violation hearings that afternoon. I carved out a couple of hours to contact my handwriting expert, Steve Flynn, a former FBI special agent, and work on the problem of how to get the samples. Steve told me that even if the author of the note had been trying to disguise his or her handwriting there would still be similarities. The sample was small, though, so he might not be able to come up with a definite match. I told him that I just needed something to point me in the right direction.

⁓ CHAPTER EIGHTEEN ⁓

I sat down at the computer and starting looking at everything and anything I could find about Cole Stephenson. There were the usual press release type things and publicity shots of him at various community events. Finally, though, my search brought up a weird link to a message board called "The Political Gossip Rag."

I saw that it was a site for people who traded gossip about politicians like others did about celebrities. Cole was only small potatoes politically, so he didn't have the amount of commentary that better known politicians had generated, but some of his proclivities had made him interesting enough to discuss. There were all kinds of rumors about him. One type of rumor kept reappearing, that he was in to kink. There was nothing first-hand though. Everyone had "heard" the story from someone else so it didn't seem very reliable — but then, I guess that was pretty much what "gossip" was. If you could believe it, though, he liked to be dominated by women and treated like a bad little boy.

Then I got to a thread that was particularly interesting. It said that rumor had it he regularly attended underground sex parties in the Philadelphia area thrown by someone named Fanny Hill. I decided to try to find out more.

There was some mention of the parties on websites for people in the area into alternative lifestyles. Even though they were underground, they were considered "open" parties in that you didn't have to be a member of a club or anything. You just had to pay a fee and have someone who the party organizer, presumably Ms. Hill, knew vouch for you. Everyone wore masks so it was anonymous and there were rumors that some of the guests were "professionals." The parties seemed to be loosely associated with a place called Gili's Cabaret. I made a note of it and figured that we may have to check it out.

It occurred to me, if you were a politician into kink you couldn't exactly just stroll into a fetish club. If you wanted to get kinky with a bunch of other people it would have to be at a private party. So, if there was any truth to the kink rumors, it would make sense that Cole might be attending these little get-togethers. An idea was forming in my head. It was kind of nutty, but then so was I.

Jess and Cam got back a little while later and I shared what I had learned with them.

"Are those parties even real?" Jess asked dubiously. "I always suspected it was some kind of urban legend."

"They're real," Cam answered. "I have a cousin who's attended them." I glanced at him with a raised eyebrow. "Not Braden," he said quickly and smiled. "Derek. He's kind of the black sheep of the family." I recalled Braden's comment that I should never meet his cousin Derek.

"Do you think he could vouch for you?" I asked.

"Uh, well, I'm sure that whoever runs them knows him, and he probably could," Cam replied hesitantly. "Even if I got in, though, how would I get Cole to give me a handwriting sample?"

"You wouldn't. Jess would. He likes to be treated like a naughty boy. So, maybe she could treat him like one." I outlined my plan for them.

"Oh no! No, no, no, uh uh, nope, forget it," Jess said.

"Oh come on! What's the big deal?" All I wanted was that she dress up like a dominatrix and spank a lecherous politician into writing down why he was a naughty boy. Was that really so much to ask?

"That can't possibly be a serious question."

"Nobody will know who you are."

"Oh! Well why didn't you say so? I have no problem attending an underground sex party and getting kinky with a perverted stranger to get a writing sample… just as long as nobody knows who I am."

"You're being sarcastic, aren't you?"

"Is this really worth it, Gabrielle?" She gave me an exasperated look but I knew that I was wearing her down.

"If it is him, I'll tell him that I have evidence against him and if he wants to maintain his political aspirations he had better never bother me or Braden again. If it isn't him, he'll never be the wiser, and I won't have to risk falsely accusing a public figure."

"How am I going to get in? I don't have a kinky cousin."

"I think you're allowed to bring your spouse," Cam said.

"I can't be the one to do it. Cole knows my voice. Are you going to help me or not, Jess?" I gave her my best pleading look — the one I reserved for those rare times when I actually got a client who was sympathetic if not actually innocent.

"Oh! Okay." She sighed. "Why not? I've never been to an underground sex party before."

"Thank you! I owe you! And thank you too, Cameron. I owe you both."

"Oh, no need to thank me Gab. Since I ran into you again my life is no longer boring." He smiled. "What are you going to tell Braden, though?"

"I don't want to lie to him. Supposedly the parties are held twice a month. He has a legal training for Pennsylvania law enforcement personnel out in Pittsburgh next weekend. He'll be away from Friday morning to Sunday morning and there's a fifty/fifty shot that there'll be a party then. I'll just be a little ambiguous about what I'm doing and where I'm going. I need you to have a man-to-man with Derek, Cam. We need details. Lots and lots of details."

"Okay. Sounds like a plan," Cam said.

"Go team," Jess said dryly.

∽ CHAPTER NINETEEN ∾

IN THE COURT OF COMMON PLEAS OF PHILADELPHIA COUNTY PENNSYLVANIA

<u>Commonwealth v. Whitley</u>

"Your Honor, Mr. Whitley is pleading guilty to indecent exposure," Braden informed Judge Channing. My client stood next to me looking very contrite. I tried not to stand too close to him. He was looking at me in a way that made me distinctly uncomfortable. Inner-Gabrielle sighed. I loved my job sometimes. And I really didn't mean that.

"You understand the charge, Mr. Whitley, and that you have a right to trial?"

"Yes, Your Honor."

"And you wish to waive that right and enter a plea of guilty?"

"Yes, Your Honor," Mr. Whitley answered solemnly. He really was a rather dignified-looking guy. He was even wearing a suit. Looks could be deceiving though.

"Mr. Pierce, please give me the facts of the case." I tried not to cringe.

"Your Honor, in the early morning hours of May third in the County of Philadelphia, Mr. Todd Whitley drove his automobile through the drive-through lane of a Burger King Restaurant on Broad Street where one LaTanya Wilson was working the late shift. Mr. Whitley placed an order and pulled up to the window. When Ms.

159

Wilson leaned out to collect his money, she saw that he was holding his genitals in his hand and he reportedly asked her, and I quote, 'Hey baby, do you want to hold my whopper?' unquote. He then drove off and Ms. Wilson noted his license plate number and contacted the authorities."

"Mr. Whitley," Judge Channing said in a reproving voice. "Couldn't you come up with something more original than *that*?" Judge Channing looked like he had a bad case of indigestion. "Don't answer that! Ms. Ginsberg?" he asked, sounding both bored and disgusted.

"Mr. Whitley has no criminal record. He's a college student studying hospitality management." Stupid frat boy. I was careful not to mention that he was an upstanding citizen. "He regrets his actions." Yeah right. Ew.

"Mr. Todd Whitley, you've indicated that you understand the charge and you wish to plead guilty. There's an agreement with the DA's office?"

"A year probation and sex offender classes, fines and costs," Braden answered.

"The court accepts the plea and Mr. Whitley is hereby sentenced to a year's probation, sex offender classes, a one thousand dollar fine and court costs." The judge banged his gavel. "Court adjourned." He got up and left without a backward glance. My client smiled a creepy smile at me and reached out to shake my hand. He had to be kidding. I gave him a friendly pat on the arm and wished him luck. Then I went over to my table to pack up my things. That was the last case for the day.

"Hey baby..." Braden smiled.

"Don't say it!" I warned. He laughed and handed me the order. "Let's leave early," I suggested. "I just want to get out of here and go scrub myself off."

"Sounds good to me. Want to bring your stuff over to my place?" he invited.

"Sure. By the way, we're sharing a room at my parent's place too, and I have to admit that I have the same Freudian issues about them hearing us, so I'm really going to try to be quiet tonight."

"That's okay. I'm kind of in a quieter mood anyway." He leaned down and kissed me gently and I smiled up at him. Suddenly, I had the urge to tell him nice things about how I felt.

"I'm glad you're coming home with me and I really do want you to meet my parents. They're pretty cool even if the rest of my family isn't."

Braden pulled me into a hug and we stood like that for a couple of minutes until I heard an "ahem" come from the direction of the bench. We both pulled back quickly and nervously looked up. Judge Channing had obviously left his glasses behind in his quest to be out of there. I was surprised to see that there seemed to be a kinder than usual, almost amused look in his eyes.

"Err, if I didn't say it before. Have a nice weekend you two."

"Thanks Your Honor," I said with a smile.

"Yes, thank you Your Honor and you too," Braden added.

"And try not to bring too many crazy cases into my courtroom next week," he added, but he couldn't quite match his usual level of gruffness. As he turned I saw something that may actually have been a smile.

* * *

At six that evening our train pulled into Penn Station and we got a cab to my parent's place on the Upper East Side. Being back in New York always filled me with energy. I loved the noise, the smells, the lights, and the people. New York just always made me feel so alive. We pulled up outside the three-story Brownstone townhouse in the east seventies and my parents were waiting out on the stoop with their arms around each other. Ben and Judy Ginsberg were such a nice couple. Braden and I got out of the cab and grabbed our bags. My father came over to help us and we schlepped our stuff onto the sidewalk as my mom paid the cabbie. Mom and dad pulled me into a ginormous hug and buried me with love. Then they stepped back and looked over at Braden with big bright smiles.

"Braden, this is my mom, Judy, and this is my dad Ben. Mom, Dad, this is Braden."

"Hello," my parents said at the same time.

I could see that they weren't completely sure what to do with the six foot three beautiful blonde gentile that their daughter had brought home, but that whatever it was, they wanted to do it right.

"It's a pleasure to meet you," Braden said, sounding very charming but also a tiny bit nervous.

My dad went over and shook Braden's hand warmly.

"The pleasure's all ours! Gabby's never brought anyone home to meet us before. You must be special to her." My dad was such a nice guy, which explained why he was willing to marry into my mom's wacky family.

My mom came over and took both of Braden's hands in hers. "Wow, you're very handsome, and a lawyer! That's nice! Please come in; let's get you off the street." We went up the steps and into the front parlor. "Have a seat; make yourself comfortable. Can I get you something? Wine, beer, juice? We have good juice! Fresh squeezed." I had a feeling she would have grown the oranges herself for him if she could have. I wandered in behind everyone else and found a seat on my own.

"Oh, I'm fine, thanks," Braden answered politely. Apparently nobody cared if I wanted juice.

"So, did you guys make reservations for us somewhere?" I asked.

"We decided that we should do Shabbos dinner here and we invited the family," my dad said.

"Please tell me you're joking."

"Gabby, sweetie," my mom said consolingly. "It's best to get it over with quickly, trust me."

"Honey, I met them on my first date with your mother." He looked at Braden. "I married her anyway." I saw Braden try not to laugh. "It's okay! You can laugh. We laugh a lot here. It keeps us sane and being sane is what separates us from the rest of Judy's family."

"Who's coming here? I demand that you tell me!"

"Uncle Ira, Aunt Ruthie and Rachel," my mom answered.

"Okay fine."

"And Bubbe of course."

"Oh great!" I threw my hands up in the air, got up and started pacing.

"You told Braden about Bubbe, right, Gab?" my dad asked, smiling nervously.

"I told him that she's blunt."

"Blunt?" My mother seemed to consider that. "That was very tactful, honey." She turned to Braden. "Braden, darling, my mother's got a dirty mind and a mouth like a sailor. She's also got no tact whatsoever. Just ignore her." She gave him a sweet smile.

"Seriously, just ignore Rose," my dad seconded. "The night that I met her, she shook my hand and asked me how many women I had schtupped. I'll be happy to translate any Yiddish that you don't understand, by the way." He hesitated. "You can probably figure that one out though."

"Uh yeah," Braden said with a laugh. For some reason he looked delighted. I think he was having fun!

"Well. Let's get your stuff up to your room. You're staying together right?" Dad asked.

"That's okay?" Braden asked.

"Oh sure! We don't care!"

"Thanks Dad," I said dryly.

"Well, I mean we *care* but we figure Gabby can make her own choices, and we'd rather see her sleeping with you than a bunch of cats." He turned and headed up the stairs, with us following in his wake. We went down the hall to my room. It hadn't changed much over the years. The queen-sized bed covered with soft pillows, the overflowing bookshelves and comfy reading chair, the framed black and white photos of Dorothy Parker and Woody Allen hanging on the wall. It was all still there.

"I'll let you two get settled. Come down whenever you're ready."

"Okay Dad." I turned to Braden. "We'll go out for dinner tomorrow."

"I'm happy to eat in. This is your Sabbath dinner, right?"

"Yeah, but we're not super religious. We light candles and break bread and drink wine but we're not going to cart you off to a synagogue or anything."

"I think it's interesting! I've had dinner on Friday nights with Adam's family before."

"You have? Well, that's great. But I should warn you, we're more like *The* Addams family."

"Stop worrying! My great-uncle Leland thinks he's still in the army even though he's seventy-eight." Braden came over and stood behind me, circling my waist with his arms. "I think your parents are great. I see where you get your sense of humor."

"I'm glad you like them." I smiled. He leaned down and kissed my neck.

"I missed you last night," he whispered. "I'm glad we can sleep together tonight."

"Me too." I turned around and pulled his mouth to mine for a deep and tender kiss. After a few moments though I pulled back.

"The peanut gallery will be here soon. We should save this for later. We'll probably need to comfort each other after they leave anyway."

"Okay," he said, tucking my hair behind my ear gently. As if on cue I heard the doorbell. I tensed up. It was time. I tried to remember my mother's words. It was best to get it over with quickly.

CHAPTER TWENTY

We walked downstairs and first I saw my Aunt Ruth and my Uncle Ira. Ruth came over to me and clutching me to her ample bosom, said in the most nasal voice and the heaviest Queens (and I don't mean the British kind) accent most people have ever heard, "Gabrielle! How awre you?"

"I'm great, Aunt Ruth. How are you?"

"Fabulous! Simply fabulous! You look amazing! Look Ira! Doesn't Gabrielle look amazing?"

"You look amazing, Gabrielle. You lost some weight huh?"

"Nah, not really. I just walk a lot, so I'm kind of like more toned, you know? Uh, let me introduce you. This is my boyfriend Braden. Braden, this is my Aunt Ruth and my Uncle Ira."

"It's a pleasure to meet you," Braden said, sounding wonderfully cultured. It wasn't hard to sound wonderfully cultured next to my Aunt Ruth though.

"Oh my gawd!" Ruth screeched. "Gabrielle brought a guy home! And he's so good-looking!" I wanted to crawl under the couch and hide.

"Well, that's a first!" Ira added. "It's a pleasure to meet you, Braden! We were starting to wonder if maybe Gabby was gay, you know?" He chuckled. "Not that there's anything wrong with that."

"There's nothing wrong with that! I know lots of gay people!" Ruth chimed in. "My hair stylist is gay and he's a lovely person!" She seemed to be apologetically explaining this to me for some reason.

"Where's Rachel?" I asked, before Ruth could name every gay person she knew.

"She and Bubbe are still outside. They're having a little disagreement and I asked them to resolve it before they came in," she said, rolling her eyes.

"Maybe we should check on them," my mom said. Yeah, no kidding. They could be out there all night. On the other hand... My mom went out front.

"Ben!" Ira said. "How's the world of big business?"

"Great, Ira! How's the dry-cleaning business?"

"Wonderful! We're the ones who keep your guys lookin' good!" My dad chuckled like Ira hadn't said that every time that he had seen him for the past thirty years.

"And what do you do, Braden?" Ira asked.

"I'm an assistant district attorney." He smiled.

"Another lawyer! Well, good for you, Gabby! You found one with a good job. We were worried you might get desperate enough to start dating your clients. So when are you getting married?" I wanted to drink bleach.

"Uh, well, we haven't been dating that long yet, Uncle Ira."

"Well, Gabby, you're not getting any younger and I don't think you want to let this one go, you know what I'm saying, kiddo?" he said in a quiet voice, like he was sharing privileged information with me.

"Ira, why don't you come with me for a minute while I check on dinner?" My dad jumped in quickly. "I want to hear everything that's going on in the dry cleaning world." Dad was such a great guy. He was totally taking one for the team. Ira followed him to the kitchen, talking serious dry cleaning talk. The front door swung open and my mother came in looking stressed. She plastered a big smile on her face anyway. She was pretty great too. My parents were really going to the mat for me.

"Gabrielle, sweetheart, look, your cousin Rachel's here!" Rachel, my thirty-two-year-old cougar cousin with the big hair, the expensive manicure and the Jimmy Choos came over and hugged me.

"Gabrielle, you look great!"

"So, do you Rach! This is my boyfriend, Braden."

"What a pleasure," she smiled. Then she turned to me and said loud enough for everyone to hear, "Wow, very hot. Is he built to scale?" My eyes widened. Braden coughed to cover a surprised laugh. And then I heard it, coming in the door, the voice of my childhood nightmares.

"Gabrielle! Dahling! Is that you?"

"Bubbe! Yes it's me." My grandmother, all four foot eleven inches of her, shuffled in, leaning on her cane. The cane was a prop, of course; she could sprint a city block when she needed to.

"I almost didn't recognize you. Probably because you never visit me. I wouldn't know your voice because you never call me either. Would it kill you to call once in a while? Maybe you could even write a letter if you were feeling particularly generous."

"I'm sorry, Bubbe." She made it to the front of the crowd and squinted up at Braden. She also had twenty/twenty vision incidentally. "Who's the Viking?"

"This is my boyfriend, Braden, Bubbe."

"Your boyfriend? We thought you were gay. Does he have a job?"

"He's a lawyer."

"A lawyer who makes money or a lawyer like you?"

"He's a prosecutor."

"So, a lawyer like you but on the right side." She squinted again. "He doesn't look Jewish."

"He's not Jewish, Bubbe."

"Why not?"

"What do you mean why not?" Rachel cut in. "Because he's not! And I've got news for you. It doesn't matter! I married a nice Jewish guy." *Oh no! Here we go!* "A doctor! Top of the freaking Jewish food

167

chain. And do you know where he is now? Shacking up with a twenty-three-year-old shiksa! That's where he is now!"

"Well, were you keeping him happy in bed?" Bubbe asked, and I started to panic.

"Ma!" my mother cut in. "How could you ask that? You're not gonna blame her because her husband cheated on her?!"

"I'll bet you any money she didn't give him oral attention," Bubbe announced.

"Uh! I don't think we should…" I tried.

"Excuse me! But a lot of women simply do not enjoy performing oral sex! I mean guys pee out of that thing!" Rachel shouted.

"See? What did I tell you?" Bubbe looked smug.

"Braden, maybe we should check on dinner," I said desperately.

"Uh," he replied. I grabbed his hand and dragged him into the kitchen where Ira was still talking dry cleaning and my dad's eyes were glazing over.

"I'm so sorry," I said to Braden and I meant it from the bottom of my heart.

"It's okay! Don't worry so much." I could hear Rachel and Bubbe yelling at one another in the other room. My mom popped her head in.

"So, Ben, sweetheart, does the brisket look done?"

"Judy! Yes, honey, why don't you help me? I don't want to impose on Ira here. Ira, why don't you go in the other room and relax?" Like anybody could relax with the cage match going on in there.

"Okay, if you don't mind."

"No! Not at all! Go! Really!" my dad pleaded. Ira grabbed a carrot stick and headed for the other room. Maybe he had learned to block them out.

"Daddy, can Braden and I please stay in here and help you too? *Please*!"

"Yes, of course sweetheart! You don't have to go back out there."

"So, Braden, I hope you like brisket," my mother said with a smile just as Rachel shouted something about how maybe Bubbe should just go and blow all the guys in her bridge club.

"I do, thanks," he said, trying not to laugh. My dad turned to face him with a look of exasperated amusement, and in that moment, Braden Pierce and Ben Ginsberg bonded.

"Okay, let's get this show on the road. Gabby, do you want to light the candles, sweetheart?" Dad asked.

"Okay. Ma, will you please make them be quiet?"

"Of course, honey." She took a deep breath. "Ben, Gabby, I love you. Braden, darling I think you're wonderful. Okay! Let's go!" she said in a voice filled with steely determination. We got into the other room and my mother put two fingers to her lips and whistled shrilly. "Everybody shut up! It's time to light the candles and welcome the Sabbath!" I sighed.

"Here you go, Braden," my dad said, handing him a yarmulke. Braden looked at it like he had just been given a gift. There weren't a lot of six foot three blonde-haired blue-eyed guys who wore Jewish skull caps, but he managed to carry it off pretty well. We went into the dining room and everyone stood by the sideboard as I lit the candles and said the blessing. I glanced up and smiled at Braden who was watching me carefully. He really found this interesting. I also saw my parents watching him. The fact that he found it interesting made them happy. Somebody up there must have been listening to the prayers because my crazy relatives stopped screaming at each other and sat down quietly. It was a Sabbath miracle.

Dinner wasn't too bad. The food was great and my relatives had the courtesy to call a ceasefire. For most of it anyway. There were a few awkward moments.

"So you two are sleeping together?" Bubbe asked.

"Ma!" my mother cut in.

"It's okay. We seem to get asked that a lot," Braden said with a smile.

"Well, it's no big deal if you are, sweetheart. God knows that Ben schtupped Judy enough before they got married. The two of them were always going at it."

"Bubbe please!" I begged. "I don't want to hear about my parents having sex at the Sabbath meal! Or ever! I need therapy now."

"Mother that is enough!" My mom was getting seriously pissed.

"Hey, at least you're out of high school not like Rachel's boyfriends," Bubbe responded giving Braden an evil smile.

"For the last time! My boyfriends are not in high school, you crazy old bag! *One* of them was a college student who was student teaching."

"Well, maybe your cousin could teach you a thing or two about how to find a boyfriend old enough to have finished college. Look at the Viking over there! I'll bet he gets plenty of oral attention!"

I almost passed out, I swear. And then it dawned on me; while he may have gotten plenty in the past, I hadn't given him any. As if sensing my thoughts Braden reached over and squeezed my hand reassuringly.

"Okay, okay Rose," my dad said, starting to sound very pissed off too. "My family's sex lives are not dinner conversation." As if wanting to be a stand-up guy too, Ira chimed in and attempted to change the subject. Unfortunately, it was Ira.

"So Gabrielle, maybe if you do good work you can get a job as a real lawyer someday."

"A public defender is a real lawyer. In fact most of them are better than the private defense lawyers," Braden corrected, sounding a teeny bit pissed himself. What a lovely family dinner.

"You hear that Ira?" Ruth asked in a chastising tone. "He didn't mean any offense Gabby! We know that getting criminals off is very important!"

Bubbe huffed. Apparently, she didn't agree.

"At any rate," Ira tried again, "you're *looking* great Gabby! You were getting kind of chunky there for a while."

"So Braden, do you have any brothers or sisters?" Rachel cut in, trying to help out.

"I have a sister who's twenty-five and a brother who's twenty-three."

"Uh oh," Bubbe said under her breath but loud enough for everyone to hear.

"What's that supposed to mean?!" Rachel shot back.

"Okay enough!" my mother shouted.

We ate in silence for a few minutes before Bubbe made one last attempt to be annoying by asking Braden if he would be learning anything about Jewish culture in the foreseeable future. Before I or anyone else, could rush in to defend the fact that he had had the audacity to be born a gentile, he himself answered that he had been thinking about doing that for quite some time, as one of his closest friends was also Jewish. My mother looked like she wanted to crawl across the table and embrace him and my dad looked like he wanted to fund a scholarship at Yeshiva University in his name.

After dinner everyone retired to the parlor and my father did something extraordinarily kind; he suggested that since Braden and I enjoyed walking so much, we should go out for a stroll around the neighborhood before it got dark. I loved my dad! We headed out into the warm New York evening holding hands.

"So I'm sure you've been to New York many times, but this is my neighborhood."

"I love this. These homes have so much character. This city has so much character." He was looking around and taking it all in.

"I think so too! Whenever I was feeling depressed about something I would take a walk and remind myself that I lived in one of the most exciting, must cultural, most interesting cities in the world and it would cheer me up." I smiled and took it all in.

"You really love it." He smiled.

"I do!"

"So why did you move to Philly?"

"I wanted some space from my family so I could learn how to be a grown-up. Besides, I like Philly too, even more now." I squeezed his hand.

We talked about what we should do the next day and decided to visit a museum and go book shopping among other things. As it got darker we walked home again, and I must say I felt much calmer than when we left. When we got back nobody was fighting, thank God. My relatives were being decently well behaved and they had the courtesy to leave not long after we got back.

"So, Braden! You survived!" my dad said with a smile.

"They were very interesting." Braden laughed.

"Clearly he doesn't know them well enough yet," my mother said dryly. "So my darling family, it's nine o'clock on a Friday evening in Manhattan. Obviously we can't just stay in the house." I liked that fact that she had included Braden in our "darling family." He seemed to like it too. It was almost cracking me up how much he was enjoying this trip so far.

"Well, kids, what do you think?" my dad asked. "Jones Wood Foundry?"

"That's a British style pub not far from here. You can sit outside," I explained to Braden.

"Sounds great," he replied.

"Okay then! Let's go get some well-deserved alcohol!" My mom laughed.

We headed out to the pub and settled in for a chat. We had a lot of fun. My parents were on a real roll, cracking all kinds of jokes, doing impressions of my relatives, telling funny stories and being very cute and flirty with each other.

"So Braden, I've been looking into your dad's political record. I'm a Democrat but I really liked what I saw. He seems to be a well-grounded guy with some really good ideas."

"My father is pretty level-headed. He's not a reactionary."

"I like that. That's what we need more of in Washington."

"Braden's family is so sweet. They were so nice to me."

"I guess that means we can't stick him with the check then, huh?" my dad joked.

"Be quiet!" I laughed.

"You should let Braden and I spend some time getting to know each other tomorrow," my dad said. "I promise to go easy on him."

"No hints!" I said. "We've only been dating for a couple of weeks. Give the poor guy a break."

"Hints? Hints about what? I don't know what she's talking about. Do you know what she's talking about?" he asked my mom.

"I have no idea what she's talking about," she said innocently.

"Incidentally, I can get you a good deal on a band and a caterer should you ever need them for anything," Dad joked. At least I think he was joking.

"So, do you want to see baby pictures of Gabby?" Mom asked with a huge grin. "She was so cute!"

This was obviously some kind of a mom thing. Maybe when I had given birth someday I would develop the Kodak moment hormone.

"Hey! I'm still cute."

"I would love to," Braden said enthusiastically.

"You *would*?" I asked, surprised. The guy who had recently told me that he wanted to nail me against the fucking wall now wanted to see my baby pictures. That was unexpected.

"We should show him the one where she took all her clothes off at that birthday party," my mom said to my dad with a smile.

"Oh my God! What, have you been holding on to that picture all these years just waiting for this opportunity to humiliate me?"

"Oh come on! It's so cute! She's shaking her naked little tuckus to Disney songs." My dad smiled at Braden who looked like he was trying not to laugh.

"What is *wrong* with you people? I finally bring a guy home and you immediately have to break out the kiddie porn?"

"Gabby! I'm sure he's seen you naked before," my mom said. Clearly my parents weren't going to stop until I had no pride left.

"Oh! Yuck — Ma! You sound like Bubbe! I'm really gonna need therapy now."

"Oh please!" She rolled her eyes and waved her hand.

"I do really want to see that picture," Braden said to my mom with a smile. Great.

We made plans to just relax in the morning. My dad and Braden could hang out and "get to know each other" whatever that entailed. After lunch, we would go to the Museum of the City of New York, then go to the Strand Bookstore, have dinner in the Village, and then go watch Shakespeare in the park. Sounded like a fun day. At least that was the plan. We got back home around eleven and Braden and I told my parents that we were going to turn in. They said that they were going to stay up a little longer and they wished us goodnight.

⚭ CHAPTER TWENTY-ONE ⚭

We got up to my room and I locked the door behind me. I wasn't taking any chances.

"So, what do you want to do now?" he asked with his hot Braden sex smile. It wasn't hard to figure out what he wanted to do now.

"I'm glad you asked. Have a seat." I gestured to the stuffed armchair near my overflowing bookshelf. He went over and sat down, looking at me expectantly. "You know what Bubbe said about oral attention?" I asked as I came over and sat on the ottoman that was resting in front of the chair.

"Yes?" He was looking very interested.

"Well, it occurred to me that while you've been very generous and giving with your oral attentions, I haven't made any effort at all to reciprocate. So, you do like that, right?"

"I'm a guy, Gabrielle. Most guys like that." I tried not to think about how many women may have diverted him in restrooms across the Greater Philadelphia Metropolitan area.

"I feel bad. I should have offered." I sounded like I was saying I should have offered to do the dishes or pick up the check.

"Gabby, it's only been a couple of weeks. It's not like we've been married for ten years and you haven't offered." He paused, looking at my expression which happened to be an amused smile. "What?"

"You called me Gabby." I smiled.

"I did? Probably because your parents always call you that."

"It's okay. You can call me that if you want. Did you have a nickname?"

"My mom and dad used to call me Brady when I was a kid."

"Brady? That's so sweet!"

"Well, you can call me Brady if you want."

"Oh lord. Adam and Mark are right. We're a disturbingly cute couple."

"It's understandable. We both have happily married, disturbingly cute parents."

"Yeah, that's pretty uncommon these days."

"It's pretty rare these days, but how did we start out talking about oral sex and end up talking about our parents?"

"I don't know but that's very disturbingly disturbing. Let's go back to the original topic. Of course, I realize that by having this conversation I've pretty much killed the moment."

"Trust me. It wouldn't be hard to revive."

"Oh yeah?" I smiled and stood up, leaning over to start kissing his neck. He took a deep breath.

"It's definitely reviving," he said with a laugh.

"Mm." I started sucking on his earlobe and slid my hands under his shirt and across his bare abs and chest. His breathing got heavier and his hands went to cup and gently squeeze my breasts. I pulled his shirt over his head and tossed it aside. Then I let my mouth move lower, nibbling a trail and tracing over it with my tongue. He leaned his head back against the chair and closed his eyes. I worked my way even lower with open-mouthed kisses, grazing my teeth lightly against his skin and then I licked his belly button, making him groan. I reached down and opened his jeans, realizing, however, that I had encountered some logistical problems. "Uh, I may need some help here."

He stood up and removed his pants and boxers, showing very clearly that the moment had been very much revived. "So I see you're up for this," I quipped.

"Oh man. That was so bad!" He shook his head.

"I've got a million of 'em. Sit down, Harvard." Harvard sat down.

"Take your shirt and your bra off," he said huskily.

"Me?"

"Yeah you." He laughed. "Who do you think I'm talking to?"

"Listen Mr. Funny Guy, I want to do this for you. You don't have to do anything for me."

"Being able to see you excites me."

"Oh, okay." I had almost forgotten. He was a boob man. I took off my shirt and bra and I could see his eyes get darker. I figured I might as well take the rest off while I was at it and so I slipped out of my shorts and panties too.

"Gabrielle, you're so beautiful."

"You're the beautiful one, Braden." I sat down on the ottoman again and leaned in to start running my tongue down his happy trail as he started to pant. I could see that he was trying not to squirm and I took pity. Building anticipation is one thing and torture is another. I wrapped my hand around him and took him as far back into my mouth as I could. He gasped and his hips seemed to rise involuntarily. I looked up at him and saw his eyes were fixed on me.

"You look so fucking hot," he said hoarsely. I slid him in and out of my mouth and used my hand to take care of the part that didn't fit. As I've mentioned before, Braden is a healthy boy, and despite reports to the contrary, my mouth isn't *that* big. His breathing started coming in harsh rasps and he reached down and pulled my hair back away from my face, presumably so that he could better see what I was doing to him. I glanced up again and saw that he looked dazed and his face was flushed. He also kept mumbling words of pleasure and encouragement to me continuously, sounding almost delirious. Remembering our encounter in the interview room, I reached down with my other hand and gently squeezed his balls making him groan with pleasure.

Eventually, I sensed that he was getting close. His hips were moving up to meet my mouth and his fingers were buried in my hair. He was breathing quickly and heavily through his mouth and I could feel the tension in his body. Suddenly, he froze. "I'm going to come!" he bit out. I kept going and he tried to pull back. "Baby! I'm..." I started to move faster, not letting him escape. He didn't finish — well his sentence anyway. He groaned louder and let out a ragged breath as his body shuddered. I swallowed quickly and he looked down at me with stunned bliss. "That was so good," he said, still breathing heavily. "My heart's beating so fast."

"You're not going to have a heart attack or something, are you?" I asked nervously. I could just picture that story on Page Six – senator's son winds up in hospital…

"No." He laughed. "But we'll have to be careful when I'm Mr. Davis' age."

"Okay. No oral attention for you when you're one hundred and five or however old he was."

"I just said we would have to be careful. Not that we had to stop completely. Now trade places with me because I want to see if you can handle my sharp tongue." Inner-Gabrielle hit the floor.

We finally made it to my bathroom to wash up for bed. Then we snuggled in together and I thought about how warm he always felt, like my own personal furnace.

"So what did you think of my crazy family?"

"I love your parents. They have a great sense of humor and they seem really down-to-earth."

"I'm glad you like them. They like you too. I can tell."

"Well, that's good. Your other relatives are pretty wild but they're funny as hell."

"You say that now."

"It'll just make your dad and me closer."

"He always wanted a son. We should sleep now. We have a big day tomorrow."

"Good night baby. I'll dream about you."

"Me too, Braden," I said quietly and leaned up to kiss him goodnight.

∽ CHAPTER TWENTY-TWO ∽

We slept late, enjoyed some leisurely morning sex, showered together and made our way downstairs, where my parents had set up a nice spread with genuine New York bagels, cream cheese, veggies and fresh fruit. There was also fresh squeezed juice and the nectar of the gods, good hot coffee. After breakfast my dad took Braden out for a walk to show him some more of the neighborhood, and presumably, to get to know him better. I decided to use the opportunity to check in with Jess and find out how Marla night with Cam had gone. I got out my cell and gave her a call. She answered on the first ring. I think she had been waiting for my call.

"You are not going to believe this, Gab!"

"Well hello to you too. The trip is going very well, thanks."

"Yeah, that's good. Listen! You are not going to believe this!"

"So you said. What is it I'm not going to believe?"

"I think that maybe she's a hooker!"

"What?!"

"Well, technically, I guess you would call her a call girl because she met rich-looking guys at the best hotels in Philly. She went in, met them in either the lobby or the lounge, got into the elevator with them and then left again, usually about a half an hour or an hour later. She met four different guys in four different hotels."

"Are you sure that's what she's doing?"

"No. Maybe she's a freelance chambermaid."

"Oh wow. Why would Marla be hooking if her family's rich?" I wondered out loud.

"Maybe they cut her off."

"That's an interesting idea. That would make her pretty desperate to land a rich husband, wouldn't it?"

"Maybe even desperate enough to try to scare off someone's girlfriend."

"Hmm. I wonder if Marla's as crazy as everyone thinks she is."

"We eventually followed her to a drag club called Gili's Cabaret."

"Wait! Gili's Cabaret? That place is supposedly associated somehow with those parties!"

"Well, that makes sense because we saw a flyer for one in there."

"A flyer? They advertise underground sex parties with flyers?"

"Hey, it's a business. They might have a Facebook page for all we know. Anyway, there is a party next weekend. And it's a costume party. You're supposed to dress up like your favorite sexual fantasy."

"Well, we can figure out what fantasy a naughty boy might be into."

"So do you think Marla, the call girl, goes to these parties?"

"Supposedly some pros do, but I don't want to put all our eggs in one basket. I think we should still treat her as a separate mission, especially since she lives right here in the city."

"Okay, I hear you. I have to admit to you, Gabrielle, Cam and I have been having fun."

"Oh yeah?"

"Yeah, this is actually kind of exciting. Should we watch her again?"

"I guess so. Maybe we can figure out a way to leave a note for her to reply to at one of these hotels or something."

"We're on it," she said, and hung up.

My mom and I sat down to talk for a little while and she made it clear in no uncertain terms that she and my dad approved of Braden. Dad and Braden got home about a half an hour later and they seemed to be happily bonding. All was well at the Ginsberg residence. Then my dad went to check the mail.

"Gabby! Come here, honey!" he called out in a weird tone of voice. Braden and I glanced at each other and went to meet him in the entranceway. I saw that my dad was holding a letter of some sort.

"What is it?" I asked warily.

"It's a letter for you, but there's no return address and no postage."

"Can I see that?" Braden asked.

"Sure." Dad held it out to Braden.

"You hold on to it and tear it open carefully. I'll come over and look over your shoulder. If it's something suspicious we don't want too many sets of fingerprints on it," said Braden, the prosecutor. My dad did exactly what Braden asked. My mind was racing. Maybe it was some kind of marketing gimmick. When I got closer my hopes were dashed as I saw that the handwriting was familiar. It said, *"You should stay away from him! Something very bad could happen if you don't!"*

"What the hell?!" my father exclaimed.

"What's going on?" my mom asked, coming in from the kitchen.

"Gabby got a threatening letter!"

"From who?!"

"It's not signed and there's no return address."

"Oh my God!"

"Mom! Don't worry! It's probably some kind of a stupid joke."

"Threatening someone is funny?"

"It may not even be meant as a threat. It's completely ambiguous. You can't tell if they're trying to warn me off because they like me, or trying to warn me off because they don't."

"The fact that there's no stamp means it obviously didn't come with the rest of the post. It must have been hand delivered," Braden added, making even me a little weirded out. If this had been a movie, lightning would have streaked across the sky and thunder would have boomed just as he said that.

"Who even knew you were here?" my dad asked.

"Just our closest friends and Braden's family. Nobody else and I'm sure that none of them would play this kind of joke." I told myself firmly that it couldn't be Cam.

"We need to report this to the police," Braden said, sounding authoritative.

"Yes! Of course!" my father agreed. "Maybe the FBI too. If someone followed her here they crossed state lines."

"Let's not go crazy here, J. Edgar," I said, rapidly feeling like this situation was getting out of control. After all, it wasn't a death threat – at least not an explicit one. Maybe my job had made me a little numb to crime but this just didn't feel all that serious to me.

"Gabby, this sounds threatening to me and I would rather be safe than sorry," my mom, who had come over to read the letter, chimed in.

"I agree," Braden added.

"That makes three of us," my dad said. "You're outvoted. We're going to report it to the police and to the FBI. We're also going to need to take precautions. We have an excellent, state of the art alarm system here. Gabby, you're going to need something like that too."

"I live in a secure building," I reminded him.

"It couldn't hurt. I'm buying you a dog too."

"Dad, I don't need a dog. I don't even know if I'm allowed to have a dog in my building."

"I'll get her a dog," Braden assured him.

"Thank you, Braden," he said gratefully, patting him on the back affectionately.

"Oh my God." I rolled my eyes.

"Of course you know that we want you two to stay together no matter what this crazy person says," my mom said, looking almost imploringly at Braden.

"Mom, we're not breaking up because of some stupid letter!"

"If anything, we feel like she's safer with you, Braden. If you had been dating longer I would suggest you move in together," my dad said with a sigh.

"You sure you didn't send this?" I asked dryly.

"That's not funny, Gabrielle," my mom chastised. She was "Gabrielling" me. Ma was stressed.

"Maybe you should spend more time at my place," Braden suggested.

"Should I bring my dog?" I asked with a smile.

"Alright, I'm going to go call Lou," my father announced.

"Why are you calling your lawyer? Do you need investment advice?"

"I just feel like he should be in on this. Maybe he knows some cops."

"Dad, he's a corporate lawyer. Braden here is a prosecutor. Don't you think he might get a little further?"

"Good point. Braden, let's go into the study and make some calls."

"Okay, Ben. I'm going to call some people in Philly too and have them coordinate with New York."

"Good idea."

Ben and Braden were on it. I went off to find the crossword puzzle. I'll be honest, I did find it very annoying and maybe a little unnerving that someone had gone through the trouble to schlep an hour and a half from Philly to New York, but I still thought it was probably one of those three losers and I couldn't see any of them being all that dangerous.

An hour later an NYPD detective and an FBI special agent were sitting in my parents' parlor. I couldn't believe that the FBI actually sent somebody. I suspected it had more to do with the fact that Braden was the son of a senator than the possibility that some schmuck had crossed state lines to harass a public defender.

I answered all of their questions but I was careful about what I said. I stressed the fact that it was very ambiguous and said that for that reason I really didn't know who it could be. I simply wasn't ready to start accusing people just based on guesswork and without any evidence. Maybe I had been a defense lawyer for too long.

Mostly, I just didn't want Braden or I getting in hot water if it turned out I accused an innocent person. After a couple hours of my life that I'll never get back, the law enforcement type people left.

"So, where are we going for dinner?" I asked.

"We'll eat in," my mom announced, heading toward the drawer with the take-out menus.

"Why?"

"I just think it's best if we stay in, sweetheart." She took out a stack the size of War and Peace.

"All night? No Shakespeare in the park?" I knew that I was whining, but come on!

"Honey," my dad chimed in. "Let's just stay home and relax. Come on, we'll watch a movie. We still have to show Braden your baby pictures anyway."

"You're going let some cowardly letter writer make you lock yourself in the house?"

"Gabrielle, I came to spend time with your parents anyway. We can have a nice time just staying in," Braden said. They were all against me. I knew there was no winning this. I went over and sat down rather ungracefully on the sofa.

"Okay, fine, but order really good food and let's watch Manhattan or something. I want Braden to have some kind of New York experience beyond bagels and Bubbe."

We ended up having Indian delivered and watching Sex and the City: The Movie, which I had obviously already seen, but as far as I was concerned, one could never get enough Sex and the City. After the movie, my mom and dad flanked Braden on either side and showed him every embarrassing picture of me they could find. If I was doing something incredibly awkward, had a really bad haircut or was wearing amazingly ugly clothes (or no clothes) it had been captured and preserved. The best ones were where all of the above applied, like at that damned birthday party.

Eventually Braden and I turned in and I had come up with something else that I had never offered but that I suspected would be a big hit. I locked my bedroom door again.

"Come over here and get naked with me in bed," I said without preamble.

"I love it when you say things like that," he said, yanking off his shirt and tossing it onto the chair. His jeans joined it seconds later. He wasn't one to waste time. I pulled off my own clothing and went to sit back against the pillows. He crawled onto the bed with me and the Harvard endowment was already looking very interested in finding out what I had in mind.

"You know I thought of something else I could do for you."

"Oh?" His voice was already starting to sound thick.

"You may have noticed that my body has changed a bit since my naked birthday party days." His eyes flew to my chest and I saw him start breathing faster. Slowly he looked back up into my eyes, a silent question hanging in the air. "Come over here, Harvard," I said throatily.

He looked so incredibly happy as he knelt over me and as I rubbed some of his favorite parts of my body against one of my favorite parts of his. His eyes were looking dazed, he was breathing hard and it was easy to see that he had fantasized about this one a few times already. Finally I pushed my breasts together tightly and he began thrusting, groaning continuously, his eyes fixed on the sight of his cock sliding between them. Here's a hint for you; for a boob man, this one is a real winner.

"Oh baby, so hot." His voice was strained and I knew he was close. "These are mine. Nobody else gets to play with them." He panted.

"That's right, baby. Nobody else gets to play with my toys either."

"No," he groaned. "Don't want anyone else. Only you."

"Come on baby. Come for me," I urged and it put him over the edge. For a boob man, the finale of this particular event is apparently almost enough to bring tears to the eyes. He collapsed onto his back groaning and panting ecstatically.

Since we seemed to have established a theme, when he had caught his breath and some blood had returned to his brain, he decided to devote concerted efforts to seeing if he could give me a happy ending just by paying my breasts a great deal of oral and manual attention. The answer, incidentally, was that he could. He found the effort so much fun that he was ready to go for round two afterward, and we explored a couple of different positions that allowed him easy access to his toys. This little Sex *in* the City party went on for a couple of hours, until we had tired each other out to the point of exhaustion. Have I mentioned that Braden and I had a very good sex life?

It kept getting better and better too. We had learned a lot more about how and where each other liked to be touched which was one of the big perks to familiarity. I found that getting him all worked up was about the most empowering, flat-out most arousing thing I had ever experienced. I loved how his eyes got darker when he wanted me. I loved the look on his face when he slid inside me. I loved the hot sexy things he said to me when our bodies were moving together, and I loved the way that he groaned and said my name when he came. I also loved how afterward, we always laid in bed snuggled up and talking.

"I'm sorry that we didn't get to do all that fun stuff we had planned," I said.

"I had a great time. Given, I would have preferred that you hadn't gotten a harassing letter, and we didn't have to speak to the police and the FBI for a couple of hours, but the rest of the time was fun."

"I'm just not all that worried, Braden. I do think it is just somebody harassing me. I know it's weird that I got this letter in New York, but we're only an hour and a half from Philly. It's not like an arduous journey to get here, you know? And maybe they were just afraid somebody in Philly would recognize them or that it would be traced back to them somehow."

"Yeah, I thought of that too. Hopefully, it's just an isolated incident, but I would feel better if you would spend a couple nights during the week at my place and let come home with you some nights too."

"I'm fine with getting to sleep with you more often."

"Maybe I should cancel the Pittsburgh trip." I immediately got nervous, but I forced myself to relax. I needed him out of town.

"You have to go, Braden. It's important. Jess will be with me and Cam is around too."

"Then I'm going to ask Mark to hang out with you too. There's safety in numbers." Great. I knew that when Braden made up his mind, he made up his mind. I had a feeling that we might be gaining a new team member and that I might have to steal Mark's cell phone so that he wouldn't be on it calling Braden within seconds of hearing my plan.

"You should come to game night tomorrow and stay over at my place."

"Okay. You know, I think that I'm really starting to understand the complexities of baseball. There's more to it than one would think. Are you laughing?"

∽ CHAPTER TWENTY-THREE ∽

The next morning I was able to convince my parents that it was probably safe to leave the house. We went out for breakfast and a walk in the park, although they made a big deal about staying "on the paths" (like I was planning to go for a jaunt through the woods.) I was very happy that at least we got to do something nice. At noon Braden and I got ready to leave. We hugged my parents and they promised to visit Philly soon. Then my dad reminded Braden of his promise to buy me a dog. Inner-Gabrielle beat her head against the wall a few times.

We were back in Philly by three and he said he would come over at six-thirty to get me because, God forbid I walk two blocks in daylight by myself. I walked into my apartment to find both Jess and Cameron waiting for me.

"So, you're not going to believe this," I said.

"You have a "you're not going to believe this" too?" she asked.

"Yeah. I got another note when I was in New York, with the same handwriting. It pretty much said the same thing as the first one."

"In New York?" Cam asked, sounding surprised. "How did anybody know you were even there?"

"Either they followed us or they heard it somewhere."

"Did your parents and Braden find out this time?" Cam asked.

"Yes, and it has been duly reported to the NYPD and the FBI."

"The FBI?" Jess asked, sounding understandably surprised.

"Crossing state lines."

"Okay." She didn't look convinced. I didn't blame her.

"And a senator's son called them."

"So they know about the first one now too?" Cam asked.

"No."

"Why not?" They both asked in unison.

"For the same reason I didn't tell them before. Just like I predicted, Braden and my dad got all protective. If I told them about the first one and my suspicions, Braden would likely have all three of those schmucks investigated. I want to do this low key."

"Is your dad hiring you a bodyguard?" Jess asked.

"No, but we're getting a new handy dandy alarm system and Braden and I will be seeing more of each other. Oh, and I almost forgot! He wants Mark to hang out with us next weekend!"

"What are we going to do about the party?" Cam asked.

"We're going to have to get him onboard. Hopefully, we can convince him to help us and not to tell Braden. It might work out even better since Cole knows your voice too and if Marla were there she would probably recognize you even in a mask. Mark may have to be the one to go in with Jess. I think that you and I should still dress the part, though, just in case we have to get close to help them."

"Derek will vouch for me and the organizer knows him. Fanny Hill is a fake name by the way. Apparently it's the name of some classic erotic novel. The woman who organizes the parties prefers to remain anonymous."

"I can't imagine why," Jess said dryly. "Derek won't say anything about the fact that I'm not really married and he won't be there so it doesn't matter if Mark goes in my place. We just have to pay the fee."

"How much is it?" I asked.

"Three hundred bucks. It would have been more if I'd have wanted to use the house services, if you know what I mean. Supposedly Fanny Hill provides professional company for guests willing to pay extra. I don't think that's common knowledge, though, even in the community."

"Fanny Hill — even if it is the name of an erotic novel that's still a stupid-sounding pseudonym. She couldn't come up with anything better than that?" Jess commented.

"What, like the Merry Madame?" I joked. "Don't worry about the fee, by the way. It's on me. Don't say I never gave you anything. What else did you find out about this party?"

"Jess told you that next week is a full costume party?'

"Yeah. If Jess is going to treat Cole like a bad little boy we should get some stern-looking school teacher clothes. Maybe you and Mark can dress up like school boys or something."

"Great," Cam said without much enthusiasm.

"What? You would have rather been a pirate?"

"Maybe." He smiled. "Would you be a wench?"

"It doesn't matter what we are, actually, since we're just dressing up in case something goes wrong and we have to try to get in or at least blend in outside this place. I should probably pick out something dominatrix-like too though."

"Anyway," he continued, "I set up a special e-mail account and I'll get the location of the party and a code that morning. That night we'll show up at nine and they give the doorman the code. They go in and from there it's just like a cocktail party except that there are rooms where people have sex and do kinky things publicly and there are other rooms where they can do them privately if they prefer. He said that we could expect to see about twenty people there."

"What if Cole's with somebody?" Jess asked.

"Then you'll have to distract her. Maybe Mark…"

"Could solicit a prostitute?" Jess asked.

"They're not all professionals."

"Right. Maybe he could just publicly screw an amateur."

"Okay. Maybe not. We'll play it by ear."

"Speaking of prostitutes, what are we doing to get Marla's sample?" Cam asked.

"Well, if her parents cut her off and she needs money she would probably be just as happy for a chance with you, Cam. You could go to her place and distract her, and Jess and I could sneak in and try to find something with her writing on."

"Um, Gab?"

"Yes, Jess?"

"When you say, "sneak in" do you just mean trespass or actual breaking and entering? And when you say, "find something," are you talking more like theft or receiving stolen property? Just asking."

"Okay, technically, this may sound kind of illegal."

"Cameron, let me just turn this into a teaching moment. When Gabrielle says something sounds 'technically kind of illegal,' that's the same thing as 'illegal'."

"Okay. I have another idea then. Anything that's thrown away is considered abandoned property. If she puts her trash out on the curb then it's not on her private property and we're not trespassing or stealing."

"You want us to dig through Marla's trash?" Cam asked, making a disgusted face.

"Fine. I'll dig through her trash. You act as lookouts. In fact, maybe we should just take her trash with us to a safer location."

"I'm not driving that night," he replied.

"Jess can drive."

"Only if we take your car, honey."

"I have a Mini Cooper."

"How much trash can she have?"

"Okay," I said, reminding myself that they were doing me a favor. "We'll take my car. You'll drive. Cam can act as lookout and I'll dig through the trash. If it seems unsafe to do so at that location I'll take her trash. Does that work for everyone?" They both agreed and I hopped on the computer to check on trash pick-up times in Marla's neighborhood.

"I think we should shoot for tomorrow night. We can go as soon as it gets dark and move fast. Hopefully, it won't take more than an hour. And if we don't get anything, then I'll just have to think of something else."

"We haven't even thought about Mrs. Mason."

"I know. I'll have to give it some more thought."

"So, do we get tonight off?" Jess asked.

"Sure, did you have plans?"

"No, how about you?"

"Braden wants me to come to game night with Mark and Adam again at his place."

"Oh, are they watching the Phillies?" Cam asked.

"I guess. Do you guys want to come?"

"Sure!" Cam said enthusiastically.

"Sure," Jess said, unenthusiastically.

At about six-fifteen Braden called up from the lobby and I buzzed him up. I went over to open the door when I heard him ring. He was standing in the hall with an adorable smile and I couldn't help being charmed and smiling back. Then I heard it. A yip. I looked down. Way down.

CHAPTER TWENTY-FOUR

"What in the hell is that?"

"This is Bruno."

"Bruno? Braden, that's a Chihuahua. Naming him Bruno won't make him a bigger dog."

"That was the name he came with."

"And whose dog is this, Braden?"

"Bruno," he said, addressing the dog. "This is mommy."

"Mommy? Braden, this isn't a baby. This is a dog. A very small dog."

"Your building had strict size requirements."

"And what do you think that Bruno would do if I were attacked? Trip the guy?"

"He would bark and alert people that you were in distress."

"He would bark and alert people that there was an annoying little yippy dog around and they should head the other way."

"Don't worry," he said, addressing Bruno. "Daddy will convince her."

"Daddy? We're the parents of a Chihuahua?"

"You never know what the future holds. It would be good practice."

"For when we had puppies?"

"Can we come in?" I stepped aside. Braden took Bruno off of his leash and he promptly checked the place out and made it his own by peeing on a rubber tree plant. Bruno, not Braden.

"Hey!" Jess exclaimed. "Here, doggy!"

"He answers to Bruno," I explained.

"Bruno?" She looked confused.

"Apparently Braden and I have a Chihuahua together."

"I hope he has primary custody," she said, following Bruno as he headed toward her room. "Wait, doggy. Don't go in there!"

"Hello, Cameron," Braden said.

"Hello, Braden. Nice dog. And, um, why?"

"She needs protection. Didn't she tell you about the letter?"

"A Chihuahua?"

"I promised her father I would get her a dog and her building doesn't allow pets over twenty lbs. Do you know how small that is? Bruno can bark as well as a big dog can. He'll alert people."

"Who's going to take care of Bruno when I'm at work? He'll be all alone. And I'll have to walk him in the evenings. He'll have to wait all day to pee." I glanced at the plant. "He'd better wait."

"I arranged for doggy day care," he answered.

"Doggy day care? Are you serious?"

"There's a place right on the way to work. You can drop him off in the morning and pick him up on the way home. He'll have other dogs to play with and the people there will walk him."

"Did you check these people out? I mean are they a good place? The bigger dogs wouldn't pick on him, would they?" I couldn't help it. I'm a Jewish mother.

"More importantly, can they get him into the right colleges?" Cam added. Braden and I gave him an unamused look.

"I checked them out. They have a good reputation."

"Well, okay, I guess. You're going to help me take care of him, though, right? It's not going to be 'go ask mommy' whenever he wants something?"

"Mommy?" Jess asked, returning with Bruno tucked under her arm and one of her slippers in his mouth.

"And are you Daddy?" Cam asked Braden with a smile.

"Of course he is! What are you implying?" I asked indignantly. Jess and Cam gave each other a look that clearly said they thought Braden and I had gone round the bend.

"So, can you convince baby Bruno here to let go of my slipper?"

"Here," Braden said, digging around in his pocket. He held out a milk bone. And I had thought he was just happy to see me. "Bruno! Daddy has a bone for you."

"Does that work with you too, Gab?" Jess asked with a laugh.

"Very funny," I replied. Bruno promptly dropped the slipper and Jess set him down so that he could go get his treat. He looked up at Braden adoringly. He was a daddy's boy.

"Okay, Gabrielle, we should get going." He paused. "Do you two want to come along?"

"Yeah, sure!" Cam said with a smile.

"What the hell," Jess said.

I grabbed my suit-bag and we all headed for Braden's place with Bruno in the lead on his stylish leash. I had a feeling that I would find all kinds of designer doggie gear at Braden's place.

* * *

I was right. I discovered that Bruno had his own leather and suede plush doggie bed, a marble bowl with his name carved into it, and enough toys to fill his own play room. How had Braden managed this in three hours? Jess and Cam made themselves comfortable in front of the TV as Braden went to assure himself that Bruno had enough water, just in case it had evaporated in the half hour since I was certain he last checked it. A few minutes later Mark and Adam rang up from the lobby and were at the door, six packs of beer in hand.

"Wow, the gang's all here," Mark said as Jess and Cam called out their greetings. Just then I heard the rapidly approaching "clickity click" of tiny nails on hardwood floors accompanied by the "yipping" that only a tiny dog can emit. Bruno had been alerted to the presence of intruders. He came full throttle, stopped short and skidded to a stop at Adam's feet, barking his little Chihuahua ass off.

"Bruno! Stop! Down! Heel! Shut up!" I tried.

"Quiet Bruno!" Braden said and Bruno immediately stopped barking and sat down.

"Bruno?" Adam asked. I had a feeling that would be a common reaction.

"Is that supposed to be a dog?" Mark asked.

"He stopped you, didn't he?" Braden asked.

"I was afraid I might step on him," Mark replied.

"Is this your dog?" Adam asked.

"I got him for Gabrielle, but I'm thinking that I'll help her take care of him. I've been joking around and saying that we're his mommy and daddy."

"Oh, that's so cute!" Mark teased.

"I hope you insisted that this dog be raised Jewish, Gabrielle." Adam gave me a stern look.

"I'm okay with that. I'm getting kind of interested in Judaism. I'm thinking about taking a class," Braden said.

"Interested as in 'hey, that's kind of cool' or as in 'I'm thinking about becoming a Jew?'" Adam wanted to know.

"I don't know. I would have to learn more about it first. You and Gabrielle seem to like it."

"But we were born this way." I explained. "We've been conditioned from childhood to pretend that a lamp that burned longer than it should have was as exciting as a visit from Santa Claus."

"I'm just thinking about taking a class to learn more. I'm not exactly a pillar of the Episcopalian church right now though. I doubt that anyone would even notice that I was gone."

"I think your parents might, but whatever. You want to take a class, I'm all for it," I said. "In fact, you want to be Jewish? That's great too, as long as it's because you really want to be and not because you're worried about Bruno growing up conflicted."

"You two are the parents of a Chihuahua and Braden's talking about becoming a Jew. This is some kind of weird dream, isn't it?" Mark asked, looking around like he expected to see something.

"Can we get out of the entryway before the beer gets warm?" I asked impatiently. We got out of the entryway before the beer got warm. Everyone settled in and we ordered pizza. We watched a pregame show and began watching the baseball game. Bruno made his rounds, encouraging everyone present to pet and pay attention to him. Eventually he settled in on a loveseat next to Braden and me.

In was an exciting game for the most part, although the Phillies pulled ahead at the end. At the bottom of the ninth inning with our team ahead by four runs I started cleaning up. As I put things away and washed some dishes in the kitchen, I felt Braden sidle up behind me and put his arms around my waist, pulling me close. He whispered in my ear.

"I was only kidding around about the mommy and daddy thing, but I have to admit that playing house with you turns me on."

"I'll have to wash dishes more often, dear." I guess it wasn't just my shorts riding up last time.

"You know darling, we've never had kitchen sex. Perhaps I could bend you over the counter and take you from behind. I'm thinking that I'm just going to pick you up and fuck you against the wall though." God, I loved it when he said stuff like that.

I glanced up at the living room area which was in plain view. "The game's almost over. Our guests will be gone soon, honey bunch."

"As soon as that door closes I'm going to make you feel so good, sweetie pie." Argh! He was killing me here!

"Well, dearest, that sounds like a sound plan for the future." I felt myself starting to sweat and my panties got damp. The Astros struck out and the game was over within minutes. Our friends stretched and stood up. My heart started racing as they headed for the door.

"Thanks for inviting us along," Cam added.

"We do it every Sunday night. Come whenever you want," Braden said. That was definite progress.

"I guess we'll play it by ear next week?" Mark asked.

"We'll be back in time," Adam said.

"But Braden might be busy making up for the loss of his Saturday night sex."

Cam offered to walk Jess home and we said our goodnights as everyone left, shutting the door behind them.

∽ CHAPTER TWENTY-FIVE ∾

Braden turned to me with his hot look and I was up against the wall in seconds with his mouth on mine, his tongue exploring possessively. His hand traveled up under my shirt and into my bra where he gently squeezed my nipple and cupped my breast. Then the other hand traveled under my skirt and into my panties, where he began stroking me.

"Mm. My baby's ready for me," he said with satisfaction.

"You gave me advance notice," I answered breathily.

He pushed my skirt up and my panties down. I slid them off as he freed himself and then he lifted me up and pushed into me as I wrapped my legs around him and gasped with pleasure. With my back braced against the wall he thrust into me deeply over and over and I started moaning deliriously. Through a lust-filled haze I suddenly heard a foreign sound. It sounded like… yipping. Oh no!

"No, no Bruno," I panted. "Daddy's not hurting mommy. Daddy's making mommy feel *so* good! Oh baby, so good!" Bruno didn't let up, though. If anything, the yipping got louder and he started running from one side of Braden's legs to the other.

"Quiet, Bruno!" Braden tried, sounding desperate, as I pushed my hips hard against him and squeezed my inner muscles tight. "Oh fuck, yes!" he groaned loudly. Bruno kept yipping louder and louder. "Bruno! Quiet! Daddy wants to enjoy this." He started moving his hips faster.

"Yes! Like that!" I cried and he started pounding into me.

"Tell me how much you love it baby," he grunted as Bruno kept yipping.

"So much! I love it so much! It feels so good!" I moaned and Bruno started jumping.

"Who's fucking you Gabrielle? I want to hear you say it!" The yipping was unrelenting and now Bruno was running in circles.

"Oh Braden! Braden! Only you!"

"You're mine, Gabrielle," he bit out, and then Bruno started doing something that transcended annoying and moved into the realm of the really weird, and not just a little disturbing. He grabbed on to Braden's leg and started pumping.

"Bruno! Jesus! Stop that!" Braden bit out, sounding distracted as he shook his leg, trying to get Bruno to let go.

"Why is he doing that?" I gasped, confused.

"I'm pretty sure he thinks this is a game."

"Only mommy and daddy get to play, Bruno!" I pleaded.

Braden took a deep breath and lowered me to the floor. He pulled my skirt back down and closed his pants over his erection. Bruno let go and looked up at him quizzically like he couldn't figure out why we had stopped playing the humping game just when it was getting good. Braden gave him an exasperated look and grabbed my hand and his keys. "Let's go."

"Where?"

"To the roof garden."

"The roof garden?! *We're* leaving?!"

"Nobody else is ever up there and it's a nice night."

We took the stairs and when we got there Braden found a dark spot and once again lifted me up and braced me against a wall. The city lights sparkled in the distance. I felt him slide into me again and start moving more slowly. He buried his mouth against my neck and pushed into me deeply while I moaned and ran my hands up and down his back. Without any further distractions it wasn't long before I felt myself get to where I needed to be. Braden sensed it and started talking to me again. This time, though, he didn't talk dirty to me. The things he said were romantic instead and they turned me on just as much.

"Gabrielle, you're so beautiful. And sweet. And sexy. It's never felt like this before. I want to lose myself in you. I want to be inside you forever."

"Braden, I need you so much." I felt myself slip over and fall into oblivion and then a couple of minutes later he let go and joined me. We held on to each other tightly as sensation and release washed over us and then we stood there panting with our foreheads pressed together.

"Braden," I said after a few minutes, "are we going to have to have sex on the roof from now on?"

"No, baby. We're going to have sex in the bedroom and Bruno is going to wait in the living room. I just had to get out of there."

"Okay. Just asking. I figured it might get cold eventually." We headed back downstairs where Bruno met us at the door and gave us a dirty look. He was obviously deeply offended that we were not willing to involve him in our sex life.

* * *

I told Braden that I had to help Jess with something the next night. That was technically true. He said that he would watch Bruno and invite Adam and Mark over to play cards and hang out again. He still wanted to spend the night together, though, so I told him that he should come by and pick me up at ten and that I would go back to his place with him. I knew that I was cutting it close but I didn't want to act suspiciously by being out late on a night before court. Besides, how much garbage could she have anyway? So the next night Bruno was off at Daddy's place when Jess and Cam and I piled into my Mini Cooper at eight-thirty and headed for Marla's townhouse. We parked down the street and strolled casually toward her address. When we were in front of it though, we encountered a little problem. The homes were narrow and attached and there were a whole bunch of garbage cans standing together. You couldn't tell which one belonged to which house. *Shit!*

"Okay, okay, think, Gabrielle," I said to myself as I put my hands on my hips and paced. "She's a single woman, so if we see guy trash it's probably not hers."

"Guy trash?" Jess asked dubiously.

"You know, stuff that a guy has that women doesn't."

"A penis?" Jess shook her head in bewilderment.

"Cam, what kind of stuff would a guy have that a woman probably wouldn't?"

"Uh, Playboy, Penthouse, cigars, Scotch. Actually, if you find that stuff let me know. I think I want to hang out with that guy."

"Well, what kind of stuff would a woman have that a guy wouldn't?" I was getting desperate.

"Tampons!" Jess yelled and clapped her hands like she was on Family Feud.

"Will you be quiet?" I hissed. "The point is we can figure out within maybe five cans which one is hers. It looks like there's an alley over there and there are street lights. I say we carry the cans back there and figure out which one it is."

"Okay, good luck with that. I'm the lookout, remember?" Cam said, walking away.

"I'm the driver," Jess chimed in.

"And I'm the trash picker. Yes, I recall the conversation, but I need your help carrying it back there." They sighed and both of them went over and picked up a can and hauled it back to the alley. I picked one up too and we soon had five cans back there. We had placed them directly under a street light and I opened the lid and started going through the first can. I was leaning into it covered in garbage myself when Jess finally broke.

"Oh Jesus, honey! I can't watch you do this anymore. Move over!" She started going through a second can. I saw Cam squirm.

"I'm not going to do this."

"So, don't. You're the lookout," I reminded him.

"I'm serious. I'm really not picking through trash."

"Ew! Is that a condom?" Jess asked.

"Ah man!" Cam made a face and kicked the base of the street light. "It's like I can *hear* my mother saying 'a gentleman picks through trash *for* a lady, Cameron'," he grumbled. "Move over!" He stormed over and ripped the lid off a third can. "I don't know if we're going to find anything we can use," he said, and suddenly a voice called out.

"Cameron? Is that you?" Cam froze. Three male shadows approached. "It's Bob – Bob Lewis."

"Bob! How are you?" Cam stood up as a well-dressed middle-aged man and his two companions approached.

"Phil, Jack, this is Cameron Clay from Findlay Clay. He's my financial planner. I trust him with all of my most important money decisions."

"Uh, I would shake your hands but…" Cam was fighting hard to maintain his dignity. Maybe he would make a good public defender yet.

"What are you doing here, Cameron?" Bob asked, seemingly noticing for the first time that his financial planner, the man he trusted with all of his most important money decisions, was at the moment picking through a garbage can.

"Um…"

"I know!" Jack said with a chuckle.

"You do?" Cam asked dubiously.

"Yes, I do. It happened to my wife just last week."

"It did?"

"Her diamond ring came off in the kitchen and wound up in the garbage. We spent an hour digging through the trash before we found it. So did your girlfriend lose something valuable?"

"Yes!" both Jess and I said at exactly the same time. We looked at each other and then said "she did" at the same time too. "You did!" I said through gritted teeth.

"I did," she said. "My uh, yearbook." *Huh?* "My high school yearbook. It must have fallen into the garbage. I'm very broken up about it." Jack looked confused. I didn't blame him.

"Well, uh, I hope you find it," he said with a nod and a smile, backing away slowly. Clearly he thought we were either nuts or on drugs. I didn't blame him for that either.

"Take care," Bob threw in, looking like he thought maybe he was missing something here and there really was a perfectly reasonable explanation for all of this. The three of them continued walking down the alley and around the block. Cam breathed a sigh of relief and then he glared at me.

"You look angry," I noted, taking an involuntary step back.

"Angry? Why would I be angry?" he asked quietly. "A multi-millionaire who trusts me to give him investment advice just caught me picking through trash and saying that we might not find anything that we could use."

I glanced at my watch. *Shit!* It was ten minutes to ten! "We have to get out of here. I told Braden I would be ready to go to his place by ten."

"Come on!" Jess said and headed for my car with Cam and I right behind her. We pulled into my parking garage at ten exactly. I thanked Cam again and apologized for the fiftieth time about Bob. He seemed to be over it. In fact I think he was starting to find it kind of humorous. He waved as he hopped into his own car and headed home. Jess and I sprinted up the stairs and tore into the lobby… where Braden and Adam and Mark and Bruno were patiently waiting.

∽ CHAPTER TWENTY-SIX ∾

I saw their faces register confusion and then, well, disgust to be honest, and I looked down. I was covered in garbage. There were gum wrappers, used napkins, bits of tinfoil and something that I hoped was a wad of gum stuck to my clothes. I looked over at Jess and she was no better. Among other things she had a Ziploc baggie stuck in her hair and there was a banana peel melded to her shorts.

"Oh, I can't *wait* to hear this," Adam said.

"I may need to take a quick shower before we go." Bruno began to whine and then he hid under a chair. Braden handed his leash to Mark and got up to walk over to me. When he got about two feet away, though, he halted.

"Oh, Gabrielle!" He made a face and waved his hand to clear the air. "Maybe not a quick one." Great. I smelled bad too. Jess walked over to the elevator.

"Might as well come on up and make yourselves comfortable," she offered.

"Uh, we'll take the stairs," Mark said with a grimace.

Twenty minutes later I was clean again and entering the living room, where Jess was already talking to the guys.

"I was just explaining how we went out to eat and I left my wallet on the tray and it got dumped into the trash and we had to check the dumpster to find it." Wow, that was a lot better than 'I accidentally threw my high school yearbook away'.

Bruno gave a happy yip and came running up to me. Braden came over hesitantly, leaned down, nuzzled my neck and inhaled deeply.

"Mm, much better. What were you two out doing tonight anyway – besides going out to eat and digging through dumpsters?"

"Gathering evidence for a case."

"What? Why were you doing that? That's what your office pays investigators for."

"It wasn't dangerous."

"Gabrielle, anything could be dangerous right now. You know that. And you wound up crawling around in a dumpster. I really don't want you doing things like that anymore." He didn't want me doing things like this anymore? Who was he, my dad?

"Oh? And you'll never go out to a crime scene or go out to interview a witness in the field huh?"

"I'm a guy," he said, like that explained everything.

"So. Female prosecutors do it too."

"Yeah, but they're not my girlfriend and they're not getting harassing letters." He was starting to sound annoyed.

"They probably get lots of harassing letters."

"Okay, have I mentioned that they're not my girlfriend?" He was definitely sounding annoyed now.

"Even before the letter, you were worrying about me going into lock-up to interview clients charged with violent crimes."

"Because you could get hurt and there are plenty of male public defenders who could do it."

"But I can do it and it's my job to do it. Next you'll be telling me that you don't want me to represent anyone charged with a violent crime in general." I was getting rather annoyed now too.

"Well, now that you mention it…"

"Braden! I'm a criminal defense lawyer. I defend criminals. All kinds of criminals. Not just criminals that you approve of."

"Well, you can't expect me not to worry or care, Gabrielle!"

"Are you guys arguing?" Jess asked.

"Are we?" I asked.

"Maybe a little but that's okay. Couples argue. We'll figure it out and we can have make-up sex later," Braden said, and Bruno yipped.

"Hey, I think the dog knows that word," Mark said, studying Bruno curiously.

"Look who his parents are," Adam said dryly. "God knows what he's been exposed to. He probably needs psychoanalysis."

"Okay, you know it's getting late, guys and we all have court tomorrow, I'm sure," Jess hinted.

"Yeah, I had better be heading home. Come on Adam, I'll drop you off," Mark said.

"Let's go, Sherlock," Braden said to me. By the time we got back to his place it was eleven. He put Bruno in the bedroom and came back into the living room area, shutting off the lights. "Look," he said and pulled me over to the window. I could see the city lights. The view was gorgeous.

"It's beautiful." I sighed.

"You're beautiful." He stood behind me and pulled me against his chest. "I'm sorry if I sounded pushy. I'm feeling very protective of you and I'm not used to that. I just don't want you getting hurt."

"I know Braden, and believe me, I love the fact that you care so much. I care about you too. It scares me that you make enemies of dangerous people every day. It's what you do, though, just like defending them is what I do. I won't knowingly put myself in any actual danger. How's that?"

"I guess it'll have to be good enough. Do you want to do this for the rest of your life?"

"I don't know. Sometimes I think so and other times I don't."

"Do you want to have real kids someday?" Wow, Braden was talking about kids. That was surprising to say the least.

"I think so. I'd like to be married first, though."

"Of course," he said, like that was a given. Wasn't this guy a major player a month ago? This was a rather quick metamorphosis. Something about it felt right, though, and I think he just sensed it too. "So you really like the lights, huh?"

"Yeah, I really do."

"I'll be right back," he said and went over to a closet. He grabbed a comforter and brought it back to where I was standing and spread it out on the floor. "Let's make love here then," he said quietly. He had never called it that before. He sank down and pulled me down beside him. Then he laid me back and kissed me sweetly and softly, my lips, my cheeks, my eyelids, my jaw, my ears, my neck, my everywhere. I sighed with both contentment and arousal. He undressed me slowly and then undressed himself, holding my gaze the entire time. Then he covered me with his wonderfully warm body and sank into me as the lights sparkled in the distance. We made love, slowly and tenderly until finally we climaxed one after the other. Afterward we laid there holding each other for quite a while before heading off to bed. Bruno was asleep doing his little Chihuahua snore and I fell asleep in Braden's arms.

* * *

The week went by quickly. By some miracle all of my cases were pretty normal. There were no confused fanny grabbers, geriatric pot-heads or armed robbers who worked the counter or offered to show ID. Just your typical run-of-the-mill felons. I had a few cases against Adam that week, which gave him the opportunity to catch up on teasing me about something besides my love life. Bruno took well to doggy day care, where he was reportedly quite popular. Braden and I were spending every evening together at either his place or mine. Bruno learned to accept hanging out in the living room and eventually forgave us for playing the humping game without him. His reward for being so understanding was that he got to sleep in the bedroom with us when we were done playing. In his own bed of course. He now had one at each of our apartments.

Unavoidably, after spending several hours on Thursday night talking in bed and making love, Friday morning arrived. Braden and Adam were flying out to Pittsburgh to avoid a five-hour drive and they were leaving at ten, so I said goodbye to him before I left for work in the morning.

"So, you'll text me to let me know you got there okay?"

"Right, and you'll text me to let me know that you and Bruno had a good day?"

"Yes, and you'll call me to say goodnight?"

"There's some kind of cocktail thing. Should I call you before or after?"

"After. Then you can just relax. You and Adam are sharing a room?"

"Yeah. I'll probably leave the party a little early so I can speak to you privately. In case I get mushy. Or horny. Or both." He kissed me and then he said goodbye to Bruno and we parted ways.

I dropped Bruno off at doggy day care and made it to the office by nine. I didn't have court that day as so many prosecutors and judges would be out of town. Jess and Cam and I were all planning to take the afternoon off to go in search of costumes and finalize plans for Operation Cole. Mark would be coming by at noon the next day.

∽ CHAPTER TWENTY-SEVEN ∾

It took some searching but we finally found what we needed at a place called Tony's Fantasy Land. It was a little scary finding out what other people fantasized about.

"Who has fantasies about being a tampon?" Jess asked, looking over a long white fleece tube.

"People are weird," I answered.

"Wasn't there a member of the royal family years ago?" Cam asked.

"Don't talk about it. The poor man will never live that down," I replied.

"What in the hell is that?" I asked.

"I believe that's a dildo, in size," Cam checked a label, "men's extra-large."

"I think I see a pattern here," Jess offered.

"Newsflash, men fantasize about being inside women's vaginas," I said dryly.

"Oh look! A naughty nurse costume. I think I like that one," Cam said with a smile.

"I don't think it would fit you." Jess laughed.

"A nun?" I asked.

"To a priest that might be pretty enticing," Cam explained.

"Hmm. Here's your pirate suit, Cam," I teased.

"And here's a wench costume. Which one of you wants to put it on for me?"

"I found one! Sexy school teacher," Jess announced.

"Do they have two of them?"

"No, just one, and one naughty school boy."

"I guess that I'll have to go for another dominatrix look," I said, disappointed.

"The S&M stuff is in the next room," Cam shared.

"You've been here before, haven't you?" I joked.

"There's a sign over the door," he said defensively.

Finally I found a pair of shiny rubber hot pants, (Who knew that hot pants came in rubber?) a patent leather bustier and some boots that I think that Gene Simmons from KISS once wore. It had a matching leather mask. I imagined that this was a very stylish ensemble in the BDSM world. Cam picked out some leather pants, a leather vest, leather hat and a collar. I really hoped that he didn't run into any more of his clients, dressed like that. We also grabbed a black wig for Jess and masks for them and for Mark. Ah, if Bubbe could see me now! When we got back to our place, after picking up Bruno of course, we ordered Chinese and went over the plan.

We would sit Mark down, tell him about the notes, describe the cast of characters and explain why we needed to be careful about suggesting anything without some kind of proof. Then we would outline our plan, which was fairly simple. Mark and Jess would go in as a couple. Jess would approach Cole, tell him he was a bad boy and that she wanted him to write down all of the nasty things he had done. If necessary, she would spank him with a ruler. Then they were out of there. How bad could that be, right? Yeah, I know. Those famous last words again.

Since it was Friday night Cam and Jess decided to go out for a drink. I stayed in and tried to relax. Bruno happily kept me company but he seemed a little perplexed about the fact that Daddy wasn't around. He kept going to the door and sniffing around the covers on Braden's side of the bed.

Wow, suddenly that sunk in. Braden had a side of the bed. We had been together for a month and we were a real couple. We had survived our first argument – even if it wasn't a very big one. We had talked about the future; we had met each other's parents and we shared a dog. Although we still argued in court, still did plenty of naughty sexy things and still engaged in plenty of snarky banter, we had also developed a very natural affection with each other and we had both acknowledged that this relationship was special and that we wanted to be together for a very long time. I knew what it meant, and I wanted to tell him, but I was still kind of scared to go there. That night I watched a documentary as Bruno snuggled into his doggy bed and I waited for Braden to call.

∽ CHAPTER TWENTY-EIGHT ∾

"Hey, sexy."

"Hey. Partying down with all the law enforcement types?"

"Yeah. They can be a wild bunch."

"Are the women hitting on you?"

"I've made it very clear that I have a girlfriend." So they were. It figured. "Why? Are you jealous?" He sounded amused.

"Of course," I admitted.

"Well now you know how I feel."

"What because a bunch of drunk MBA types tried to pick me up at O'Malley's?"

"No, because Cameron was the first guy you were ever with." *Oh, that.* Suddenly, I realized that Braden hadn't only become more possessive lately because he was worried about me. He was jealous, and amazingly enough, he felt a little insecure. I wanted to reassure him. I was going to work up the nerve to say "those words" soon.

"That was years ago and it was only one time. I didn't even have a happy ending — in any way."

"You didn't?"

"No, I had no idea what I was doing and it was slightly uncomfortable. Besides, Cameron and I were both beer buzzed. It was very much a college hook-up, nothing at all like what you and I have together. I've told you before, you're the best partner I've ever had. You're the first guy who can get me there just by being inside me."

"Really?"

"Yeah, and not only that, but I've never had more than one happy ending in a night and I've had up to six with you."

"Seven," he corrected.

"You counted?"

"I just happened to notice."

"It's not just your technical skills. You and I always seem to be in sync."

"Well, while I will admit that does kind of make me feel better, I wasn't just talking about sex, Gabrielle. Obviously you must have cared about him or you wouldn't have slept with him, whether you were beer buzzed or not, not the first time."

"He was my friend and I was infatuated with him. I was eighteen years old."

"Now you're both grown up and he's your friend and he works with you every day. What if you start to feel something for him again?"

"Braden, eight years ago I had a crush on a cute boy. Now I have much deeper feelings for an incredibly sexy man – and just for the record, I mean you, not Cam."

"Well, that's good to hear because I don't want to lose you."

"You're not going to. I'll be with you as long as you can put up with me."

"I'm never going to stop wanting you, Gabrielle." This conversation was getting very intense. As if on cue, I heard a voice in the background.

"Hey Braden! Are you done with your phone sex yet?"

"You can come in!" Braden called out. I thought I heard a door close. "I didn't expect to see you back here tonight."

"I gotta sleep, man. Besides, I couldn't remember her name and it felt kind of awkward after she gave me such a great…"

"Still on the phone here, dude," Braden interrupted.

"You're still on the fucking phone? You just saw her this morning. You might as well just hand her your balls right now." Then in a louder voice he called out, "Hi Gabrielle!"

"Please tell Adam that I said hello and that I can hear him even when he's not shouting."

"She said hello and she can hear everything you're saying."

"Terrific. So your girlfriend knows that I'm a dick."

"She knew that that already," Braden replied.

"Did you tell her you missed her?"

"I think I got this, Adam."

"Did you tell you love her?"

"I really don't need your help here."

"Ah, Braden's in love," Adam teased. "All the women at the G Lounge are probably crying into their vodka."

"Will you please go occupy yourself somehow? Take a shower, brush your teeth, study the Crimes Code. Just leave me alone for a minute so I can say goodnight to my girlfriend."

"Goodnight Gabrielle!" Adam called out.

"I'm sorry about that," Braden apologized.

"Don't worry about it. I'm not dating him. Listen, I'm going out with Jess, Cam and Mark tomorrow night. I'm not sure what time I'll be home."

"Call me no matter what time. And text me or call whenever you want during the day. I might even be able to wrap up early tomorrow. If I can maybe I'll switch to an earlier flight."

"Okay, I will."

"I should say goodnight while he's still in the bathroom, because I do really want to tell you that I miss you." He hesitated for a second. "And that I love you." Oh my God. Oh my God. Oh my God. He said it! Calm, Gabrielle. My heart started hammering. I wanted so much to be with him at that moment.

"I miss you and I love you too." My voice shook a little because the emotions I was experiencing were so powerful that they almost overwhelmed me. "So much."

"Goodnight, baby."

"Goodnight. Sweet dreams

* * *

215

The next day at noon Mark sat in our living room listening while I laid out the whole story. I told him about the notes, the suspects, and our efforts thus far to collect evidence. Then I laid out the plan. Finally, I paused and Mark spoke up.

"So, let me get this straight. You met three obnoxious people at Braden's fundraiser, and when you got a couple of anonymous notes saying that you should break up with him, or something bad might happen, you assumed that one of those three wrote them."

"Because while each one of them had an interest in seeing us break up, nobody else did, and it wasn't common knowledge that we were dating then."

"So, instead of just telling the cops, and letting them handle it, you decided instead to try to get handwriting samples yourself, because you were worried that there would be a backlash if you said you suspected one of these people."

"Right."

"And in pursuit of that evidence you convinced Fred and Ethel here to follow private citizens and dig through garbage with you." He glanced at Jess and Cam like he wondered just what in the hell was wrong with them.

"Well, yeah. You know I'm mostly doing this because I don't want Braden or my parents to worry anymore, right?"

"Uh huh. And now you want *me* to wear a costume and go to an underground sex party with you so that Jess can dominate some kinky politician into giving her a sample of his handwriting."

"It's for a good cause."

"And you think that one of my closest friends, who also happens to be your boyfriend, is going to think that there's nothing wrong with this plan?"

"I'm not going there to have sex with anybody! I'm not even going in. I think this guy will actually do this if Jess even just orders him to. As soon as she gets the writing we're gone. I send it to my expert, he either eliminates Cole or gives me ammunition to tell him to leave me the hell alone. This is a way to possibly get someone to stop harassing me without dragging Braden or his family into it."

"Don't even try to make this sound reasonable, Gabrielle. I can't believe that you didn't tell Braden about the first note."

"Mark, I don't want him to get himself into a difficult position. If I just had a little something to back up my suspicions it would be a whole different story. Don't you understand? I'm doing this because I care about him. I don't want him worrying about me all the time and I want people to leave us alone without getting him sued."

"What if we get this sample and it's not this guy. What then?"

"I don't know. I'm not sure I'm up to digging through trash again. I think I'll just give it this one try. He's the one who it would be most controversial to wrongly accuse anyway. If it isn't him I'll just probably turn everything over to the cops and let them deal with it."

"And you're going to tell Braden about all of this?"

"Yes – I will."

"I still don't think that he's going to be okay with you doing this."

"I can't just make Jess do this herself."

"Okay look, I'll go along with this under one condition. Even though you may be dressed up to blend in you stay back unless absolutely necessary. I don't want you anywhere near this place unless we have no other choice. We can stay in communication with each other by cell."

"Okay, it's a deal. We'll park a few blocks away and we'll stay in the car unless you need us."

❧ CHAPTER TWENTY-NINE ❧

That night at eight forty-five, we were all dressed in our best fantasy wear from Tony's. Jess and Mark made quite a pair. She was wearing a skin-tight skirt that came down to her ankles but was slit up the back almost to her bottom. She had on a high-necked old-fashioned-looking ruffled blouse like a Victorian school teacher might wear, fishnets, boots with high heels, a black wig and a Mardi Gras-type mask. She was carrying a ruler and she had some folded paper and a pen stuck into a garter. Mark also wore a mask but his was plainer – sort of Lone Ranger-esque. He was dressed like an English school boy in a striped tie, knee socks, matching shorts, blazer and cap. He looked like that guy Angus Young from the band ACDC. Cam and I just looked kinky.

We arrived near the location of the party, an abandoned warehouse down by the docks. It was a rough neighborhood, so I was armed with pepper spray. We took my car and parked it several blocks away as we went over everything one last time.

"Okay, you guys have the code and we watched the video of Cole online a thousand times, so hopefully you'll be able to recognize him," I said.

"I'm going to walk up to him and tell him he's a bad boy and needs to be punished," Jess said.

"I'll stay near you the whole time," Mark assured her.

"I get him to write 'I've been a bad little boy because' and then tell him to list the reasons."

"If he won't do it you tell him you'll spank him with your ruler," I added.

"We get the sample and we get the hell out of Dodge," Mark finished.

"We're here if you need us and we can come in to help you if necessary," Cam offered.

"We'll try to stay in touch by phone as much as possible," Jess said.

"Okay, team. I think it's go time. I just want to thank you all for doing this."

"Yeah, right, Lucy," Mark replied. "When Ricky finds out he's probably going to have my ass."

"I'll tell him I made you do it. Good luck." He sighed and rolled his eyes at me, then he and Jess got out of the car and started walking in the direction of the warehouse as Cam and I sat nervously waiting. Ten minutes later I had a call from Jess.

"We're in. There was no problem with the doorman and the code worked fine. Everyone is standing around mingling right now and we think we've spotted Cole. Oops, gotta go."

"They're in and they're mingling. They've spotted him." We sat waiting for a couple of minutes quietly and then Cam spoke up in a slightly hesitant voice.

"So Gabrielle, you and Braden are pretty serious now, huh?

"Yeah, we are. We're very happy together and very compatible."

"That's good. I want you to be happy. I'm really sorry that I hurt you back in college."

"I know you are. It wasn't all your fault though. I had a big crush on you. I should have told you that before we… beforehand. I should also have told you that I was a virgin."

"Yeah, that was the thing that freaked me out the most. I did really feel something for you — more than friendship — but you were so nice and so sweet. I had just messed up my relationship with Braden and I was pretty down on myself at the time. I didn't think I deserved somebody like you and then when I realized what you had just given me, I didn't feel worthy, you know?"

"So you're saying it wasn't just a casual hook up to you either?"

"No, it wasn't but I couldn't really deal with my feelings at the time. When you didn't want to see me anymore at all I was really depressed. I realized that I fucked up royally, yet again, and I didn't want to make it worse, so I just left you alone."

"Cam. I never knew. I figured you didn't want to have to deal with me pining for you and I was just so embarrassed."

"I wasn't a really great communicator."

"I know it's none of my business but why did you hook up with Marla when she was dating Braden?"

"Braden was sick of her and on the verge of breaking up with her. She knew that and she figured if she made him jealous it might make a difference. I was out drinking with a bunch of my friends one night and Marla started hitting on me. I knew Braden didn't have any feelings for her and I knew she was just using me. I was pretty drunk and she convinced me to go off into a dark corner with her while she applied her oral skills. I felt really shitty about it as soon as I sobered up the next day but word had already gotten back to Braden. He and I had an argument. He said he could care less who Marla blew but he was mad that I had betrayed him and made him look stupid. I got defensive. I was immature. Whatever. The point is, it wrecked our friendship."

"It seems like you're getting along pretty well now."

"And I want to keep it that way. He's my cousin and he and I were good friends once. I'm still attracted to you, Gabrielle, but I really do want you to be happy and I want Braden to be happy too."

"You'll meet somebody, Cam. You're a great guy."

"To tell you the truth, I've enjoyed spending time with Jess and I do find her very attractive too. I think maybe I should explore that a little, if she were interested that is."

"I think she would be if she knew that you were interested in her. Make sure you communicate." "I'm glad that I've worked things out with you and Braden. That makes me feel a lot better." Just then a call came in.

"We got it!" Jess whispered excitedly.

"You got it?" I almost couldn't believe it.

"Yeah, but I don't think I'm going to be able to get it out of here. They're careful about what you carry in and out. I had to hide the phone and we've been getting some weird looks."

"*You've* been getting weird looks? At a kinky party?"

"Because we're not, you know, engaging."

"Oh."

"Look, we may actually need to sneak out of here. Meet us at the back of the building in case we need help. We may have to come out a window and I'm not sure what's back there."

"Shit!"

"Don't worry. Just meet us."

"Okay. We're on our way."

"They may have to come out a back window. They want us to meet them at the back of the building."

"Okay, make sure you bring the pepper spray. This isn't exactly the Upper East Side." We walked toward the warehouse, circled wide to avoid the bouncers in the front, and crept as quietly as we could to the rear of the building, crouching behind some boxes. I looked up and saw a window open. In the next minute Mark jumped out and Jess started through. Suddenly, I heard a voice shouting.

"Hey! What's going on?"

I stood up and called out, "We're over here!" Mark caught Jess as she dropped to the ground and held her hand as the two of them bolted in our direction. I heard more voices at the front of the building and it sounded like they were directing someone to come after us. We ran like hell, no easy feat in stilettos, incidentally. A group of burly bouncer-like guys swarmed around to the back of the building as we took off for the spot where we had left the car. Unfortunately when we got there, the spot was empty. Have I mentioned that this was a bad neighborhood?

"My car!" I cried.

"Are you sure this is where you parked it?"

"Yes!" I could hear voices in the distance. "What the fuck?! Why are they still looking for you?"

"Gabrielle, this is an illegal gathering and there are important people here. We just snuck out the fucking window. That may cause them some concern."

"Well, then we have no choice." I took out my phone.

"Who are you calling?" Cam asked.

"The police. We're about to give them an anonymous tip." I called it in and we set off on foot trying to get as far away as possible before the cops arrived and raided the place. We ran until we were all out of breath. Finally, we paused to rest in an alleyway.

"Okay," Mark panted. "I say we call a cab from here."

"Hey! Isn't that your car?!" Jess cried. I looked up. It was the Mini Cooper about three blocks away! Somebody had just boosted it for a joyride! We ran toward it and dove in. I pulled away with my tires squealing and headed home. Fifteen minutes later the four of us, bedraggled and sweating, were staggering into the lobby of our building, when I heard a voice. *Oh shit.* Ricky was home early from the club.

"And I thought the garbage was good," Adam said, sounding amazed.

"Gabrielle?!" You know, I had never actually heard Braden sound incredulous before. "Why are you dressed like that?!" He looked over at Cam. "Why are *you* dressed like *that*?!"

"Mark? Is that you?" Adam asked, cracking up. "Nice shorts, man." It wasn't long before he was actually doubled over with laughter. I hoped that he peed himself.

"Baby! What the *fuck* are you doing now?!" Braden was not laughing.

"There's an explanation for this," I said in a timid voice.

"Does it involve something kinky that you and Cameron were doing together?"

"No!" All four of us started trying to explain at once.

"Let's go up to your place," Braden said loudly over the top of the noise. This was also the first time I had heard him sound absolutely furious.

We all got on the elevator rather uncomfortably and rode in silence as a MUZAK version of Send in the Clowns played in the background. We entered my apartment to the sounds of joyful yips. At least Bruno was happy to see me. We went into the living room where everyone sat down and Bruno jumped up by Braden. He was happier to see him. I think that Bruno had clued into the fact that Daddy was the more stable parent.

"I know that you're probably going to beat the shit out of me, Braden, and I accept that," Mark said, sounding resigned. "But if it makes any difference, I did everything that I could under the circumstances to keep her safe."

"He did!" I backed him up. "This wasn't his fault. I made him do it."

"And I want you to know that Gabrielle and I didn't do anything together," Cam said desperately. "I swear to God, Braden! I didn't touch her!"

"So, why are you dressed like that?"

"Because we were trying to get a handwriting sample," he explained.

"And for that you had to dress like one of the Village People?" Adam asked.

"The person whose sample we needed was at an underground sex party," Jess offered helpfully.

"At a *what?!*" I had also never heard Braden yell before.

"She didn't go in!" Mark said in a panicked voice. "Only Jess and I did. They just wore costumes in case they had to come in to help us."

"Help you to do *what?!*"

"Get out after I spanked Cole Stephenson into giving the sample," she answered.

"The state congressman?" Adam asked. "Wow, Gabrielle, you really *are* dangerous."

"That's all I did – when they crawled out the window and the bouncers started coming after us – I told them where to run so that they could get away. That's all." My voice was starting to quaver. I hated seeing Braden this upset.

"Oh that's all, huh?" Braden stood up and plowed his fingers through his hair and started pacing angrily. "You promised me that you wouldn't knowingly put yourself in danger and you lied to me."

"I didn't lie to you! I didn't think it would be dangerous!"

"Why would you even do this?"

"Because you and my parents are worried about me. I didn't want you to worry. I honestly believed that either Marla or Cole or possibly Mrs. Mason was the anonymous letter writer. I figured if I just had a little proof I could tell them to back off."

"Why couldn't you just have told me that, or told the police that?"

"Because if you had them investigated it could cause a backlash for you and your family. I didn't want to see that happen over a couple of stupid notes."

"A couple? You got more than one?"

"I didn't want you to worry. I thought that if I told you that I had gotten another one, and I told you who I suspected, you might do something rash."

"*I* might do something rash?! You went to a fucking orgy dressed like the fifth member of KISS!"

"My plan worked! We got the handwriting sample from Cole!"

"Did you know that Marla's a call girl by the way?" Jess asked.

"She's a *what*?!"

"Don't worry about that now!" I glared at Jess. "I just wanted to find a way to make the letter writer leave me alone so that you wouldn't worry. I love you and I don't want to cause you stress." Finally his expression softened a little.

"Well, I happen to love you too and if you don't want to cause me stress then you can try actually talking to me rather than assuming that you know how I'll react to something. From now on, and I *mean* this, Gabrielle, you will *not* keep this kind of information from me. Do you understand?"

"Yes. Braden, baby, I'm so sorry."

"Do you *promise* me?"

"Yes. I promise you."

He paced some more and raked his fingers through his hair some more. We all sat quietly, not wanting to say anything to make him any more agitated. Finally he stopped pacing and turned to face me with a very determined look.

"Okay, you really want to make sure that I don't worry about you?"

"Yes, of course."

"And you love me?"

"Yes! So much." I could feel tears start to sting my eyes.

"Then marry me." *Huh?*

"Did you just ask me to marry you?"

"Yes. And believe me, it never would have occurred to me that one day I would be proposing in front of four other people to someone dressed as a dominatrix. Yet here I find myself. And the fact that I'm still standing here extending this offer should tell you something, Gabrielle."

"It does!" I smiled with incredible, almost irrational, joy as I felt the tears completely filling my eyes. "I thought that my dad was the only guy in the world romantic enough to knowingly marry into pure insanity just because he really loved somebody."

"So is that a yes?"

"Yes!" I ran over to him and hugged him tightly. I heard a yip and Bruno ran over and started humping Braden's leg.

⌾ CHAPTER THIRTY ⌾

"Mazel tov. Does this mean you're going to convert?" Adam asked.

"Who cares about that? Does it mean you're not going to kill me?" Mark wanted to know.

"What it means is that Gabrielle won't be digging through garbage or attending underground sex parties anymore. Well, unless I go with her. It also means that if someone is harassing her because they're hoping that she'll leave me, they'll probably just give up."

My happy balloon promptly burst. "That's why you asked me to marry you? So that you can keep an eye on me and keep me out of trouble?"

"No. I asked you to marry me because I love you and I want to be with you always, you nutty broad. The fact that I might be able to keep you out of trouble is just a perk."

"So why are you guys back early?" Jess asked.

"Because Braden missed his girlfriend too much," Adam answered.

"We finished up the programs we were scheduled for and I was able to get us an earlier flight. There wasn't anything of any importance to us going on tomorrow," Braden replied, glancing at Adam.

"Because Braden missed his girlfriend too much," Adam repeated.

"Right now I would like my girlfriend to come back with me to my place, but I would like her to please go change her clothes first so that my doorman doesn't think I'm bringing home a hooker. By the way, what were you saying about Marla?"

"I'll tell you about it on the way," I said, heading off to my room to change. I was back in five minutes in yoga pants and a tee-shirt.

"Come on Mata Hari, let's get out of here," Braden said. We said goodbye to everyone and headed back to his place with Bruno.

Along the way I told him about Marla and the real story about the garbage. He was pretty shocked but he still laughed when I told him about Cam's client showing up. At least he didn't sound angry anymore. It was starting to sink in slowly that he had proposed. I understood it on an intellectual level but I don't think that it had really hit me yet. I decided that he had been through enough stress because of me and I was going to comfort *him* with a nice massage and a bath together. When we got to his apartment I headed straight for the bathroom and started filling the tub, throwing in some eucalyptus bath oil. The scent was supposed to relax you. Bruno ran off to check the apartment for whatever Bruno always checked it for.

"Hey," I called out to him. "Come here and let me not confront you."

"I could use a lot of non-confrontation," he said, poking his head in the door and starting to peel off his clothes. He looked really good peeling off his clothes incidentally.

"It must be very traumatic for a former player to ask somebody to marry him," I teased.

"You have no idea." He smiled. I took my clothes off too while he watched with a look that was becoming less relaxed by the second. So much for the scent of eucalyptus oil.

"You sit in front of me and scoot down. I want to rub your back and shoulders. You seem tense," I said and he actually laughed out loud.

"Ya think? I wonder why."

"Well, I may cause you some tension but I also know how to relieve it." I slipped into the wonderfully warm water and sighed. He slipped in with me and sat between my legs, leaning back against me.

"Mm. I like the way your chest feels all slippery up against me," he murmured, wiggling around a little. I started massaging his shoulders and he made a sound like a lion purring.

"I missed you," I said quietly in his ear while plying him with gentle little kisses.

"I missed you too." His shoulders were loosening up and he was sounding much more content.

"You're sure you want to marry me?"

"Yes. I may want a 'do-over' on the proposal though. I think if I try really hard I could probably make it more romantic than that," he said with a laugh.

"It will make a great story for the grandkids."

"Oh yeah sure. How did you ask grandma to marry you, grandpa? Well, it was the night that she attended the orgy dressed like a dominatrix… By the way, when we tell our parents we might want to skip that part."

"Our parents! Oh my God, that's right. Do you think your parents are going to object because we haven't been together long?"

"Are you kidding? My parents love you. They'll be thrilled speechless. My dad knew he wanted to marry my mom after their first date anyway."

"Really?"

"So did your dad."

"He did? After meeting Bubbe?!"

"Yeah." He laughed. "That's true love, I'll tell you."

"So, he told you that, huh?"

"Both of them told me that when I had my man-to-man relationship talks with them. They'll probably both suggest that we have a long engagement anyway though. I'm okay with that as long as you move in with me."

"Jess won't have a roommate."

"She'll find another one and we can afford to cover your rent until she does. Now, how about if you comfort other parts of me," he said taking my hand off of his shoulder and placing it on a part of his body that was quite unrelaxed at the moment. I reached over for a bath sponge and began giving him a massage of a different kind. His breathing got heavy and he started to groan. I loved watching him get really aroused. "Sit on my lap," he said in a thick voice. I changed position and thoroughly enjoyed the look of bliss on his face as he slid inside me.

"I love you Braden," I gasped as he raised his hips and pushed into me harder.

"I love you too. Kiss me." I kissed him and lost myself in all of the wonderful sensations.

By the time we had both completely released our tension the water had cooled so we got out, toweled off and headed for bed. Bruno was asleep in his doggy bed already as Braden and I snuggled in and fell asleep holding each other.

* * *

The sound of Braden's cell phone on the bedside table woke us up the next morning. He reached over to pick it up as I groggily glanced at the clock. It was 9a.m. We had slept really late. It sounded like he was talking to either Adam or Mark.

"It's on now? Okay, yeah. I'll call you later." He hung up and reached for the remote to the TV mounted on the wall. "Apparently an underground sex party got raided last night and a few notable local personalities were picked up."

"A few?" Who had been there besides Cole, I wondered. Braden clicked on the news and we sat watching in shock as the full story unfolded.

Police say that the raid was the result of an ongoing investigation into the operation of illegal sex parties.

"Ongoing investigation my ass!" I said angrily. Braden shushed me.

Among those arrested were Pennsylvania State Representative Cole Stephenson. There was a shot of Cole with his head down walking to a car flanked by a couple of high-priced local defense attorneys. *Socialite, Marla Benton...*

"Marla *was* there! She must have been working the party!" It was a nice added bonus.

And society matron Veronica Mason, who may possibly have been the organizer of the party, known as Fanny Hill.

"Mrs. Mason! Holy shit! The whole gang was there!" I couldn't believe what I was hearing.

"Well, it looks like you'll get access to handwriting samples from all three of your suspects. I'm sure they wrote out some kind of statement. If not, though, I'll get a subpoena. It shouldn't be too hard now."

"I'll give Steve Flynn a call and see what the earliest he'll be looking at them would be. I'm not expecting today, since it's Sunday."

I was wrong though. Steve was available later that afternoon if we could get something from the arrest the previous night. Braden got on the phone with his office and found out that all three had made brief written statements, so the samples were ours. We made arrangements to meet Steve at the Roundhouse, Philadelphia police headquarters at three.

"I can't believe that nasty frigid woman was hosting sex parties," Braden said, shaking his head. "I hope it doesn't reflect badly on the foundation that she was a donor."

"I doubt it, but it will give Alan something to keep him busy." I remembered how stressed he had seemed when the journalists started questioning him about my dad and I felt kind of sorry for him. But then that was his job.

"What do you think will happen to them?"

"I think they'll hire high-priced defense lawyers, who aren't half as good as public defenders, but who will still manage to get them off with probation. Then I'm sure that all three will write books that will hit the New York Times bestseller list and they'll do the talk show circuit. It's probably the best thing that's ever happened to them."

"Poor Felicity."

"Oh come on Gabrielle. She can't stand her mother and this will probably make her the coolest Goth chick on the scene."

"Maybe you're right. Now that the letter writer is probably in custody, do you still want to get married?"

"For the final time, yes! Don't you?"

"Yes, definitely. I love you and I'm sure that I want to be with you. I'm just still kind of shocked that it happened so fast."

"I'm not. I knew from the first date too."

"You did?"

"Yeah, do you want to hear about it from my perspective?"

"Actually I do. The male mind fascinates me. So tell me about our first date through your eyes."

"The first thing I noticed, being male, was that you looked incredibly hot. You're very attractive dressed for court, but with your hair down, dressed in a short skirt with bare legs, you look amazing."

"I would have thought you would have noticed that my shirt kind of showed off my boobs."

"That goes without saying. You know how I feel about those." He glanced down happily for a moment and then continued, "I could feel the sexual tension between us and it was turning me on from the very beginning."

"I could feel it too."

"I probably would have been totally distracted by thoughts of nailing you, if it weren't for the fact that you said that you liked walking in the city in the evening because you always felt like something exciting was about to happen. I just found that really cool and I couldn't think of anybody else who would say something like that."

"Really?"

"Yeah, and then when you told me later that you wanted to have hot sweaty monkey sex with me, that was it. I was done for and I knew it."

"I'm sure lots of women have made you that offer."

"Not that way." He laughed. "And we talked for hours and found out that we had a lot in common. The biggest thing, though, was the places you took me. Anybody who could see true quality beyond superficial appearances was one classy chick in my opinion. And I could also see that you were a kind person without being condescending."

"That's so sweet. I knew you were a classy guy, and a good one, from how you acted in court." "Last but not least, when I kissed you and you were so responsive, you almost drove me out of my mind. In another five minutes I probably would have begged you to invite me in. And speaking of inviting me in, my morning friend is visiting." He gave me a slightly lecherous smile. Bruno didn't even stir. He had become so accustomed to Mommy and Daddy having hot sweaty monkey sex that it didn't even phase him anymore.

Later that day we sat across from Steve Flynn as he carefully examined the samples.

"What do you think?" I asked.

"Well, I can't be one hundred percent certain, of course, but it's my opinion this note was not written by any of these three people. I don't have the original from New York for comparison yet, but what I see in the facsimile just confirms that. Your anonymous letter writer is likely a different individual."

I was stunned. I was so sure that it was one of those three. All kinds of thoughts raced through my head. How had some other person even known we were together? What was their motive? How had they known where we were in New York? For a brief second Cam came to mind. He had confessed that he was still attracted to me but he had sounded completely sincere about being happy for us. No, it wasn't Cam. My gut told me it wasn't. So, who was it then?

"Baby, don't worry," Braden said putting his arm around me. "We'll make sure that there's a full investigation and you're going to move in with me and we're going to get married and everything is going to be fine. Nobody is going to bother us."

"Okay." I smiled at him even though I was worried that those sounded like more famous last words.

Do Gabrielle and Braden live happily ever after? Who is the anonymous letter writer? Will Jess and Cam get together? Will Marla, Cole and Mrs. Mason end up doing reality TV? How will Cousin Rachel like Drew? Will Bubbe be allowed to attend the wedding? Would Mr. Harris the shoplifter be back for the July Fourth picnic season? These questions and many more will be answered when Gabrielle and Braden's story concludes in *The Home Court Advantage* coming later this year.

Acknowledgements

A special thanks to author Kym Grosso who patiently gave me help when I knew nothing about how to become a writer, and to my editor, Julie Roberts, for her patience (does anyone see a pattern here?) and her fabulous sense of humor. Thanks to Carrie Spencer for designing not one, but two, amazing covers for me, and all of the indie authors who came before me. Thanks to Tara Sivec, Courtney Cole and Emma Chase, all of whom wrote fabulous funny and sexy books and were kind enough to accept my fan-girl adoration and my friend requests on Goodreads. Thanks to my lovely beta readers who were so helpful and to all of the readers, fellow authors, and bloggers who have stuck with me on my author pages through this whole process. As always, to my wonderfully patient husband for not kicking me to the curb while I was writing this book, to my mom for always being my number one fan, and to my beautiful children for being so damned loveable. Finally, thanks to all of my Neurodiverse peeps for your support and your strength. Flap on my friends flap on!

About the Author

N.M. Silber is a former public defender who hung up her power suit and put away her sensible pumps to become an author of contemporary romance novels. She used her experiences in the criminal court system as a starting point to build her interesting cast of characters and her humorous story lines. She is a firm believer that funny can be sexy and sexy can be funny and the brain is her favorite erogenous zone. She lives in the Philadelphia area with her patient husband and two beautiful sons.

For more information visit:

nmsilber.com,

www.facebook.com/NMSilber

@NMSilber on Twitter

14560909R00137

Printed in Poland
by Amazon Fulfillment
Poland Sp. z o.o., Wrocław